THE TRIUMPH OF CAESAR

THE
TRIUMPH
OF
CAESAR

A NOVEL OF ANCIENT ROME

STEVEN
SAYLOR

MINOTAUR BOOKS ✹ NEW YORK

THE TRIUMPH OF CAESAR. Copyright © 2008 by Steven Saylor. All rights reserved. Printed in the United States of America. For information, address St. Martin's Press, 175 Fifth Avenue, New York, N.Y. 10010.

www.minotaurbooks.com

Design by Dylan Rosal Greif

The Library of Congress has catalogued the hardcover edition as follows:

Saylor, Steven, 1956–
    The triumph of Caesar : a novel of ancient Rome / Steven Saylor.—1st ed.
        p.   cm.
    ISBN-13: 978-0-312-35983-6
    ISBN-10: 0-312-35983-7
    1. Gordianus the Finder (Fictitious character)—Fiction.   2. Caesar, Julius—Fiction.
  3. Rome—History—Republic, 265–30 B.C.—Fiction.   I. Title.
    PS3569.A96T75   2008
    813'.54—dc22

        2008003668

ISBN-13: 978-0-312-55699-0 (pbk.)
ISBN-10: 0-312-55699-3 (pbk.)

First Minotaur Books Paperback Edition: July 2009

10 9 8 7 6 5 4 3 2 1

To Keith Kahla,
a true friend of Gordianus from the very beginning

THE TRIUMPH OF CAESAR

I

"I heard that you were dead."

Such a brusque comment from Caesar's wife might have offended me had I not heard it already from so many others since I returned from Egypt to Rome, where everyone had apparently given me up for dead.

Having sent a slave to summon me, Calpurnia had received me in an elegant but sparsely furnished room in her house not far from mine on the Palatine Hill. There was only one chair. She sat. I stood and tried not to fidget while the most powerful woman in Rome looked me up and down.

"Yes, I'm sure one of my agents told me you drowned in the Nile," she said, gazing at me shrewdly. "Yet here you stand before me, Gordianus, as alive as ever—unless those Egyptians have learned to bring the dead back to life, not just mummify them." She fixed her chilly gaze on my face. "How old are you, Finder?"

"Sixty-four."

"No! Have the Egyptians found a way to restore a man's

youth? You look very fit for a man your age. You're ten years older than my husband, yet I daresay you look ten years younger."

I shrugged. "Great Caesar carries the weight of the whole world on his shoulders. His enemies have been destroyed, but his responsibilities are greater than ever. The worries and cares of the world's master must be endless. My humble life has taken a different course. My obligations grow less, not more. I've had my share of strife, but now I'm at peace with the world and with myself. For the time being, at least . . ."

Having been summoned by Caesar's wife, I had to wonder if the tranquillity of my life was about to be sorely disrupted.

"When did I last see you, Gordianus?"

"It must have been almost exactly two years ago, just before I left for Egypt."

She nodded. "You went there because your wife was unwell."

"Yes. Bethesda was born in Egypt. She believed that she could be cured of her illness only by bathing in the waters of the Nile. The cure apparently worked, because—"

"Yet you spent most of your time in the city of Alexandria, along with my husband," she said, showing no interest in Bethesda's cure.

"Yes. I arrived in the midst of the civil war between Queen Cleopatra and her siblings. During the siege that confined Caesar to the royal palace for several months, I was trapped there as well."

"Where you became quite friendly with my husband."

"I had the privilege of conversing with him on numerous occasions," I said, evading the topic of friendship. My feelings toward Caesar were more complicated than that.

"Eventually, my husband was victorious in Egypt, as he's been victorious in every other campaign. He put an end to the civil strife in Alexandria . . . and installed young Cleopatra on the throne."

She spoke the queen's name with a grimace; Caesar's adulterous love affair with Cleopatra, who claimed to have borne his child, was a favorite topic of every scandalmonger in Rome. The grimace deepened the wrinkles on her face, and Calpurnia suddenly looked much older than when I had last seen her. She had never been a beautiful woman; Caesar had not married her for her looks but for her respectability. His previous wife had embarrassed him by falling prey to gossip. "Caesar's wife," he had declared, "must be above suspicion." Calpurnia proved to be hardheaded, pragmatic, and ruthless; Caesar had entrusted her to run his network of spies in the capital while he fought his rivals on distant battlefields. There was nothing frivolous in either her manner or her appearance; she made no effort to flatter her face with colorful cosmetics or her figure with elegant fabrics.

I looked about the room, which reflected the taste of its occupant. The walls were stained deep red and somber yellow. Instead of depicting an image from history or Homer, the impeccably crafted mosaic floor displayed an array of interlocking geometric patterns in muted colors. The furnishings were exquisite but few—woolen rugs, bronze lamp holders, and the single backless chair made of ebony inlaid with lapis tiles in which my hostess sat.

It was not the reception hall of a queen; those I had seen in Egypt, bright with gold and dripping with ornaments, their dazzle intended to intimidate all who entered. And yet, in fact if not in name, Calpurnia was now the queen of Rome; and Caesar, having defeated every rival, was its king, though for now he preferred the venerable title of dictator, the office our ancestors created so that a strong man could rule the state in times of emergency. But if rumors were true—that Caesar intended to make the Senate declare him dictator for life—how was he any different from the kings of olden days, before Rome became a proud republic?

"Caesar is in danger," Calpurnia said abruptly. She clasped her hands tightly in her lap. Her face was taut. "Great danger. That's why I've called you here."

The statement struck me as so peculiar that I laughed out loud, then checked myself when I saw the look on her face. If the most powerful man on earth, the victorious survivor of a brutal civil war that had wreaked havoc across the whole world, was in danger, what could Gordianus the Finder do to protect him?

"I'm sure that Caesar can look after himself," I said. "Or if he wants my help, then he can ask me—"

"No!" Her voice rose sharply. This was not the dispassionate, coldly calculating Calpurnia I knew but a woman touched by genuine fear. "Caesar doesn't realize the danger. Caesar is . . . distracted."

"Distracted?"

"He's too busy preparing for his upcoming triumphs."

I nodded. There were to be four triumphal processions in the days to come. The first, to celebrate Caesar's conquest of Gaul, would take place three days hence.

"Caesar is consumed with the planning and arrangements," she said. "He intends to give the people a series of spectacles such as they've never seen before. Small things fall below his notice. But small things can grow to be great things. They say the Nile crocodile begins life as a creature hardly bigger than my little finger."

"Yet it very quickly it grows into a monster that can bite a man in two."

"Exactly! That's why I've called you here, Gordianus—you have a nose for danger and a taste for finding the truth." She raised a finger. The gesture was so slight I barely noticed it, but an alert slave standing just outside the doorway hurried to her side.

"Bring Porsenna," said Calpurnia.

The slave departed without a sound. A few moments later, a gray-bearded man entered the room. He wore the yellow costume of an Etruscan haruspex. Over a bright tunic was a pleated cloak fixed at his shoulder with a large clasp of finely wrought bronze. The clasp was in the shape of a sheep's liver marked into numerous sections, with notations in the Etruscan alphabet etched into each section—a diviner's chart for locating omens amid the entrails. On his head the haruspex wore a high conical cap, held in place by a strap under his chin.

Haruspicy was the Etruscan science of divination. From ancient days, Rome's neighbors to the north worshipped a child-god called Tages, who had snakes for legs. Long ago, Tages appeared to an Etruscan holy man in a freshly plowed field, rising from the dirt and bearing books filled with wisdom. From those books the science of haruspicy was born.

Even before Rome was founded, the Etruscans were examining the entrails of sacrificed animals to predict every aspect of the future, from the outcome of great battles to the next day's weather. They were also adept at interpreting dreams and at finding meaning in various phenomena. Lightning, freakish weather, strange objects fallen from the sky, and the birth of monstrously deformed animals were all attempts by the gods to communicate their will to mankind.

Haruspicy had never become a part of Rome's official state religion. To determine the will of the gods, Roman priests consulted the Sibylline Books and Roman augurs observed the flight of birds. (Roman priests sacrificed animals, to be sure, and offered the blood and organs to the gods, but they did not presume to predict the future from this pious activity.) Nevertheless, despite its unofficial status, the ancient Etruscan art of divination persisted. Believers consulted haruspices for guidance in personal and business affairs, and in recent years even the Senate had taken to calling upon a haruspex to read the entrails of a sacrificed beast before beginning the day's debate.

One of the charms of haruspicy was the fact that its practitioners used the Etruscan language in their rituals. Nobody spoke Etruscan anymore, not even the Etruscans, and the language is so different from every other language that the sound of it alone conveys an exotic, otherworldly quality.

Even so, there were plenty of nonbelievers who scoffed at what they considered outmoded superstitions practiced by charlatans. Cato, leader of the opposition's last stand against Caesar in Africa, once remarked: "When two of these yellow-clad buffoons meet in the street, babbling in their incomprehensible tongue, it's a miracle that either can keep a straight face!" Of course, Cato had come to a terrible end, enduring perhaps the most wretched of all the deaths suffered by Caesar's opponents. All Rome would no doubt be reminded of the grisly details during one of the upcoming triumphs.

According to my son Meto, who had served with him for many years, Caesar, too, took a dim view of haruspicy. At Pharsalus, all the omens went against Caesar, but he ignored them and went to battle anyway, completely destroying the forces of his chief rival, Pompey. Caesar made a show of observing the old ways of divination, but when the haruspices weighed against him, he had only contempt for them.

From everything I knew of her, I would have assumed that Calpurnia placed no more faith in haruspicy than did her husband—yet here stood a haruspex in his gaudy yellow garments and peaked hat, looking at me with a smug expression on his face.

"This is the one they call the Finder?" he said to Calpurnia.

"Yes."

Porsenna nodded vigorously, causing his pointed hat to poke the air like a comical weapon in a mime show. "Indeed, this is the very man I saw in my dreams. This is the one who can help you, Calpurnia—the only one."

She raised an eyebrow. "Before, you said the *other* fellow was the man to help me—and we both know how that turned out."

"Yes, but I was right then as well, don't you see? Because *that* man, despite his misfortune, was the one to lead us to *this* man. Divination does not always guide us straight to the truth, like the furrow of a plow. Sometimes it meanders, like a stream. No matter. As long as we follow the precepts of Tages, we surely arrive—"

"What 'other fellow' are you talking about?" I said. "And what is it you want from me, Calpurnia? When your messenger summoned me, I came here at once. How could I refuse? Before I left for Egypt, you dealt with me honestly and fairly, and I owe you my respect for that, above and beyond your station as the dictator's wife. But I must tell you right now that if you intend to offer me some commission that involves poking into dark corners, uncovering ugly secrets, getting someone killed—or getting myself killed!—I won't accept it. I'm finished with that sort of thing. I'm too old. I won't have my tranquillity disturbed."

"I can pay you handsomely."

So she *did* intend to employ me for some sort of intrigue. I sighed. "Fortunately, I don't need your money. I would advise you to call on my son Eco—he does that sort of thing nowadays; and he's younger than I am, faster, stronger, probably twice as clever. Eco is away from Rome at the moment—a commission has taken him down to Syracuse—but as soon as Eco returns—"

"No! It's *you* we must have, Finder," said Porsenna. "Tages has decreed it."

"Just as the god previously decreed that you turn to that 'other fellow' you spoke of—the one who met with 'misfortune'? I don't like the sound of that."

Calpurnia made a sour face. "You'll at least hear me out, Gordianus." It was a statement, not a question, uttered in a tone to remind me that I was in the presence of the most powerful woman in Rome.

I took a deep breath. "What is it you want from me, then?"

"Seek the truth. Only that. And why not? It's your nature. It's the thing you were born to do; the gods made you thus. And when you find the truth, I wish you to share it with me—and with no one else."

"Truth? I thought you had Porsenna to find that for you."

She shook her head. "Haruspicy functions at one level. A fellow like you functions at another."

"I see. Instead of sifting through entrails, I dig in the dirt."

"That's one way of putting it. We each must use whatever skills we possess, do whatever is necessary . . . to save my husband's life."

"What is this threat to Caesar?"

"I was first alerted by my dreams—nightmares so terrible that I sought out Porsenna to interpret them for me. His divinations confirmed my worst fears. Caesar is in immediate and very terrible danger."

I sighed. "I'm surprised, Calpurnia. I thought you were not the sort to act on dreams or omens. Others, yes, but not you."

"You sound like my husband! I've tried to warn him. He scoffs at my fears."

"Have you introduced him to your haruspex?"

"No! Caesar knows nothing about Porsenna, nor must he ever know. It would only further arouse his skepticism. But I assure you: Caesar has never been in greater danger."

I shook my head. "Surely Caesar has never been in *less* danger. All his enemies are dead! Pompey, beheaded by Egyptians who wanted to please Caesar. Ahenobarbus, driven to earth and speared like a rabbit by Marc Antony at Pharsalus. Cato, driven to suicide in Africa. The survivors who were pardoned by Caesar, like Cicero, have been reduced to cowering sycophants."

"Yet some of them must wish Caesar dead."

"Some? Many, I should think. But wishes are not daggers. Have these men the will to act? Caesar thinks not; otherwise, he wouldn't have pardoned them. I trust his judgment. The man has been courting danger all his life, and getting the better of it. Once, in Alexandria, I stood beside him on a quay when a flaming missile from an enemy ship came hurtling straight toward us. I thought that missile was the end of us—but Caesar calmly assessed the trajectory, stood his ground, and never flinched. And, sure enough, the missile fell short. Another time, in Alexandria, I watched his ship sink during a battle in the harbor, and I thought he would surely drown. Instead he swam, wearing full armor, all the way to safety." I laughed. "Later, his only complaint was that he had lost his new purple cape—a gift from Cleopatra."

"This is not a laughing matter, Finder!"

Was it my mention of Cleopatra that rankled her? I took a deep breath. "Of course not. Very well, when you say Caesar is in danger, what exactly do you mean? Is there a particular person you suspect, or some particular group? Is there a conspiracy against him?"

"I don't know."

I frowned. "Calpurnia, why am I here?"

"To help me save Caesar's life!" She had begun to slump but now sat stiffly upright, grasping the arms of the chair with white knuckled hands.

"How?"

"Porsenna will be our guide."

I shook my head. "I won't take instructions from a haruspex."

"Your orders will come from me," said Calpurnia sternly.

I sighed. Caesar was not yet a king, and the republic's citizens were not yet his subjects, yet Caesar's wife seemed incapable of accepting a direct refusal. Perhaps I could lead her by argument to see that employing me was simply not to her advantage.

"I acknowledge your sense of urgency, Calpurnia, but I don't understand what you want from me. What would you have me do? Where would I begin?"

Porsenna cleared his throat. "You can start by retracing the steps of the man we called upon to do this work before you. He delivered written reports to us."

"I take it this fellow came to a bad end. Yes, from the looks on both your faces, a very bad end! I don't care to follow in the footsteps of a dead man, Calpurnia." I directed my gaze at her, pointedly ignoring the haruspex, but it was Porsenna who replied.

"Those footsteps might lead you to the man's killer," he said, "and knowing who killed him might lead us to the source of the threat against Caesar. The fellow must have discovered something dangerous, to have paid for it with his life."

I shook my head. "Dreams, divination, death! I don't like anything about this affair, Calpurnia. I respectfully decline to become involved."

Porsenna was about to speak, but Calpurnia silenced him with a gesture. "Perhaps, if you saw the dead man. . . ." she said quietly.

"I don't see how that would make a difference."

"Nonetheless." She rose from the chair and proceeded toward a doorway. Porsenna indicated that I should follow. I did so reluctantly, with Porsenna behind me. I disliked the haruspex from first sight and didn't like having him at my back.

We walked down a long hallway, passing rooms as simply decorated as the one in which Calpurnia had received me. The house seemed empty; Calpurnia's slaves were trained to remain out of sight. We crossed a small garden ornamented by a splashing fountain with a splendid statue of Venus—Caesar's reputed ancestor—standing naked upon a gigantic seashell.

A man was sitting in the shade of the garden. He wore the voluminous toga of a pontifex, with its extra folds gathered and tucked in a loop above his waist. His mantle was pushed back to show a head of perfectly white hair. The old priest glanced up as we passed and gave me a quizzical look. I thought I saw a family resemblance to Calpurnia. His words confirmed it.

"Who have you brought into the house now, niece? Another spy? Or worse, another soothsayer?"

"Be quiet, Uncle Gnaeus! This is my affair, and I shall handle it as I see fit. Not a word to Caesar, do you understand?"

"Of course, my dear." The priest rose to his feet. He was a bigger man than I had thought. He took Calpurnia's hand. "Did I speak harshly to you? It's only because I think you're troubling yourself over nothing. You allow this haruspex to excite your fears, and insist on drawing others into this foolishness, and now we see where it leads—"

"I know what you think, Uncle Gnaeus. But if you cannot say words of support, say nothing!"

This served to silence Gnaeus Calpurnius, who dropped Calpurnia's hand and returned his gaze to me. He seemed to regard me with a combination of pity, scorn, and exasperation. I followed Calpurnia out of the garden and back indoors, glad to escape the old priest's scrutiny.

We walked down another long hallway. The rooms in this part of the house were more cluttered and less elegantly furnished. Finally we arrived at a small chamber, dimly lit by a single window high in the wall. It appeared to be a storage room. Odds and ends were piled against the walls—a rolled carpet, boxes full of blank parchment and writing materials, chairs one atop another.

In the center of the room, a body had been laid upon a makeshift bier. Flowers and spices had been strewn around it to mask the inevitable scent of putrefaction, but the body could not have been lifeless for more than a day, for it was still stiff. Presumably the corpse had been discovered after rigor began, for the petrified body retained the posture of an agonizing death, with shoulders hunched and limbs contracted. The hands were clutching the chest at a bloodstained spot directly over the heart. I avoided looking at the face, but even from the corner of my eye I could see that the jaw was tightly clenched and the lips were drawn back in a hideous grimace.

The body was clothed in a simple tunic. The darkened bloodstain was vivid against the pale blue fabric. There was nothing particularly distinctive about the garment—it had a black border in a common Greek key pattern—yet it seemed familiar to me.

"Where did you find the poor fellow?" I said.

"In a private alley that runs alongside this house," said Calpurnia. "The slaves use it to come and go, as do a few others—like this man—who don't wish to call at the front door."

"A secret entrance for your secret agents?"

"Sometimes. He was discovered at dawn, lying on the paving stones just outside the door."

"The body was already stiff?"

"Yes, just as you see him now."

"Then he had probably been dead—and lying undisturbed—for at least four hours. That's when rigor begins."

"That's certainly possible. To my knowledge, no one used that passageway during the night, so he could have been lying there since sundown. I presume he came here to tell me something, but before he could rap at the door—"

"Someone stabbed him. Are there more wounds?"

"Only this one."

"So he died of a single stab wound to the heart." His assailant must have been very lucky, or very quick, or else must have known the victim. How else could someone draw close enough to land such a perfect blow?

"Was there a trail of blood in the passageway?"

"No. He fell where he was stabbed." Calpurnia shuddered.

"His tunic . . . looks familiar," I said, feeling uneasy.

"Does it? Perhaps you should look at his face."

I stepped closer. The scent of flowers and spices filled my nostrils. My heart pounded in my chest. My mouth was dry.

"Hieronymus!" I whispered.

I I

Although his features were contorted almost beyond recognition, there could be no doubt. It was my friend Hieronymus, the Scapegoat of Massilia, who lay dead upon the bier. His teeth were bared in a grimace and his eyes were wide open.

"This was your agent? Hieronymus?"

Calpurnia nodded.

I shook my head in disbelief.

It had been three years since I'd met him in Massilia, when the city was besieged by Caesar. Following an ancient custom, the Massilians chose a citizen upon whom they would lavish every imaginable luxury until the day they cast him from the Sacrifice Rock as an offering to the gods to avert catastrophe. Hieronymus had been selected for the role, not as an honor but as a way to get rid of him once and for all. His father had been a powerful man who lost his fortune, then committed suicide. Hieronymus began life at the very top of Massilian society, then found himself at the bottom. His very existence was an embarrassment to the city's ruling class, who valued nothing but success and despised nothing more than failure. His caustic wit had not won him any friends, either.

Hieronymus saved my life in Massilia. When I returned to Rome, he came with me and took up residence in my household. After I left for Egypt, he struck out on his own; so my daughter, Diana, told me, saying she had run into him occasionally in the city. But since my return, I had not heard from him. This did not surprise me, as Hieronymus was something of a misanthrope. Nor had I sought him; I had become such a hermit that it took a summons from Caesar's wife to get me out of my house. I assumed our paths would cross sooner or later, if he was still in the city, and still alive. Amid the chaos and confusion of the long, bloody civil war, Hieronymus was just another friend of whom I had lost track.

Now I had found him again, lying lifeless on a bier in the house of Caesar's wife—who was telling me that Hieronymus had been her spy. The notion was absurd!

Or was it?

In a flash I saw how such a thing must have happened. Having resided with me, observing how I made a living and hearing my stories of past investigations, how like Hieronymus to conclude that any fool could do the same. What skills were required, except perseverance and cheek? What resources were needed, beyond a circle of knowledgeable informants, many of whom Hieronymus had already met through me? He knew I had dealt with Calpurnia shortly before my departure and that I had come away from those dealings with a great deal of money. After I left for Egypt, he must have approached her and offered his services.

"But why did you hire him?" I asked. "What sort of information could Hieronymus possibly have obtained for you? He was an outsider, a foreigner. He spoke with a Greek accent. He could never pass as a citizen."

"He had no need to be anything other than himself," said Calpurnia. "His notoriety opened doors."

"Notoriety? The man shunned society."

"Perhaps, but society did not shun him. Everyone in Rome had heard of the Scapegoat. And as Hieronymus quickly discovered, once he began making the rounds, there was hardly a household in Rome that wouldn't admit him if he paid a call. He was a curiosity, don't you see? Exotic, mysterious—the famous Scapegoat of Massilia, the sacrificial victim who was never sacrificed. In times such as these, a man who can cheat death is a man people want to meet. The superstitious hoped that some of his good fortune might rub off. The curious merely wanted to take a good look at him. And once he was admitted to a household, Hieronymus could be quite charming—"

"Charming? He had a tongue like a viper!"

"Amusing, then. Never at a loss for an epigram. Very erudite."

This was true. As a child, before his father fell into ruin, Hieronymus had received an excellent education from his tutors. He could recite long passages from the *Iliad* and knew the Greek tragedies by heart. When he chose to show off his learning, it was usually to comic effect—an ironic rejoinder, a whimsical metaphor, an absurdly high-flown bit of poetry that deflated the self-importance of his listener.

"I suppose Hieronymus was something of a character," I admitted, "and a good companion, when you got to know him.

I can see how he might have been accepted in the households of your friends . . . and your enemies."

I looked down at his face. It seemed his grimace had softened a bit. Was the rigor beginning to pass? I looked at his long, gangly limbs; at the pale, thin hair on his head; at the narrow strip of wispy beard that outlined his sharp chin. What a bitter irony, to survive a terrible fate in his native city, only to meet death in a such a manner—alone, in a dark alley, far from home.

"Hieronymus, Hieronymus!" I whispered. "Who did this to you?"

"We don't know who killed him," said Calpurnia quietly, "or why. It might have been any of the subjects on whom he's been delivering reports. Perhaps, Gordianus, if you were to read those reports and pursue the threads that Hieronymus was following, you might discover who killed him."

I grunted. "And in the meantime, I'd be doing just as you wish—following in Hieronymus's footsteps and looking for threats to Caesar." How brazenly she played upon my sympathies to get what she wanted from me! "Why can't you deduce for yourself what Hieronymus discovered? You say he delivered reports. I presume you've read them. You must know what he was up to."

Calpurnia shook her head. "Like all informants, Hieronymus was never entirely forthcoming. It's human nature to hold something back—for the next meeting, the next payment. Hieronymus was more . . . frustrating in that regard than most of my agents. I knew he wasn't telling me everything, but, given his unique potential, I decided to be patient with him. Perhaps if I had been less indulgent and more demanding, he might still be alive."

"Or we might at least know who killed him," said Porsenna. I glared at the haruspex until he lowered his eyes.

"Don't blame Porsenna," said Calpurnia. "No one recruited Hieronymus. He sought me out to offer his services."

"And your soothsayer—the man who claims to see the future!—advised you to take him on. And now this: the end of Hieronymus." Tears filled my eyes. I refused to shed them while they watched. I averted my face. "Leave me alone with him," I whispered. After a pause, I heard the rustling of their clothing as they left the room.

I touched the corpse's brow. The rigor had begun to release its grip. I straightened the fingers of the bloodstained hands that clutched his chest. I straightened his legs. I smoothed the grimace from his face and closed his eyes.

"Hieronymus!" I whispered. "When I arrived in Massilia—friendless, miserable, in terrible danger—you took me in. You protected me. You shared your wisdom. You made me laugh. I thought I saw you die, there in Massilia, but you returned from the dead! You came with me to Rome, and I was able to repay your hospitality." I shook my head. "It's hard to see a friend die once. Now I've had to bear your death twice! For now you truly are dead, my friend."

I ran my fingers over his. What long, elegant hands he had!

I stood silently for a while, then left the room. Calpurnia and Porsenna were waiting for me in the next room.

I cleared my throat. "These written reports . . ."

Porsenna had already fetched them. He held up a leather tube for carrying scrolls and parchments.

Begrudgingly, I took the collection of documents from Porsenna. "I'll begin reading these tonight. If I have questions,

I'll expect you to answer them. If there seems to be a chance that I might discover how Hieronymus died . . . and who killed him. . . ."

Calpurnia could not suppress a smile of victory.

"But I'll take no payment from you, Calpurnia. And I'll take no directions from your haruspex. Whatever I discover, I may share with you—or I may not. I work for myself, not for you. I do this for Hieronymus, not for Caesar."

Her smile faded. Her eyes narrowed. She considered for a moment, then nodded her assent.

On my way out, I passed her uncle, who still sat in the garden. Gnaeus Calpurnius clutched his priestly robes and glared at me.

There was not a cloud in the sky and the sun was at its zenith as I left the house of Calpurnia and crossed the Palatine Hill. I moved through a bright, glaring world without shadows. The thick, hot air seemed to eddy sluggishly around me. The windowless walls of the houses of the rich, colored in shades of saffron and rust, looked hot enough to scorch my fingertips.

The month was September, but the weather was hardly autumnal. When I was a boy, September was a month for playing amid fallen leaves and donning cloaks to ward off the chill. No more; September had become the middle of the summer. Those who knew about such things said the Roman calendar was flawed and had gradually fallen out of step with the seasons. The problem was worse now than ever before; the calendar was a full two months behind the place where it should be. Autumn festivals, spring festivals, and summer feast days were still celebrated according to the calendar but made no sense. There was something absurd about making sacrifices to the gods of the harvest when the harvest was another sixty days in the future, or celebrating the parole of Proserpine from Hades when there was still frost on the ground.

Was it only old-timers like me who felt acutely the absurdity of our disjointed calendar? Perhaps the young simply took it for granted that September had become a month of long sweltering days and short nights too hot for sleeping; but to me, the broken calendar represented a broken world. The civil war, which had spread to every corner of the Mediterranean from Egypt to Spain, was over at last, but amid the wreckage lay the centuries-old republic of Rome. We had a calendar that could no longer reckon the days and a Senate that could no longer govern.

But we also had Julius Caesar, and Caesar would put everything right. So his supporters claimed; so Caesar promised. He would rebuild the Roman state, making it stronger than ever. He had even pledged to fix the calendar; according to rumor, the details would be announced at the conclusion of his upcoming triumphs, after which the requisite number of days— two months' worth—would be added to the current year, and the forthcoming year, with newly proportioned months, would commence in harmony with the seasons and the passage of the sun.

But could Caesar repair the broken people of Rome? Even the gods cannot restore a severed hand or a plucked-out eye to a body maimed by warfare. Others, whose bodies might show no signs of damage from violence or deprivation, had nonetheless been changed by the fear and uncertainty that hung over their lives for so many years, while Caesar and Pompey struggled for dominion. Something about those men and women was not as it had been before, not quite right. No doctor could diagnose their nameless disease, yet it burned inside them nonetheless, changing them from the inside out. Like the calendar, they still functioned, but no longer in harmony with the cosmos.

Even Calpurnia might be numbered among these invisible victims. The confederate of Caesar and mistress of his spy ring in the capital—rigorously logical, ruthlessly pragmatic—now confessed to being driven by dreams. She allowed a haruspex to conduct her affairs, and was doing so behind her husband's back.

I came to the Ramp, the long, straight, tree-lined path that led down to a gateway between the House of the Vestals and the Temple of Castor and Pollux. I descended from the quiet calm of the Palatine to the hubbub of the Forum. Senators and magistrates attired in togas swept by me, followed by their retinues of scribes and sycophants, looking like little Caesars with their noses in the air, their posture and gait projecting an attitude that the world would come to an end if anyone dared to prevent them from reaching whatever meeting they were headed for. Their self-importance seemed all the more absurd, considering that Caesar's victory had rendered them irrelevant. The Senate had reconvened, but everyone knew that all power flowed from Caesar. His approval was needed for all important decisions. He held the key to the Treasury. He had bypassed elections to personally appoint the magistrates. He had parceled out the provincial governorships to his friends and supporters, and was busily filling the scores of vacancies in the Senate with creatures of his choosing. Some of these new senators, to the shock of old-timers like myself, were not even Romans but Gauls, men who had betrayed their own people to join Caesar and who were now receiving their rewards.

Yet the business of the Forum carried on as if the civil war had never occurred. Or at least it appeared to be so; for the Forum was suffering from the same invisible malady that plagued the populace of Rome. On the surface, everything seemed to be back to normal. Priests made sacrifices on temple steps, Vestals tended the eternal hearth fire, and ordinary citizens sought redress from the magistrates. But below the surface, everything was askew. People were simply going through the motions, knowing that nothing was quite right, and might never be so again.

I listened to snatches of conversation from men passing by. Everyone was talking about Caesar:

". . . may yet step down. That's the rumor I heard."

"Return to private life, as Sulla did? Never! His supporters wouldn't allow it."

"Nor would his enemies. They'd kill him!"

"He has no enemies left, or none worth considering."

"Not true! Pompey's son is said to be in Spain right now, rallying a force to take on Caesar."

My son Meto was in Spain, serving in Caesar's forces, so my ears pricked up at this.

"If that's true," came the response, "Caesar will squash young Pompey like an insect! Just wait and see. . . ."

". . . and Caesar may even name a new month after

himself—the month of Julius! There's to be a complete revision of the calendar, done with the help of astronomers from Alexandria."

"Well, it's about time—no pun intended!"

". . . and the whole thing will go on for four straight days, I heard."

"Not four days in a row, you silly man! Four triumphs, yes, but each with a day between. We'll need those days of rest, to recover from so much drinking and feasting."

"Imagine it! Four full-scale processions, plus public banquets for everyone in Rome, followed by plays and chariot races and gladiator games—I don't see how Caesar can afford to put on such a spectacle."

"He can't afford not to. After all we've put up with, the people of Rome deserve a celebration! Besides, he has all the money in the world—literally. His conquests have made him the richest man in history. Why shouldn't he lavish some of the booty on us?"

"I'm not sure it's right, celebrating with triumphs to mark the end of a civil war. So much Roman blood was spilled."

"It's not just about the civil war. Have you forgotten his victory over Vercingetorix and the Gauls? The triumph for that is long overdue. And another triumph will be for putting down the revolt of Pharnaces in Asia, and that's certainly well deserved."

"Granted, as may be the triumph for defeating King Ptolemy in Egypt, although that wasn't exactly a Roman conquest, was it? More like settling a family feud. The king's sister Cleopatra kept her throne."

"Because she conquered Caesar!"

"They say the queen is in Rome right now, here to watch her rebel sister, Arsinoë, paraded in chains and put to death to cap the Egyptian Triumph."

"Yes, yes, triumphs for Caesar's victories in Gaul and Asia and Egypt—no one can complain about those. But what about this triumph that's planned for his victory in Africa? It was fellow Romans he fought there. Poor Cato! Who could raise a cheer about the way he died?"

"Oh, you might be surprised. The Roman mob loves to see a big man brought down, especially by a bigger man. And if Cato was the best general the opposition could put up after Pompey was killed, then they deserved to lose."

"You! You, there! What's that you're saying? My brother fought for Cato, you piece of scum, and died at Thapsus. He was a better Roman than the likes of you, you slandering pig!"

From the corner of my eye I saw the beginnings of a scuffle, and hurried on.

Passing beyond the public buildings of the Forum, I entered a maze of streets crowded with shops offering every sort of merchandise and service. Closest to the Forum were the more respectable eateries, tailor shops, fullers, craftsmen, and jewel merchants. Further on, the atmosphere grew progressively seedier and the clientele less affluent. I saw fewer togas and more tunics. This was the Subura district, notorious for its rough taverns and brothels. Nowadays it was thronged by Caesar's veterans, many of them maimed or bearing hideous scars. Under the midday sun they gathered outside taverns, drinking wine, and gambled in the streets, casting dice made from bones.

I saw a group of street performers putting on a show for a little crowd that had gathered. Unlike their colleagues in the theater, such troupes sometimes include female performers; the ones in this company were notable for their ample breasts, barely contained in tight, sheer gowns. The sketch was more pantomime than play, featuring a balding letch dressed as a Roman commander (his armor was made of tin) and the most buxom of the actresses, who wore a cheap imitation of the tall Egyptian headdress called an atef crown, and very little else. The performers were obviously meant to be Caesar and Cleopatra, and their buffoonish interaction grew progressively more suggestive. After a few obscene puns, including a comparison of Caesar's intimate anatomy to that of a Nile river-horse (the creature Herodotus called a *híppos potámios*), Cleopatra extended her arms, planted her feet well apart, and broke into a ribald dance. Every part of her body jiggled wildly, while her towering headdress remained rigidly upright and perfectly motionless; I suddenly realized it looked more like a phallus than an atef crown.

I found the dance both arousing and hilarious, all the more so because I had dealt with the real queen in Alexandria, who was nothing like her imitator. A more self-possessed young woman than Cleopatra I had never met; believing herself to be the living incarnation of the goddess Isis, she tended to take herself quite seriously, and the idea that she would ever perform such a lurid dance was as delightful as it was ludicrous. An alms collector for the troupe saw me laughing and quickly hurried over, extending a cup. I contributed a small coin.

I moved on, looking for the street where Calpurnia had told me I would find Hieronymus's apartment.

Years ago, when I lived in a ramshackle house on the Esquiline Hill above the Subura, I had walked through this neighborhood almost every day. I had known its meandering alleys like the veins on the back of my hand. Nowadays I visited the Subura less often, and much had changed over the years. The tall, crowded tenements, some of them soaring to six stories, were so cheaply constructed that they frequently collapsed and almost as frequently burned down. New buildings were quickly thrown up to take their place. Entire streets had become unrecognizable to me, and for a while I became lost.

Then, in the blink of an eye, I found myself in front of the very building I was searching for. It was unmistakable. "Brandnew and six stories tall," Calpurnia had told me, "with a fresh yellow wash on the walls, a public fountain at the corner, and an eatery on the ground floor." She owned the building. A part of her arrangement with Hieronymus had been to supply him with free lodging.

Calpurnia had told me I would find a slave posted in the tiny vestibule. He was there partly for the security of the tenants but also to make sure they didn't start cooking fires in their rooms or carry on any business that was too dangerous or too illegal. I encountered an unshaven young man so scruffily dressed that he might have been a beggar who had wandered in off the street, but the suspicious look he gave me was definitely that of a watchman.

"You must be Agapios," I said. "My name is Gordianus. Your mistress sent me." For proof I showed him a bit of sealing wax into which Calpurnia had pressed her signet ring. For a symbol she used the profile of King Numa, with his flowing beard and priest's mantle. The Calpurnii could trace their descent from Calpus; he was one of the four sons of pious King Numa, who lived more than six hundred years ago and was the founder of many religious rites and priesthoods.

He bowed obsequiously. "What can I do for you, citizen?"

"You can show me to the room where Hieronymus of Massilia lived."

The young slave caught my use of the past tense and shot me a curious look, but he said nothing. He turned and motioned for me to follow him up the stairs.

Usually the choicest apartments in such tenements are located in the middle floors, high enough to escape the noise and odors of the street but not so high that climbing the stairs becomes an onerous challenge, or jumping from a window in case of fire means certain death. I had expected to find Hieronymus's apartment on the second floor up, or perhaps the third, but the sprightly watchman bounded up one flight of stairs after another. I found myself huffing and puffing and called to him to slow down, but he had disappeared from sight.

I followed at my own pace and eventually caught up with him on a landing. He was miming boredom by examining his cuticles.

"Hieronymus lived all the way up here?" I said. "I should have thought—"

"Not on this floor. One more flight up."

"What!"

"You have to take this final flight of steps, over here."

Why had Hieronymus left my home for such a place? This tenement was not as squalid as some, but was it really an improvement on the comfortable quarters I had provided for him?

The last flight of stairs delivered us not, as before, to a landing with dark hallways leading to numerous apartments but to a single door with an open skylight above. Under the bright sunshine, the watchman produced an iron key and opened the door.

The room was sparsely furnished, but the rugs and chairs were of good quality. The space was brightly lit by unshuttered windows on either side. A doorway appeared to lead to another room. Another doorway opened onto a terrace that entirely encircled the apartment. I stepped outside.

"A rooftop apartment?" I said.

"The only one. The tenant had it all to himself."

Hieronymus had done well for himself, after all. The space and seclusion would have suited him, and the vista would have reminded him of his pampered days in Massilia. This was one of the tallest buildings in the Subura, and the view was virtually unimpeded in all directions. Beyond the Forum there was an excellent view of the Capitoline Hill with its crown of magnificent temples and monumental statues.

I leaned forward, peered over the parapet, and felt a bit dizzy, gazing down at the tiny figures in the street below.

"How well did you know him?" I said.

"The tenant? Not at all. He kept to himself."

We stepped back into the apartment. "Did he have visitors?"

"Never. You speak of him in the past tense. Is the tenant—?"

"You can go now, Agapios. Leave the key with me, so that I can lock the door as I leave. In fact, I'll keep the key."

"But tenants always leave their key with me when they go out. I don't have another."

"Good."

"But the mistress—"

"I have authority from Calpurnia. I showed you the seal."

"So you did," said the slave, cocking an eyebrow. "All very

mysterious!" He paused in the doorway and turned back. "You know, for a graybeard who can barely manage the stairs, you're not bad looking." He skipped lithely down the steps and vanished.

I stood, confounded for a moment. It had been quite some time since a young slave of either gender had flirted with me. I blinked and caught my reflection in the polished square of copper hung on the wall beside the doorway. Hieronymus must have used it for checking his appearance before leaving his rooms. The full lips set into a frown, the knitted brow, the flattened nose (a boxer's nose, Bethesda called it) all projected a stern countenance. The silver-streaked hair and beard were kept short and neatly trimmed; that was my daughter, Diana's, doing. There was perhaps a certain gentleness about the eyes, a suggestion of the callow youth I once had been, a lifetime ago.

I watched a trickle of sweat run down my forehead onto my nose. All the heat of the building rose to these rooms, which were baked by the sun as well. I grunted and wiped the sweat away, then shrugged at the figure in the mirror and set about exploring Hieronymus's lair.

I walked from room to room and searched the usual places. I lifted the rugs. I checked the chairs for false bottoms and rapped on the legs to see if they might be hollow. I rummaged though the trunk that contained his clothing. There were a few cups and jars and other containers; they held only wine or olive oil for the lamps. I examined the narrow bed, the straw mattress, the coverlets and the cushions. He kept his valuables in a little box under the bed. I found some coins and a few trinkets, but not much else of value.

Hieronymus had kept a small collection of books. The

rolled-up scrolls were neatly inserted into a tall pigeonhole case against one wall. Most of the scrolls were identified by little tags with titles and volume numbers written on them: Eirenaios's *History of Massilia,* Fabius Pictor's *History of Rome,* the *Epigrams* of Appius Claudius the Blind, and so on. Perusing the bookcase from top to bottom, I came upon a whole row of scrolls that had come from my own library, including a rare copy of Manius Calpurnius's *Life of King Numa.* Cicero had given it to me many years ago. I couldn't remember ever lending it to Hieronymus. When he vacated my house, he must have borrowed it—if "borrow" was the correct word.

Feeling a bit peeved, I pulled the scroll from its pigeonhole and unrolled it, wanting to check its condition. The scroll was intact, but several loose pieces of parchment had been rolled up inside it. I removed these extraneous pages and saw that they were covered with writing in Hieronymus's hand. I had only to scan a few lines to realize that I had found what appeared to be a private journal, kept hidden inside the scroll of *Numa.*

I felt a sudden chill. I sensed a presence in the room and slowly turned around, almost certain I would see the lemur of Hieronymus standing behind me.

I saw no one. I was alone.

Still, I felt an uncanny sensation of being watched, and in my head I seemed to hear Hieronymus's voice: "How predictable you are, Gordianus! You saw your precious copy of *Numa* and felt compelled to check at once that I hadn't damaged it—you did exactly as I intended! You found my private notes, intended for my eyes only, while I lived. But now that I'm dead, I wanted you to find my journal, Gordianus, tucked inside your precious *Numa* . . ."

I shuddered and put the pieces of parchment aside.

I looked through all the other scrolls, but found no more hidden documents. There was one scroll, however, that piqued my curiosity. It was quite different from anything else in the bookcase. It was not a work of history or poetry or drama. It was not even a book, properly speaking, but a collection of odd-sized pieces of parchment stitched together. The various documents did have a common theme: astronomy, if I could judge the enigmatic notations and drawings rightly. The movements of the sun, moon and stars, and the symbols used to represent them, were not things I knew much about. Hieronymus's taste in reading had not run to the scientific, yet these notations appeared to have been made by his own hand.

I gathered up the scrolls which had belonged to me. I decided to leave the other scrolls, for the time being, except the astronomical miscellany, which I wanted to study further. I added that scroll to the others I was taking, along with Hieronymus's private journal.

I stepped outside the apartment and locked the door behind me.

I I I

"You went to that woman's house, *alone?*" Bethesda greeted me in the vestibule with her hands on her hips. "You should have taken Rupa with you for protection. Or at least the two troublemakers, if only to get them out of my hair." She referred to our two young slaves, the brothers Mopsus and Androcles, who were not quite boys anymore but not yet men, either.

"Protection? I hardly needed any. People say the city is quite safe now, with Caesar back in residence and his officers in charge, and with half the citizenry dead or in exile. Caesar himself is said to go strolling about the city with no bodyguard at all."

"Because Venus protects him. But what goddess looks after you?" Bethesda scowled at me. "You're an old man now. Old men make tempting targets for cutthroats and thieves."

"Not as old as that! Why just today, a young slave engaged in a rather obvious and completely unsolicited flirtation with me. Said that I—"

"She probably wanted something from you."

"As a matter of fact—"

"Promise me you won't stir from the house again without taking someone with you."

"Wife! Did we not survive the civil war and the darkest days of the chaos here in Rome? Did we not survive a terrible storm at sea, and a rocky landing in Egypt, and a separation of many months, and my own intention to drown myself in the Nile, when I mistakenly thought that you must have met such a fate? How can you suggest that no gods watch over me? I've always assumed that my life must be providing them with considerable amusement; how else can you explain the fact that I'm still alive?"

She was not impressed. "The gods may have been amused when you were Gordianus the Finder, always sticking your nose where it didn't belong, exposing so-called great men and women as conniving thieves and killers, daring the Fates to strike you down. But what have you done to amuse them lately? You sit at home, play with your grandchildren, and watch the garden grow. The gods have grown bored with you."

"Bethesda! Are you saying that *you* are bored with me?"

"Of course not. Quite the opposite. I hated it when you were always putting yourself in danger. It seems to me that now is the best time of our lives, when you've finally settled down and no longer have to work. You belong in the garden, playing with Aulus and looking after little Beth. Why do you think I became so upset when I found that you'd left the house to go visit that woman and taken no one with you for protection?"

Tears welled in her eyes. Since our return to Rome, it seemed to me that a change had come over her. What had become of the strangely aloof young slave girl I had taken as my concubine, then married? Where was the self-contained, autocratic matron of my household, who kept a cool exterior and never showed weakness?

I took Bethesda in my arms. She submitted to the embrace for a moment, then pulled away. She was as unused to being comforted as I was to comforting her.

"Very well," I said quietly. "In the future, I shall be more careful when I leave the house. Even though the house of 'that woman,' as you insist on calling her, is only a few steps away." I decided not to tell her about my excursion to the seedy, dangerous Subura.

"You'll be going back there, then?"

"To Calpurnia's house? Yes. She's asked for my help."

"Something dangerous enough to pique the gods' interest in you, no doubt?" said Bethesda tartly, having recovered from her tears. "Something to do with all those scrolls you've brought home with you?" She eyed the bag slung over my shoulder with the suspicion of those who have never learned to read.

"Yes. Actually . . . there's something I need to tell you. Something I need to tell everyone. Can you gather the family in the garden?"

They reacted more strongly to the news of Hieronymus's death than I had anticipated.

Bethesda wept—perhaps that *was* to be expected, given her new propensity for tears—but so did my daughter, Diana. At the age of twenty-four, she was quite the most beautiful young woman I had ever known (even allowing for a father's prejudice), and it pained me to see her loveliness marred by an outburst of weeping.

Davus, her hulking mass of a husband, held her in his brawny arms and wiped the mist from his own eyes. The last time I had seen him weep was when Bethesda and I arrived home unexpectedly from Egypt and found that everyone feared that we were dead. Poor Davus, thinking we might be lemures, first was scared half out of his wits—of which he had few enough to spare—then cried like a child.

Their five-year-old son, Aulus, was perhaps still too young to understand the cause of their grief on this occasion, but seeing his mother in tears he joined in with a piercing wail that set off an even more piercing cry from his little sister, Beth, who had recently learned to walk and tottered to his side.

My son Rupa was the newest addition to the family (by adoption, as anyone could tell by seeing the two of us side by side; he had the blue eyes, golden hair, and muscular frame of a handsome Sarmatian bloodline). Rupa had hardly known Hieronymus. Nonetheless, caught up in the family's grief, he opened his lips and, despite his muteness, let out a sound of despair as poignant as any line ever uttered by Roscius on the stage.

Even the young slaves, Mopsus and Androcles, who could usually be expected to exchange taunts at any sign of weakness, bowed their heads and joined hands. The brothers had been very fond of the Scapegoat.

"But, Papa," said Diana, fighting back her tears, "what was he doing in Calpurnia's employ? Something to do with Massilia? Hieronymus hardly had the personality to be a diplomat. Besides, he swore he would never go back there."

I had decided to tell them as little as possible about the specific nature of Hieronymus's activities for Calpurnia. To be sure, I was not certain myself exactly what Hieronymus had been up to; I had not yet read the reports Calpurnia had given me. Beyond that, I saw no need for any of them to know such details, especially Diana, who more than once had expressed a desire, bordering on an intention, to someday do exactly what Hieronymus had done—to follow in my footsteps as a professional ferret for the rich and powerful of Rome. Even with her keen mind and a protector like Davus, such a dangerous activity was hardly suitable for a young Roman matron.

"Perhaps he was working for her as a tutor. Hieronymus was smarter than just about anybody!" This came from Androcles, who had been very impressed by all the stories Hieronymus could recite.

"It couldn't be that," said Bethesda, sighing through her tears. "Calpurnia has no need for tutors; she's never given Caesar a child. The woman is famously barren."

"But Caesar has a son, even so, doesn't he?" offered Mopsus, doggedly following his younger brother's chain of thought. "He had a son by Queen Cleopatra, a little boy about the same age as Beth. And they say Cleopatra is in Rome right now, to witness Caesar's Egyptian Triumph, and she brought her little boy, Caesarion, with her." His face was lit by the glow of deductive success. "I'll wager Calpurnia wanted Hieronymus to be Caesarion's tutor."

Even Davus, as thick as he is, knew better than this. He laughed. "I hardly think that Caesar's Roman wife would want to engage a tutor for the son of Caesar's Egyptian mistress!"

He was right, of course. But what *was* Calpurnia's attitude toward Cleopatra and, more especially, toward the child Cleopatra claimed to be the son of Caesar? I had seen Calpurnia grimace when she spoke the queen's name, but she had said not a word, harsh or otherwise, about Cleopatra. Mopsus and Androcles were clearly far from the mark with their speculations about Hieronymus, but could the Scapegoat's death have had something to do with Cleopatra, nonetheless? I felt a stab of eagerness to begin reading the reports Calpurnia had given me as well as Hieronymus's private journal.

But first, there were practical considerations to be dealt with. I had told Calpurnia that I would assume responsibility for Hieronymus's funeral rites. I dispatched Rupa and the slave boys with a cart to fetch his body. Diana, with Davus to accompany her, I sent to pay a call on an undertaker near the temple of Venus Libitina. I had used the man's services before. He would supply slaves to wash the body and anoint it with oil and perfumes, and deliver a wreath of cypress for the door and a funeral bier with garlands for my vestibule. He would also enter the name of Hieronymus in the official registry of the dead and make arrangements for his cremation.

Bethesda busied herself with preparing the evening meal. We would eat that night in honor of the memory of our departed friend, Hieronymus of Massilia.

Left to myself, I withdrew to the garden and sat on a chair in the afternoon shade. With the scrolls beside me, and with a much-desired cup of wine close at hand, I began to read.

I began with the documents Calpurnia had given me. The reports from Hieronymus—there were a great many of them—had been neatly arranged into sections under the names of various persons. Most of these people were familiar to me, and I could see why Calpurnia thought it worthwhile to keep an eye on them.

I turned to the reports regarding Marc Antony.

Antony had been one of Caesar's most trusted officers during the conquest of Gaul. Later, he fought beside Caesar at Pharsalus in Greece, where Pompey was routed. When Caesar pursued Pompey to Egypt, he sent Antony back to Rome to keep order. Because Antony's return occurred shortly after I left for Egypt myself, I had not been present during his tenure as master of the city.

Governing the city for month after month, while Caesar defeated his enemies and quelled unrest abroad, had been no easy task. The wartime capital was plagued by shortages and riven by factional violence. Antony had forbidden citizens to carry arms, but this ban was universally ignored. Gangs had ruled the streets by day; common criminals had ruled the city by night.

Added to the general violence had been the growing unruliness of the lower classes, many of whom expected Caesar to abolish all debts and (in their wildest dreams) to redistribute the vast properties of the defeated Pompeians to the poor. Stirred up by one of Caesar's youngest officers, the radical firebrand Dolabella, a mob had gathered in the Forum to call for debt relief. Antony explained that he had no authority to grant their demands; they would have to wait for Caesar's return. The mob rioted. Antony, determined to keep order, dispatched soldiers to clear the Forum. By the end of the day, more than eight hundred citizens were dead. The city was calmer after that.

When Caesar finally returned and learned of the massacre, one of his first actions was to publicly berate Antony for the heavy-handedness of his rule—and to heap praise on Dolabella, the instigator of the mob. Caesar's actions may have been purely pragmatic, a bid to regain the favor of the lower orders. Still, his rebuke of his longtime protégé must have stung. Shortly after Caesar's return, Antony vanished from the public arena.

So much, from hearsay, I knew about the situation between Caesar and Antony. What else had Hieronymus discovered?

I scanned the notes written in Hieronymus's elegant hand. He went back and forth between Latin and Greek. His Latin was a bit stiff, but his Greek was almost absurdly elevated, full of Homeric flourishes, recondite references, and complicated puns. All this made for slow and difficult reading; glancing at the massive volume of material, I groaned at the idea of trying to read it all. I was surprised that Calpurnia had tolerated such prose.

Translating in my head, I tried to strip away Hieronymus's stylistic indulgences, looking simply for the facts.

Antony currently resides in Pompey's old house, called the House of the Beaks, in the Carinae district. . . .

How could that be? I remembered the day, shortly after my return to Rome, when Caesar announced that Pompey's entire estate would be sold at public auction to benefit the Treasury. He had charged Antony with conducting the auction, a formidable task. Pompey's house was stuffed with so many precious items, looted from his many campaigns of conquest, that simply making an inventory would pose a logistical challenge. But so far as I knew, there had been no auction. Yet Antony himself was living in the house of Pompey, according to Hieronymus.

Had Caesar given Antony the house outright, and with it Pompey's treasures? That seemed unlikely. Rewarding a favorite with so much plunder would be a slap at the mob, many of whom were in desperate straits and still ready to agitate for a radical redistribution of wealth. It would also smack of the arrogant favoritism that Sulla had practiced when he was dictator, and Caesar would never wish to be compared to Sulla.

I read on.

Antony divorced his second wife (and first cousin), the lovely Antonia, some time ago. He is living, quite openly, with his lover, the even more beautiful Cytheris. There can be no question of marriage, of course. An aristocrat like Antony, no matter how dissolute, could never marry a mere actress, especially a foreigner from Alexandria. . . .

News of Antony's divorce came as no surprise. I had met Antonia before I left for Egypt. She was a bitter woman. Her marriage had not been happy, thanks largely to Antony's open affair with Cytheris, whom I had met also. "Even more beautiful" than Antonia, Hieronymus had written, but when I tried to picture Cytheris, the impression in my mind was not so much of her face as of her sheer sexual allure—a tangled mass of auburn hair; flashing hazel eyes; a loose gown that could barely contain her voluptuous breasts; and, most especially, the way she had of moving, executing even the smallest gesture with a dancer's sinuous grace.

Everything that one hears about the parties Antony and Cytheris have been throwing in Pompey's house is true. These events are

*obscenely lavish. If there are food shortages in Rome, one would
never guess from looking at Antony's table. Pompey's famous stock
of expensive wines? Almost gone! Antony and Cytheris have done
their share to empty the amphorae, but they've had plenty of help
from every thirsty actor, dancer, street mime, and juggler in Rome.
(Cytheris knows everyone connected to the theater.) She has told me
I have a splendid voice for declaiming Greek, and says I should have
gone on the stage.*

I laughed out loud at this sudden intrusion of Hieronymus's
vanity into his report. It seemed that my friend had not only
managed to get himself invited into Antony's house but also
had won plaudits from Cytheris. I could easily imagine him
reciting a racy bit of Aristophanes at one of the couple's raucous gatherings, after warming his throat with a draft from the
dwindling store of Pompey's fine vintages.

I quickly scanned the rest of the material about Antony. The
details seemed to be as much about the spy as about the spied
upon—Hieronymus reported that one of his puns had made
Antony laugh so hard he spat out a mouthful of wine, and recounted at length a verbal duel in which he got the better of a
faded actor with rouged cheeks. I grew weary of the ornate
prose and found the documents increasingly difficult to read. It
seemed to me Hieronymus was intentionally filling space to pad
reports that had contained very little actual information. He
would not be the first confidential informant to pull such a
trick. As long as Calpurnia kept paying (and Antony kept inviting him back), why not stretch out the accounts as much as possible, even if he had nothing of importance to report?

I wondered if his private journal had been as prolix. I set

aside the material about Antony and picked up the scraps of parchment I had found in Hieronymus's apartment.

I saw at once that the prose was indeed different—it was entirely in Greek, with some passages succinct to the point of abbreviation, like the shorthand code invented by Cicero's secretary, Tiro.

I saw my own name and stopped to read the passage.

Beginning to think dear old Gordianus was a bit of a puffed-up charlatan. This "finder" business not remotely as difficult, or as dangerous, as he always made it out to be. The tales he used to tell, portraying himself as the fearless hero on a relentless quest for the truth! Half of those stories were probably made up. Still, if he's truly dead, as people say, I shall miss the old windbag. . . .

My face turned hot. If the lemur of Hieronymus was present, watching me, what would he say now about the danger of this sort of work?

I shuffled through the notes, looking for other mentions of my name, but instead I found this:

At last, I have hit upon it! Calpurnia's fears, which I had begun to think absurd, may be well-founded, after all—and the menace to Caesar will come at a time and from a direction we did not anticipate. But I could be wrong. Consequences of a false accusation— unthinkable! Must be certain. Until then, not a word in any of my official reports to the lady and her soothsayer. I dare not write my supposition even here; what if this journal were to be discovered? Must keep it hidden. But what if I am silenced? To any seeker who finds these words and would unlock the truth, I shall leave a key.

Look all around! The truth is not found in the words, but the words
may be found in the truth.

An icy chill swept through me. Apparently Hieronymus had
discovered something of deadly importance, after all. But what?

It appeared he had even foreseen his death and anticipated
the discovery of his journal. But what was the key he spoke
of—a real key or a metaphorical one? "Look all around!" he
wrote, yet I had searched every corner of his rooms and found
no key, nor anything else of obvious significance. "The truth is
not found in the words, but the words may be found in the
truth." More of his irritating, self-indulgent wordplay!

Mopsus appeared in the garden to announce that dinner was
ready. I put aside the scraps of parchment and rose from my
chair, glad to feel the warmth of the last rays of the sun on my
face.

I V

I stayed up late that night, reading for as long as the lamps had oil to burn. My eyes are not what they were, and neither my brain nor my body can boast the stamina they once possessed. Deciphering Hieronymus's ornate handwriting and his cluttered prose, especially by dim lamplight, wearied me to exhaustion. The great majority of documents remained unread when I finally succumbed to a few hours of restless sleep.

Before breakfast, I stepped into the vestibule to view the body of Hieronymus. All had been properly done, according to Roman custom. Washed, perfumed, and dressed in a spotless tunic, surrounded by fragrant garlands, he lay upon a bier with his feet toward the door, his upper body slightly elevated so that any visitors could see him at once from the entrance, where a wreath of cypress had been hung on the door to signal the household's grief.

No doubt the Massilians had their own way of doing these things, but Hieronymus had rejected his native city, and it seemed to me that Roman rites would be proper.

I gazed for a long moment at his face, which was peaceful in repose. In death, his features gave no indication of the tart words that could issue from that mouth of his, within which now lay the coin to pay his passage to the underworld.

"Puffed-up," he had called me, and "charlatan," and, worst of all, "windbag." Indeed! Yet, gazing at him, I could feel no resentment. Tears welled in my eyes, and I turned away.

After a breakfast of farina prepared in the Egyptian manner, with bits of dates and a sprinkling of poppy seeds—since our return from the Nile, Bethesda had prepared nothing but Egyptian dishes, revisiting all the favorites of her childhood—I set out, with Rupa at my side. If I were to discover the reason for Hieronymus's murder, I had to begin somewhere. The house of Pompey, where Antony now resided, seemed as good a place as any.

The so-called Great One had owned several houses in Rome. I was most familiar with his magnificent villa with gardens on the Pincian Hill, outside the city walls. The house claimed by Antony was within the walls, in the very heart of the city. People called it the House of the Beaks, because the vestibule was decorated with metal ramming beaks from ships captured by Pompey during his illustrious campaign to rid the sea of piracy some twenty years ago. Only the choicest of these trophies were displayed; it was said that Pompey captured some 846 ships. The House of the Beaks was located in the Carinae district, on the southwestern slope of the Esquiline Hill above the valley of the Subura.

The most prominent monument on the slope of the Carinae was the Temple of Tellus, the earth goddess. We passed it on the way to Pompey's house, and Rupa indicated, by a nod and gesture, that he wished to step inside for a moment. I could guess his reason. Tellus is celebrated during sowing and harvest, for accepting seed and giving forth grain, but she is also worshipped for receiving the dead, for all things return eventually to the soil. Rupa still mourned his older sister, Cassandra, whose death had brought him into my family. No doubt he wished to put a coin in the temple coffers and say a prayer for the departed spirit of Cassandra.

I waited outside on the temple steps, remembering Cassandra in my own way.

Just as Rupa emerged, I saw a litter coming up the hill, heading in the direction of the House of the Beaks. Through a break in the yellow curtains, I caught a glimpse of the occupant. It was Cytheris, lounging on a pile of rust-colored cushions that complemented her auburn hair and exquisite complexion. Cytheris had known Cassandra, and Rupa, back in her days as a dancer in Alexandria. If I moved quickly, I might make it appear that we had run into her by chance. A meeting that seemed fortuitous rather than premeditated was often to be preferred in my work—as I had more than once told Hieronymus. Had he absorbed that lesson, or had he considered it hot air from a windbag?

I grabbed Rupa by the arm (insofar as my hand could lay claim to such a massive limb) and hurried down the steps to intercept the litter, which was making slow progress through the crowded street.

Things could not have gone more to my liking. While I pretended to look the other way, Cytheris spotted the two of us and called out.

"Gordianus? Hello there! Can it truly be you? Back from

the dead? But it must be, because that big blond demigod beside you can only be Cassandra's little brother. Rupa!"

She pushed aside the curtains and, not waiting for a slave to assist her, bounded from the litter. The flimsy gown she was wearing seemed more suitable for staying in than going out, and the hug she gave Rupa, pressing her small body full against him, caused him to blush to the roots of his golden hair. But when Cytheris threw back her head in a laugh of sheer delight, Rupa did likewise, though the sound that emerged from his throat was something between a bray and a bleat.

"But this is too delicious!" she said, turning her attention to me. "One heard that you were dead. Oh, dear, is it awful of me to say that aloud? I'm sure I must be flouting some superstitious rule of silence. But really, it's such a surprise. You were off in Alexandria, weren't you? Along with Rupa? But now you're back! What are you up to, here in the Carinae?"

"Well . . . we were just stopping here at the Temple of Tellus, so that Rupa could say a prayer for his sister." This was the truth, after all.

"Ah, yes, Cassandra . . ." Cytheris and Cassandra had been close in their younger days, when they were both street performers in Alexandria. "But you must come with me, both of you. You must tell me all about Alexandria. It's been ages since I was there, but some days I still wake up with the salty smell of the harbor in my nostrils. Come with me to the House of the Beaks, and we'll share some wine in the garden."

Are you watching, lemur of Hieronymus? I thought. *Take notes! I had intended to make your death the reason for my visit, as the bearer of sad news, but this is much better. To all appearances, we have met by chance, and my visit to the house of Antony is Cytheris's idea, not my own. I shall mention your death only in passing. . . .*

Slaves scurried to assist Cytheris back into her litter, but she shooed them away and beckoned to Rupa. With a single sweep of his arms he lifted her up and deposited her among the cushions. While Cytheris rode, we walked beside her. The litter bearers restrained their pace, in deference to my slow, uphill progress.

Like many houses of the rich in Rome, Pompey's old residence presented an unostentatious face to the street. The portico was small and there was little in the way of ornament. But once we passed through the front doorway, I saw how the house had come by its name. The vestibule was enormous—one could have fitted a more humble house inside it—and the display of ramming beaks was dazzling. Some were very crudely fashioned, little more than man-sized lumps of bronze with a pointed end. But some were amazing works of art, fashioned to look like griffins with ferocious beaks or sea monsters with multiple horns. They were fearsome objects, intended to wreak havoc on other ships, but strikingly beautiful. I pondered for a moment the degree of artistry that is lavished on spears and swords and other weapons, to make pleasing to the eye a thing designed to cause death and destruction.

"Hideous, aren't they?" said Cytheris, noting my fascination. "Antony dotes on them like children. He has names for them all! You'd think he had captured them himself. He says that someday he may build a fleet of warships and use the best of these to ornament them."

"His own fleet of ships? Caesar might have something to say about that."

. . . Caesar." She made a wry face.

walked through the house it appeared to me that the
been depleted of some of their furniture and orna-
here were niches without statues and walls where
paintings had been removed. It had the half-vacant feeling of a
house where someone is moving in or moving out.

Completely secluded from the street, the garden at the center of the house was unusually large and splendid, full of fragrant roses in bloom and pebble-strewn pathways decorated
with fountains and statues. Set amid the little arbors of myrtle
and cypress were many dining couches piled with plump cushions. Clearly, the occupants of the house spent a great deal of
time in this space, which could accommodate many guests.

Cytheris led us to a secluded corner, collapsed on a couch
with a sigh, and gestured for Rupa and me to do likewise.
There was no need to call for wine. A slave bearing a tray with
a pitcher and cups appeared before I had time to settle myself.

"So, Gordianus, tell me *everything* about your stay in Egypt.
Are the Alexandrians as mad as ever? Do they still hate Romans? Did you meet Cleopatra?"

"Yes, yes, and yes."

"Really? I keep telling Antony he should invite her here,
since she's in Rome for a visit, but he says it wouldn't do. He'd
be embarrassed to present his concubine to a queen, I suppose,
but Antony says it's because Caesar is still disputing his claim to
this house."

"Yes, I was curious about that. I thought the House of the
Beaks and all its contents were to be sold at a public auction, to
benefit the Treasury."

Cytheris laughed. "Oh yes, there's going to be an auction—

but don't bother to come, because Antony's already given the best things to our friends. Every time we throw a party, no one is allowed to leave without a piece of silver or a rare scroll or whatever else they're up for carrying. Antony tells me, 'I'd rather your actor friends end up with Pompey's spoils than some rich banker friend of Caesar's.' Have a look around, Gordianus, and see what you might like to take home with you. Rupa's big and strong. He could probably carry that statue of Cupid over there."

"You *are* joking?"

"Are you not a friend, Gordianus? You've met Antony, haven't you?"

"A few times, over the years."

"And doesn't he like you? Antony likes everyone. Well, everyone except Cicero. Antony says Caesar should have executed Cicero after Pharsalus, instead of pardoning him. 'Shows just how little my opinion counts with Caesar these days,' as poor Antony says. But you were going to tell me about Alexandria, Gordianus. If you're going to earn that Cupid, you'll have to cough up an amusing anecdote or two."

"I'm afraid my time in Egypt was not particularly amusing."

"But you must have had many adventures. You were there for months, and right in the middle of that nasty little war between Cleopatra and her brother, with Caesar showing up to play kingmaker. You must have had a brush or two with death—or perhaps a dalliance with one of the queen's handmaidens?" Cytheris raised an eyebrow.

"Well, I suppose I could tell you about the narrow escape we had from a rioting mob, when we had to find our way through a secret passage beneath the tomb of Alexander the Great. . . ."

Cytheris sat forward. "Yes! That's exactly the sort of tale I want to hear! Hilarion, bring more wine. We must keep Gordianus's throat well lubricated."

I regaled her with that story, and thought of a few more incidents in Alexandria that might amuse her, and then steered the conversation back to the subject of the house.

"How beautiful it is, here in your garden. And what a splendid house this is. No wonder Pompey loved it. But I still don't quite understand; does Antony own the house or not?"

The wine had relaxed her considerably. She spoke freely. "That depends on whom you ask. When Caesar saw that Antony was dragging his heels, they exchanged some harsh words. Caesar pressed the matter. 'Throw a final party there if you must, then auction the damned place and get out!' But Antony wouldn't budge. He was quite blunt. 'The way I see it,' he told Caesar, 'I deserve this house as much as anyone. I did my part to bring down Pompey, no less than you, and this is my reward!' The two of them have carried on a pissing match about it ever since. Officially, Caesar insists on an auction, but I think he may have finally given up, or maybe he's just too busy arranging his upcoming triumphs to keep pestering Antony. So Antony's plan now is to hold some semblance of an auction— toss out Pompey's moth-eaten togas and get rid of the dented silver—then declare that the auction is done and go on living here. I want to redecorate the whole place, anyway. Pompey's wife had dreadful taste in furniture."

What a long way Cytheris had come, from working as a street dancer in Alexandria to cohabiting with one of the world's most powerful men. An actress and a foreigner, speaking ill of Pompey's wife and brazenly living in Pompey's house, in defiance of Caesar himself!

"But surely," I said, "Antony must realize how this might look to those who accuse Caesar of betraying the common people. They might say Caesar's behaving like Sulla, allowing a henchman to distribute the spoils of war to a small circle of favorites rather than using them for the common good."

"The common people aren't that stupid. Every gossip in Rome knows that Antony is keeping the house against Caesar's wishes."

"But I should think that's even worse, from Caesar's point of view. The people will see that he allows open defiance. A dictator can't afford to tolerate disobedience. It makes him look weak."

Cytheris smiled. "No, it makes Antony look like a spoiled brat, and Caesar like an indulgent parent. Is he not the father of the Roman people now? And isn't Antony his most brilliant protégé, a little stubborn and reckless at times but worth a bit of spoiling in the long run? Never mind that the two of them are hardly speaking at the moment. That will pass."

Was this really what Cytheris believed? Or was she glossing over a deeper anxiety? Had Caesar become a menace to her world?

And what were Antony's feelings? To me, he had always seemed a bluff, brash fellow, completely open about his likes and dislikes, an unlikely candidate for conspiracy. But anyone who had risen as high as Antony undoubtedly possessed the instinct for self-preservation at any cost that characterized such men and women. Just how serious was his falling-out with Caesar?

Even as these questions flashed through my mind, Cytheris

spotted him across the garden, smiled, and waved. Antony came striding over, wearing a tunic that was a bit more brief than many would consider seemly; it certainly showed off his brawny legs. The rumpled yellow garment looked as if he might have slept in it, and there was a long wine stain down the front. He looked and moved as if he might be slightly hungover. He cast a curious, heavy-lidded glance in my direction, then bent forward to plant a kiss on Cytheris's cheek. She whispered something in his ear—my name, no doubt—and he gave me a halting nod of recognition.

"Gordianus . . . yes, of course, Meto's father! By Hercules, how long has it been?"

"Since our paths crossed? Quite some time."

"And yet, they cross again." Was there a glint of suspicion in his bleary eyes? Antony's face combined the poet and the brute, making his expression hard to read. He had a harsh profile, with his dented nose, craggy brows, and jutting chin; but there was something gentle about the curve of his full lips and a soulful quality in his eyes. I would have called him a bit homely, but women seemed to find his looks fascinating.

He grunted and held out his hand. A slave put a cup of wine in it. "Where is Meto nowadays? I suppose he must be back in Rome, for . . ." He was surely going to say "the Gallic Triumph," for Meto had served Caesar in Gaul, as had Antony, but his voice trailed away.

"No, Meto is in Spain, I'm afraid."

Antony grunted. "Scouting the extent of young Pompey's forces, no doubt. You and Meto were both in Alexandria, weren't you, while Caesar was there?"

"Yes," I said.

"But now you're back."

"Can you believe it?" said Cytheris. "We met by chance outside the Temple of Tellus. And this is Rupa, who's Gordianus's son now. Rupa is an old friend from my days in Alexandria."

"Ah, yes," said Antony, "all roads circle back to Alexandria, it seems. I shall have to return there myself someday. But I seem to recall hearing . . . yes, I'm certain someone told us that you were missing in Egypt and presumed to be dead, Gordianus. Now who was it who told us that? I can recall standing in this very garden, and somehow your name came up, and some fellow . . . Cytheris, help me remember."

"Oh, I know!" she said. "It was the Scapegoat."

"Scapegoat?"

"The Massilian. You know—Hieronymus. He's the one who told us the rumor of Gordianus's demise. He seemed quite upset. He hardly ate or drank a thing that night."

"Ah, yes . . . Hieronymus . . ." Antony nodded. "An odd character, that one. I thought he was another of your actor friends, my dear, until you explained where he came from. Claims to be a friend of yours, Gordianus."

"Hieronymus," I whispered. "So you knew him?" *What a stroke of fortune, that they should be the first to mention him, not I.*

"Oh, yes, the Scapegoat is one of Cytheris's pets." Antony did not sound entirely pleased.

"Come, Antony, Hieronymus never fails to make you laugh. Admit it! Such a naughty tongue that fellow has."

"Actually, I'm afraid I have some bad news about Hieronymus." I tried to make my face and voice register the emotion one feels when confronted, suddenly and unexpectedly, with

the task of delivering sad news. I glanced at Rupa. His muteness made him a good companion for this investigation; he
would never blurt out anything to give me away.

"Hieronymus is dead," I said bluntly.

"Oh, no!" Cytheris's surprise seemed genuine. Of course,
she was a trained actress.

Antony was harder to read. He furrowed his forehead and
narrowed his eyes. "When did this happen?"

"Two nights ago."

"Where? How?"

"He was stabbed, in an alley on the Palatine." This was true,
if deliberately vague.

"By whom?" asked Antony. He had once been charged
with keeping order in Rome; news of a crime seemed to pique
his interest.

"I don't know. It happened at night. There seem to have
been no witnesses."

"How distressing!" said Cytheris. "Who would have wanted
to kill poor, harmless Hieronymus? Was it a thief? I thought the
days of robbery and murder in the streets were over."

I shrugged and shook my head.

"We must send a garland for the bier," said Cytheris. "The
body . . . ?"

"Hieronymus lies in my vestibule."

"Yes, beloved, send a garland," said Antony. "I'll let you take
care of that." He squinted and shielded his eyes from the sunlight. "You'll have to excuse me now. Suddenly my head is
pounding. No need to get up, Cytheris. Stay here in the garden
with your guests."

But she was already on her feet, gazing at him sympatheti-cally and reaching out to gently stroke his temples. I saw it was time to go.

"Thank you for the wine and the hospitality. I should return to my house now, in case anyone comes to pay his re-spects to Hieronymus."

Antony nodded. "Let me know if you discover anything else about his death."

"If you wish. I realize how busy you must be, with Caesar's triumphs approaching. I believe the first, to celebrate his con-quest of Gaul, is the day after tomorrow. I know from Meto what an important role you played in that war."

Antony scowled. "Be that as it may, I shall *not* be taking part in the Gallic Triumph."

"No? But you were a cavalry commander at Alesia, weren't you? When Vercingetorix led a night attack against the Roman besiegers, it was only your swift response that saved the situation."

Antony grunted. "Your son told you about that, did he?"

"Caesar himself says so, in those memoirs of his. Surely you'll be riding in a place of honor, the first mounted officer behind Caesar's chariot? And I should think you would be among the privileged few to witness the execution of Vercinge-torix in the Tullianum."

"I'm sure they can manage to strangle the wretched Gaul without me. Do you know, Cytheris, I think we'll hold the auction that day, right here in the street outside the house. Let's see if we can lure any of the revelers away from the parade route to come gawk at Pompey's pinky rings and bedroom slippers."

"But surely Caesar himself will insist that you take part," I said.

"Caesar is a selfish, ungrateful—" Antony caught himself. "For months, after Pharsalus, I was left on my own, in charge of this unruly city, without any instructions from Caesar."

"To be fair, Caesar was trapped inside the royal compound at Alexandria, with no way to send word," I said.

"For part of that time, yes. But once he'd broken out, and defeated Ptolemy, did he hurry back to Rome? No, he took a leisurely trip up the Nile with Cleopatra. While he was sight-seeing and doing who knows what else with the queen, I was facing an angry mob here in Rome, not even knowing whether Caesar was alive or dead! The situation was quite precarious, let me tell you! And Dolabella deliberately made it worse. It wasn't enough that the boy was sleeping with my wife—from whom I am now divorced, thank the gods. Oh, no! Dolabella insisted on promising wholesale debt relief to the poor, saying it was just what Caesar would have wanted. He raised the hopes of the rabble, whipped them to a frenzy, and pitted them against me. Do you know what he called that gathering he organized in the Forum? A demonstration. I called it a riot. If I hadn't ordered my men to restore the peace, there would have been a complete breakdown of order in this city, utter chaos, with looting and murders everywhere. I did what I had to do. But when Caesar finally returned, and heard all the complaints, did he thank me? Did he praise me, reward me? No! He scolded me in public— humiliated me!—and embraced Dolabella, saying what a good, clever boy he was to show such sensitivity to the needs of the poor."

This was just the kind of spontaneous response I was

hoping for. How might I goad him to further candor? I frowned and feigned surprise at his vehemence. I clucked my tongue. "Dolabella, that naughty fellow, sleeping with your Antonia! Presumably he did so behind the back of his own dear wife?"

"The pathetic Tullia, Cicero's whelp? Dolabella divorced her—after finally getting her pregnant. But don't trick me into saying that cursed name again."

"What name?" I ventured.

Antony narrowed his eyes and glared at me, suspicious now that I was deliberately taunting him.

"Ah, you mean Cicero," I said. "I realize that the two of you have been bitter enemies for a long time. But Caesar saw fit to pardon Cicero, did he not?"

Antony gritted his teeth. "Yet another example of Caesar's outrageous—" He caught himself. He pinched the bridge of his nose, grimaced, turned around, and left without another word.

"Oh, dear," said Cytheris. "I'm afraid you set him off."

"I hadn't realized the situation between Antony and Caesar was so delicate."

"It's not as bad as it sounds, truly." She shook her head. "These headaches he's suffering—they worry me. It's not what you think. It isn't the drinking that causes them. It's the pressure he's under."

"A man like Antony must have much on his mind."

"Not enough, these days. That's the problem! These headaches never plague him when he's in the thick of things, having to contain a riot or lead a cavalry charge. It's the idleness afterward that brings them on. It's as if he's still releasing the pressure, after all those months of stress, running the city as

Caesar's surrogate, facing one crisis after another, not knowing if Caesar would ever come back. It took a toll on him. Who can blame Antony if all he wants now is to throw parties and drink and sleep until noon?"

"Who can blame him, indeed?" I said.

V

As Rupa and I departed from the House of the Beaks and made our way back to the Palatine, I experienced a distinct sensation of being followed.

Over the years I have learned to trust this sensation; it never misleads me. Unfortunately, my skill at spotting a stealthy pursuer has diminished over the years, even as my skill at sensing one has grown more acute. At one point, I asked Rupa to lag behind a bit, to see if we could outstalk my stalker, but the ruse didn't work. I arrived home safely but with the disturbing sensation of having been followed and no idea who had done so or why.

I retired to the garden, found a shady spot, and resumed my reading of Hieronymus's reports and his private journal. There was little in them to hint at any danger that Antony might pose to Caesar; mostly Hieronymus listed in great detail who attended the parties at the House of the Beaks; what they wore, ate, and drank; and what they gossiped about. After my single interview with them, I could have done a better job of reporting on Antony's state of mind and speculating on any dangerous motivations that might be attributed to Cytheris.

Hieronymus had uncovered something dangerous enough to get himself killed. It would appear he harbored no particular suspicions of Antony, and yet that very fact raised an alarm. How had Hieronymus put it? "The menace to Caesar will come at a time and from a direction we did not anticipate." To judge by his reports, Hieronymus had not anticipated any menace from Antony and Cytheris—or had he grown suspicious only when it was too late to save himself?

I scribbled a few of my own notes toward assembling a report to Calpurnia, then skimmed more of the material. Which of Hieronymus's paths should I retrace next?

I decided to talk to Vercingetorix as soon as possible. In two days, the man would be dead.

Since his defeat and capture at Alesia six years ago, the former leader of the Gauls had been kept a prisoner. Had the civil war not intervened, Caesar would long ago have staged his Gallic Triumph, and Vercingetorix would be dead. Thus it had been since the earliest days of the Republic: when a victorious Roman general celebrates a triumph, his most prominent captives are paraded in fetters; and at the conclusion of the procession, they are taken to the dungeon chamber called the Tullianum and strangled to death, to the delight of the gods and the glory of Rome.

Now the time had come for Caesar's triumph, and for Vercingetorix to face his destiny.

It was hard to see how the captured leader of the Gauls could pose any threat to Caesar—surely he was kept under strict guard—yet Calpurnia had arranged for Hieronymus to see him, so she must have considered him a possible menace. Looking through Hieronymus's notes on their single meeting, I saw references to the Gaul's appearance and state of mind, but the most important question was not addressed: Had Vercingetorix been allowed any contact at all with friends and family? If he had been kept in complete seclusion, as I suspected, then he could not be plotting against Caesar, nor have any knowledge of a plot. On the other hand, even during the most controlled visits from the outside he might have exchanged information in code or might simply have given inspiration to his visitors by a show of fortitude. Caesar had done his best to undermine any remaining Gallic resistance, partly by rewarding those who cooperated, but there must be many Gauls who hated him fiercely and wished him dead.

Hieronymus had not remarked on the question of outside contacts with Vercingetorix, perhaps because Calpurnia already had that information. Mostly he ruminated on the special attributes he possessed for winning the captive's trust:

The two of us have something in common, after all. As the Scapegoat in Massilia, impending doom hung over me every day, every hour. I tasted the torment that V. faces as his final day draws near. Because I escaped the Fates, he may deduce that I received special dispensation from the gods. For a man in his circumstances, it will be natural to draw close to me, hoping that some of that favor might rub off on him.

"Hieronymus, Hieronymus!" I whispered, shaking my head. "You cheated the Fates for a time, but no man escapes them forever. The doomed Gaul still lives, while you lie on a bier in my vestibule. Did he have anything to do with your death?"

"Papa?"

Diana stepped into the garden. The sunlight sparkled and glimmered upon her dark hair. I was struck anew by her beauty—inherited entirely from her mother—but her face was grave.

"What is it, daughter?"

"There's a visitor who's come to pay respects to Hieronymus."

"So soon?" Word of his death had already begun to spread, then, faster than I expected. The official entry had been registered by the undertakers, of course, and there are gossip vultures who follow those lists daily. Or had someone in Calpurnia's household spread the news? "Who is it?" I asked.

"Fulvia. She says she'd like to speak to you."

"Of course. Would you show her to the garden yourself, Diana? Have the boys bring refreshment."

My association with Fulvia went back many years. It was safe to say that she was the most ambitious woman in Rome. But what had she gained by her ambitions except a widow's garments? First she married the rabble-rouser Clodius, whose mobs terrorized the city; but when Clodius was murdered on the Appian Way, Fulvia, as a woman, could do nothing with the tremendous political power her husband had harnessed. Then she married Curio, one of Caesar's most promising young lieutenants. When the civil war began, Curio captured Sicily and pressed on to Africa—where King Juba of Numidia made Fulvia a widow again and took Curio's head for a trophy. When I last saw her, before my departure for Alexandria, she was still beautiful, but bitter and brooding, lacking the one thing a woman in Rome needed to exercise power: an equally ambitious husband. In Alexandria, a woman like Cleopatra may exercise power alone, but Romans are not Egyptians. We may revert to having a king, but we have never submitted to the rule of a queen.

So far as I had seen, Fulvia did not figure in any of Hieronymus's reports to Calpurnia. Her ambitions thwarted, she had become irrelevant. But if Hieronymus had not visited her, why was she coming to pay her respects? Even as I recalled Hieronymus's reference to a threat "from a direction we did not anticipate," Fulvia stepped into my garden.

Appropriately for such a visit, she was dressed in a dark stola, with a black mantle over her head. But she had been similarly dressed when I last saw her, in mourning for Curio. Perhaps she had never put off her widow's garments. She was now in her late thirties; her face was beginning to show the strain and suffering she had endured over the years, but the fire in her eyes had not gone out.

Fulvia spoke first, as if she were the hostess and I the guest. That was like her, to take the initiative. "It's good to see you, Gordianus, even if the occasion is a sad one. I had heard—"

"Yes, yes, I know—that I was dead."

She smiled faintly and nodded.

"But you must have known that wasn't the truth, Fulvia. Surely you knew the moment I arrived back in Rome, from your famous network of all-seeing, all-hearing spies. I seem to recall, at our last meeting, that you boasted to me that nothing of importance could occur in Rome without your knowledge."

"Perhaps your return to Rome was not of sufficient importance."

I winced. Was this sarcasm? Her expression indicated that she was simply stating a fact.

"You came here to pay respects to Hieronymus?"

"Yes."

"Did you know him well?"

She hesitated an instant too long, and chose not to answer.

"You didn't know Hieronymus at all, did you, Fulvia?"

She hesitated again. "I never met him. I never spoke to him."

"But you knew *of* Hieronymus—who he was, where he went, what he was up to?"

"Perhaps."

"And somehow you knew about his death, ahead of nearly everyone in Rome, and of the presence of his body in this house. How could that be? I wonder. And why should you care enough about this stranger Hieronymus to come pay your respects?"

She drew back her shoulders and stood rigid for a moment, then released her tension with a short laugh. "It's a good thing I have nothing to hide from you, Gordianus. With only two eyes and two ears, you perceive all. What a gift you possess! Very well: I know who Hieronymus was, because I have men who watch the House of the Beaks and report back to me on everyone who comes and goes—including your old friend, the so-called Scapegoat."

"And your men were watching this morning, weren't they? They saw me arrive, with Cytheris, and at least one of them tracked me when I left. I *knew* someone was following me! The fellow must be very good. Try as I might, I couldn't trick him into revealing himself."

"That's quite a compliment, coming from Gordianus the Finder. He'll be flattered."

"And when your spy saw the cypress wreath on my door, he knew there must be a dead body in my vestibule."

"The death of Hieronymus is a matter of public record now. My man had merely to check the registry."

"And that gave you the pretext for this visit."

"Yes. But I see now that I needn't have bothered with a pretext. I should simply have come to you . . . as a friend."

This was exaggerating our relationship, but I let it pass. "And as a friend, what would you ask of me, Fulvia?"

"Why did you visit Antony's house today? Who's employing you to spy on him?"

My response was equally blunt. "Do your men merely watch the comings and goings at the House of the Beaks, or does someone follow Cytheris wherever she goes?"

Fulvia did not answer.

"Because, if one of your men *was* following Cytheris, he could tell you that she met me quite by chance outside the Temple of Tellus and invited me on the spot to come home with her."

"I don't believe it. If you met Cytheris in the street, it didn't happen by chance but because you wanted it to happen. You were at Antony's house today because you meant to be there, Gordianus. And that would happen only because someone has hired you to investigate Antony. Either that or you're acting entirely on your own—in which case you must suspect that Antony had something to do with your friend's death."

"Couldn't it simply be that I wished to inform Antony and Cytheris of Hieronymus's demise, knowing that he had been a guest in their home in recent months?"

She wrinkled her brow. "Perhaps." Her shoulders slumped. She was suddenly tired of sparring with me. I realized she was standing in the hot sunlight.

"Please sit, Fulvia, here beside me in the shade. There should be some wine on its way. I wonder where those useless boys have got to. . . ."

As if they had been lurking out of sight, waiting to be prompted, Mopsus and Androcles appeared at once, one bearing a silver pitcher and the other two cups. At least they had the good sense to bring the best vessels. Hopefully they also had brought the best vintage.

At the sight of them, Fulvia expressed surprise, then smiled. "My, how they've grown! They're almost a big as my son, Publius."

I had almost forgotten that the boys had once belonged to Fulvia; I acquired them from her in the course of my investigation into the murder of her first husband. I saw now why the boys had hung back; they were still in awe of their former mistress, and why not? I was a little in awe of Fulvia myself. Androcles approached her with downcast eyes and offered her a cup. Mopsus was equally shy when he poured from the pitcher.

"They've served me very well," I said. "They went to Egypt with me, and kept me company in Alexandria. You may go now, boys."

After daring to raise their eyes to catch a glimpse of Fulvia's face, the two of them withdrew from the garden.

The wine was very good, a Mamertine vintage that was almost as smooth and delicate as a fine Falernian. I thought Fulvia might comment on it, but she said nothing. No doubt she took such quality for granted.

"As I see it, Fulvia, the question is not why I was at Antony's house this morning. The question is, why are you keeping such a close watch on him?"

She studied me over the rim of her cup. "Was this your first contact with Antony and Cytheris since your return?"

"Yes."

"And what did you make of their little household?"

"They seem very comfortable with each other."

"Were they . . . amorous?"

I smiled. "Not in my presence. If you're asking if they carried on like sex-mad lovers, the answer is no. To be candid, Antony seemed a bit hungover. I think he may have been asleep when I arrived. But Cytheris was lively enough."

"Cytheris!" Fulvia spoke the name with disdain. "Well, at least she's achieved her goal of getting him to divorce Antonia."

"I think Antonia may have done her part to make that happen, carrying on with Dolabella."

"Indeed. Well, their marriage is over, and that's what matters. Now it's just a matter of prying him away from that dreadful actress."

"You intend to marry Antony?"

"Yes."

"But does *he* intend to marry *you*?"

"We've discussed the matter at some length." She spoke as if they were negotiating a business partnership or planning a military expedition. "We agree on the advantages of such a marriage. We also agree on our . . . compatibility . . . in certain other areas. I am in every way woman enough to satisfy a man like Antony." She said this defiantly, as there might be some doubt. "I was a passionate wife to Clodius, and to Curio, as well a good partner. Why Antony thinks he must hold on to that creature, I can't understand. He actually proposes that I should agree to some formal arrangement for keeping her, letting her live in one of Antony's houses and draw an income, as if she were a second wife. When my mother heard that . . . well, the repercussions were not pleasant for anyone."

I remembered the gaunt, white-haired Sempronia, who was every bit as ambitious as her daughter but less charming.

"As for those who say I brought ill fortune to my previous husbands, and would bring ill fortune to Antony as well—"

"Who says such a thing?"

"Cytheris, of course. But it's a lie and a slander to suggest that I carry a curse. Given the times we live in, is it any wonder that two men who dared to raise themselves above the pack were struck down?"

I tended to agree with Fulvia, but it seemed prudent to change the subject. "What about Antony's falling-out with Caesar?" I said.

"The situation is ridiculous! And totally unnecessary. Cytheris is behind it, of course. She's the one who talked him into settling in at the House of the Beaks. She's made it their little love nest, where they can entertain her dubious circle of foreign dancers and acrobats."

"Dubious foreigners . . . like my friend Hieronymus?" I said.

"I'm sure they welcomed him into their circle because he had a certain freakish appeal—the Scapegoat who cheated death."

"On the contrary, Hieronymus could be quite witty and entertaining."

"Of course. I didn't mean to speak ill of your friend, Gordianus. But a woman like Cytheris is not to be trusted. She cares only for her own advancement. Everyone else is merely a stepping-stone, including Antony."

It occurred to me that Fulvia might be describing herself. "So your marriage to Antony . . . ?"

"Our plans have not been finalized. He won't be pinned down. He's behaving like an irresponsible boy, rejecting the sensible advice of the two people who care most about his career and can do most to help him, Caesar and myself. He's spurning us to carry on with that—that Alexandrian whore!"

"Perhaps Antony is not such a good match for you, after all. If he lacks sound judgment . . ."

"No. He's come this far, and he'll go much, much farther. He's the man I should have married in the first place. We both know that; we've known it for years. But circumstances simply never fell out that way. I married Clodius, and he married that first wife of his, that nobody. . . . I can't even remember her name. Then the Fates led us both to a second marriage but not to each other—I to Curio, Antony to Antonia—and our mutual destiny was postponed . . . until now. I am a widow again; Antony is divorced. Now is the time. It will happen. It *must* happen."

I shrugged. "The gods have a habit of thwarting even our most reasonable expectations."

"No! Not this time. It will happen because I will make it happen. Antony *will* achieve the destiny he deserves . . . and so will I."

I sighed. I feared it would not be the gods who denied Fulvia her desire but another mortal: Antony. There is nothing so unsure as the plans we make that rely on the sensible behavior of another human being.

"I gather, Fulvia, that you intend to 'save' Antony—from Cytheris, from himself. But what if Antony refuses to be saved?"

Her face lengthened. "Was that your impression, from your visit to the House of the Beaks?"

"Not exactly. I was there to talk about Hieronymus, not Antony." This was not entirely true, but the fact was that I had nothing useful to tell her about Antony's future plans, at least regarding the women in his life. "I do know that he won't be taking part in the Gallic Triumph, but I'm not sure if that was Caesar's decision or Antony's."

She shook her head. "He should be in the very front line, just behind Caesar. The whole city should see him and remember the part he played in conquering the Gauls. He offended many people when he was in charge of the city, but if they could be reminded of his sacrifice, his bravery, his loyalty—what a squandered opportunity! This rift with Caesar . . . it must be ended, one way or another!" The light behind her eyes suddenly flared, like flames fanned by a hot wind.

She closed her eyes, as if to hide their intensity from me. "At least I shall be able to take some satisfaction from the African Triumph, eight days from now. King Juba claimed my husband's head as a trophy; now Juba is dead, his kingdom belongs to Rome, and Caesar shall parade Juba's little son as a captive."

She abruptly rose and made ready to go, adjusting her mantle and gathering the folds of her stola. "As always, Gordianus, your candor is greatly refreshing. This city is full of flatterers and outright liars! Sometimes I think you must be exactly what that monster Cicero called you, 'the most honest man in Rome.' "

I smiled. "That was a rare compliment from Cicero, and I'm not sure he'd repeat it nowadays." I spoke carefully; if anyone hated Cicero even more than Antony did, it was Fulvia. "I haven't seen Cicero in a very long time."

"Not since you returned from Egypt?"

"No."

"I see. Then you don't know what the old goat is up to?"

"No." I raised an eyebrow.

She laughed shrilly. "It's too delicious! But I don't think I'll tell you. I'll let you find out for yourself. You won't believe it— what a fool that old scoundrel Cicero has made of himself."

I followed her out of the garden and into the vestibule. She paused for a moment to gaze at the body of Hieronymus.

"I truly am sorry about your friend," she whispered, and then stepped outside, where a retinue with a litter awaited her in the street.

I watched her depart. Hieronymus had jotted no notes about Fulvia in his reports or his journal, but he had also spoken of a menace from an unexpected quarter. It was Fulvia's ambition that Antony must be made to fulfill his destiny, at any cost. Before that could happen, his rift with Caesar must be ended— "one way or another," as Fulvia had stressed.

V I

After Fulvia's departure, I sent a message to Calpurnia, telling her I wanted to be admitted to visit Vercingetorix in his cell the next day. She sent a message back to me before sunset. Apparently she had been able to arrange my visit at a moment's notice—and without Caesar's knowledge, since she cautioned me to tell no one, lest he learn of it. The extent of her authority continued to surprise me.

It occurred to me that Calpurnia was the woman Fulvia wished to become. How could that happen, as long as Caesar was alive?

That night at dinner with the family, I recounted some of my conversation with Antony and Cytheris but kept to myself anything that might embarrass (or simply displease) Calpurnia should it spread beyond my house. It was not that I doubted the discretion of my loved ones, but in my experience, words once uttered have a way of taking flight, as if acting on their own volition. I was struck again at Rupa's suitability to act as my companion and bodyguard. He heard all but could repeat nothing.

My body was weary. I would have slept with the sun, but restless thoughts kept me awake. The prospect of meeting the leader of the Gauls on the last full day of his life filled me with trepidation. The interview would almost certainly be unpleasant, in one way or another, and I found myself wishing I could avoid it altogether.

Unable to sleep, I left my bed. The night was warm. Crickets thrummed in the garden. I stepped into my library, lit a lamp, and did my best to peruse the difficult handwriting of Hieronymus. Previously, I had intentionally skipped over the entries having to do with Cicero, assigning them a low priority. For one thing, I had no wish to read about Cicero—if Hieronymus had thought *me* a windbag, what in Hades had he made of Cicero?—and for another, it seemed to me that Cicero was the unlikeliest of assassins. But Fulvia's reference to him had piqued my curiosity.

Over the years, my relations with the great lion of the Roman law courts had been mixed. Over thirty years ago, I ferreted out the truth for Cicero when he took on his first major case, defending a man accused of parricide in the gloomy days when Sulla's shadow covered Rome. I nearly got myself killed more than once in the course of that investigation, and Cicero had faced considerable danger as well, daring to take on one of the dictator's most dangerous henchmen in the court. His surprising success had redounded to the enduring benefit of us both.

But Cicero's meteoric rise in the political arena had revealed a darker side of his character. He was perfectly willing to sacrifice the reputations and even the lives of his rivals to attain success, though he was careful to do so by using (some would say twisting) the law. As he grew in fame and power, I hardened my heart toward Cicero. But when men like Caesar and Pompey elbowed him off the political stage, their terrifying ruthlessness made Cicero, even at his worst, look benevolent. My feelings about him had softened, but I had never quite patched up the strained relations between us.

Could Cicero be the menace to Caesar?

When civil war loomed, Cicero had wavered between Caesar and Pompey for as long as he possibly could, and would have avoided choosing either side had such an option been possible. Ultimately he sided with Pompey and the old establishment and fought against Caesar. After a resounding victory, Caesar saw fit to pardon Cicero. Since then, the great orator, whatever his true feelings about the new dictator, had kept his mouth shut.

I could no more easily picture Cicero as a conspirator than I could picture Antony, for different reasons. If Antony was too brash and outspoken, Cicero was too cautious and indecisive. And, to his credit, he was a true defender of the republican virtues of debate, compromise, and consensus; a man like Cicero would pursue every possible legal channel, no matter how tortuous or tenuous, rather than resort to violence. But had not Caesar's victory closed all political and legal avenues of challenge to his authority? What was a true republican to do when faced with the prospect of a dictator for life?

These were strange days. If Calpurnia could fall under the spell of a haruspex, if Antony the man of action could wile away his days in a drunken stupor, if an Alexandrian dancer could take up residence in Pompey's house, could Cicero become a murderous conspirator?

What had he been up to in my absence and since my return to Rome? What had Fulvia been hinting at? Having kept so completely to myself, I truly had no idea. When I read the details in Hieronymus's report, my jaw dropped.

Could it be true? Marcus Tullius Cicero, the most pious advocate in Rome (now that Cato was dead), the defender of staid virtue and old-fashioned family values, had divorced his wife of more than thirty years and married his ward, a girl named Publilia—who was only fifteen!

Strange days, indeed! I laughed out loud, imagining Cicero married to a teenager. This I would have to see with my own eyes.

Laughter released the tension in me. Suddenly I was very sleepy. I extinguished the lamp and stumbled to bed, where Bethesda huffed and sighed and spooned her body to accommodate me beneath the thin coverlet.

The first Roman prison, called the Carcer and located at the foot of the Capitoline Hill above the Forum, was built hundreds of years ago by Ancus Marcius, fourth king of Rome. According to legend, it was the sixth king, Servius Tullius, who excavated a subterranean cell in the Carcer, which forever after bore his name: the Tullianum.

This dreadful word evoked dankness; darkness; an inescapable pit; a place of hopeless, helpless waiting for death. Yet it was also a word that politicians and military men uttered with pride, for the Tullianum had been the final destination of many of Rome's fiercest enemies over the centuries, where they met their end at the hands of a Roman executioner.

It had been the practice, begun by the kings, to parade their captives in a triumphal procession, stripped of all insignia and symbols of worldly status—sometimes stripped naked entirely—the better to demonstrate the utter humiliation of their defeat and the contempt of their conquerors. After being paraded for the amusement of the Roman populace, less important captives were destined for slavery. The more important were strangled in the Tullianum. Afterward, their bodies were thrown down a flight of steep steps to the Forum, so that the crowd could view their corpses.

As I made my way with Rupa across the Forum, heading for the Tullianum, all around us we saw preparations for the Gallic Triumph to be held the next day. Along the parade route, reviewing stands with awnings were being erected to accommodate important personages, and areas where vendors usually hawked their wares were already being cleared to make room for the anticipated crowds. From atop the Capitoline Hill I could hear the echo of workers shouting amid a din of hammering and creaking wood; a bronze statue of Caesar had been installed across from the Temple of Jupiter, and the scaffolding around it was being removed for its official unveiling the next day.

At the western end of the Forum, with the steep slope of the Capitoline looming above us, we came to a flight of steps carved out of the stone. Two guards stood at the foot of the steps. I produced the pass I had received from Calpurnia—a small wooden disk with the seal of her ring impressed in red wax—and they let us pass without speaking a word.

The narrow steps ascended steeply. Behind us, the Forum was a jumble of columns, rooftops, and public squares. At some distance to the northeast, in a newly developed area adjacent to the Forum, I could see the glittering, solid marble Temple of Venus erected by Caesar in honor of his divine ancestress and the patroness of his victories. The temple had just been completed; it faced a vast open square surrounded by a colonnaded portico that was still under construction, with the pedestal in place for a monumental equestrian statue of Caesar. The Temple of Venus was to be dedicated on the last day of Caesar's four triumphs, providing a divine climax to the celebrations of his earthly conquests.

Such lofty thoughts fled when we came to the heavily guarded entrance to the Carcer. Again, the guards looked at my pass from Calpurnia and said nothing before admitting me. Rupa was made to wait outside. The heavy bronze doors swung open. I stepped into the Carcer, and the doors clanged shut behind me.

The chamber, perhaps twenty paces in diameter, had stone walls and a vaulted stone roof. The only natural light and ventilation came from a few small windows high in the wall facing the Forum, which were crisscrossed with iron bars. The place stank of human excrement and urine, as well as the odor of putrefaction; perhaps there were dead rats trapped in the walls. Even on a warm day such as this, the place was dank and chilly.

The warder, a grizzled bull of a man, insisted on seeing my pass again. He scowled at the pass, then at me. "Shouldn't be doing this," he muttered. "If the dictator finds out . . ."

"He won't find out from me," I said. "And I presume the dictator's wife has paid you quite well enough to keep your mouth shut."

He grunted. "I can hold my tongue. No one will know you were here—as long as you don't do anything stupid."

"Like try to help the prisoner escape? I'm sure that's impossible."

"Others have tried. And failed." He smiled grimly. "But I was thinking more along the lines of helping him escape his fate."

"By dying, you mean? Before Caesar has the chance to execute him?"

"Exactly. In this case, a dead Gaul is a useless Gaul. You wouldn't try to pull a trick like that, would you?"

"You've seen the seal I carry. What more do you want?"

"Your word as a Roman."

"As a Roman who sneaks behind Caesar's back and consorts with others who do the same?"

"Loyalty to Caesar isn't necessarily the same as loyalty to Rome. You don't have to be Caesar's lackey to have a sense of honor as a Roman."

I raised an eyebrow. "Who would have guessed? A Pompeian is in charge of the Tullianum."

"Hardly! I don't shed tears for losers. Couldn't do this job, if I did. Just swear by your ancestors that you're not up to something."

"Very well. By all the Gordianii who came before me, I swear that I have no intention either to harm or to help Vercingetorix."

"Good enough. And don't get yourself killed! I wouldn't be able to explain that either."

"Killed? Isn't the prisoner chained?"

The warder lowered his voice. "Druid magic! They say he can cast the evil eye. I never look him in the face. I put a bag over his head whenever I have to go down there and slosh his feces down the drain hole."

With that pleasant image in my mind, I sat on a wooden plank attached to a thick, padded rope; it was like a crudely made swing that a boy might hang from a tree branch. The warder handed me a small bronze lamp with a single wick, and then, using a winch, he slowly lowered me though a hole in the floor. This was the only entrance to the Tullianum.

As my head passed below the rim of the hole, I descended into a world that was darker, danker, and even more foul smelling than the room above. An odor of mold, sweat, and urine filled my nostrils. The dim lamplight faded to darkness before it could reach the surrounding walls. Below me, as I slowly descended, I heard the scurrying of rats. I looked down. I couldn't see the floor. For a moment I almost panicked; then I caught a glimmer of reflected lamplight on the glistening wet stone floor that drew nearer and nearer until my feet made contact.

"All steady?" the warder called down from above. "No, don't look up at the hole! You'll get vertigo. Besides, the light will blind you. Close your eyes for a bit. Let them adjust."

Closing my eyes was the last thing I intended to do in that place. I stepped away from the rope, holding it to steady myself, and raised the lamp so as to illuminate the chamber without dazzling my eyes. Slowly I began to perceive the dimensions of the place. It seemed larger than the chamber above, but perhaps that was an illusion of the darkness.

Huddled against a wall, I saw a human figure. The lamplight reflected dully off the chains binding his wrists and ankles. He wore a filthy, ragged tunic. His hair and beard were long and tangled. When he turned his face toward me, the lamplight flashed in his eyes.

So this was Vercingetorix, leader of the Gauls, the man who

had accomplished the almost impossible task of unifying the fiercely independent tribes under a single command. He had very nearly succeeded in throwing off the Roman yoke, but Caesar's tactical genius and sheer good luck defeated him in the end. Caesar's utter ruthlessness had also played a part in his victory. Even my son Meto, who loved Caesar, was haunted by the cruelties inflicted on the Gauls—villages burned, women and children raped and enslaved, old men hacked to death. During the revolt of Vercingetorix, Caesar laid siege to the city of Avaricum and took no prisoners; the entire population—forty thousand men, women, and children—were massacred. Caesar boasted of this atrocity in his memoirs.

The last stand of the Gauls had been at the fortress of Alesia. Vercingetorix believed he could hold the position until reinforcements arrived, then destroy the Roman legions with the combined armies of the Gauls. But the reinforcements were insufficient, and the Roman choke hold on the fortress proved impenetrable; the starving survivors were ultimately forced to surrender. A Roman commander would have killed himself, but Vercingetorix rode out from Alesia and surrendered to Caesar. If he thought that Caesar would treat him with honor and respect, he had been mistaken.

Vercingetorix must still be a young man—Meto told me the Gaul was only a teenager when he began his campaign to unify his people—but I would never have guessed it from the broken figure huddled against the wall, the gaunt face sharply shadowed by the lamplight, or the haunted eyes that flashed like shards of obsidian.

"Is this the day?" he whispered hoarsely. His Latin had a strong Gallic accent.

"No. Not yet," I said.

He pressed himself against the wall, as if he wished to disappear into the stone.

"I'm not here to harm you," I said.

"Liar! Why else are you here?"

If he could see my face, I thought, he might be reassured. I held the lamp before me. The light shone into my eyes. He could see me, but I could no longer see him in the darkness.

His breathing quickened. The chains rattled. When I flinched and stepped back, he barked out a noise that must have been a laugh.

"*You* fear *me,* Roman? That's rich! After all the beatings you've given me . . ."

"I'm not here to beat you. I only want to talk."

"Talk about what?"

"I'm a friend of a man who came to visit you not too long ago."

"A visitor? No one visits me."

"He was a Massilian. His name was Hieronymus."

"Ah!" I heard him breathe in the darkness. There was a rattle in his throat, as if phlegm had settled in his lungs. "The Scapegoat, you mean. I wasn't sure if he existed or not. I thought perhaps I only dreamed about him."

"Hieronymus was real. He was my friend."

"Excuse my poor Latin, Roman, but I think you're speaking in a past tense."

"Yes. Hieronymus is dead."

More breathing in the darkness. More rattling from his throat. Then an explosion of laughter. He muttered something in his native tongue.

I shook my head. "What are you saying?"

"The man who was famous for cheating death is dead. And I, Vercingetorix, am still alive. At least I think I am. For all I know, this is the Roman underworld. And yet I don't remember dying. . . ."

Unable to see his expression or gauge the tone of the words cloaked by his thick accent, I couldn't tell whether he was serious or not. I felt an urge to see his face, but I kept the lamp before me, illuminating myself. As long as he could see me and look into my eyes, he might keep speaking.

"I think I like that idea—that I'm already dead," he said. "That means the ordeal is over. The thing I dreaded so much, for so long—it's behind me now. Yes, that's good. And for all I know, you're the Roman god of the dead, here to welcome me. Pluto is the name, I think. Isn't that right?"

The darkness grew thick around me. The dank air chilled my lungs. "Yes," I whispered. "Pluto . . . is the name."

"So, Hieronymus the Scapegoat arrived in Hades ahead of me. Too bad for him! He seemed to be having such a good time, being alive in the world. When he visited, I made him tell me all about the parties he went to. He described the houses of the rich and powerful, the sweet-smelling gardens, the banquets with food of every sort piled high. Oh, yes, the food!" In the darkness, I heard his stomach grumble.

"Can this be right?" he whispered. "Does a dead man's empty belly groan in Hades?"

I couldn't tell if he was joking, mad, or simply spinning a fantasy, as men do in unbearable circumstances. I only knew that he was speaking freely, which was what I wanted.

"Yes, Hieronymus loved life," I said.

"How did he die?"

"He was stabbed."

"Ha! By a jealous husband? Or some great warrior he insulted?"

"I honestly don't know. You say he was your only visitor?"

"Yes."

"No one else has come to see you?"

"No one except the warders."

"But you weren't always kept in the Tullianum, were you?" Usually the prison was only for those awaiting imminent judgment or execution.

"No. For a long time—months and months, years and years—I was kept here and there, in cages and boxes and holes in the ground. Moved from one of Caesar's estates to another, I presume, to keep my followers from knowing my whereabouts."

The siege of Alesia had ended more than six years ago. With that victory, Rome's conquest of Gaul was complete. Normally, Caesar would have returned to Rome to celebrate his triumph over the Gauls as soon as events allowed, certainly within a year or two; but his quarrel with the Senate and the eventual civil war had intervened. Vercingetorix should have been executed years ago. Instead he had been kept in captivity all this time, living a nonlife while awaiting a terrible death. No wonder he seemed more a ghost than a man.

"How did they treat you, in those cages and holes?"

"Not badly. No, not badly at all. I was fed well enough. Kept reasonably clean. Beaten only when I tried to escape or made other trouble. They needed to keep me alive, you see, for

Caesar's triumph. You can't humiliate a dead man by parading him through the Forum. You can't inflict suffering on a corpse. No, they needed to keep me alive, indefinitely, so they never starved me and they never beat me beyond my endurance. They made sure I had no way to kill myself. They even sent a physician once or twice, when I was ill.

"Then everything changed. The time grew near. They brought me to Rome. I knew, when they lowered me into this pit, that I would never come out again until the day of my death. They began to starve me. They beat me, for no reason. They tortured me. They made me sleep in my own waste. For Caesar's triumph, they didn't want a strong, proud Gaul walking upright through the Forum. They wanted a broken man, a cringing, pathetic creature covered in filth, a laughingstock, an object of ridicule, something for children to jeer at and old men to spit on."

He suddenly lurched forward, pulling his shackles taut. I gave a start and almost dropped the lamp. "Tell me I'm right!" he cried. "Tell me you're Pluto and the ordeal is already over! They say the dead forget their troubles when they cross to the underworld and drink from the river Lethe. Have I drunk from the river? Have I forgotten the day of my death?"

My heart pounded in my chest. My hand shook, causing the lamplight to flicker. "Who knows what you've forgotten? Tell me what you *remember*, Vercingetorix. Tell me . . . about the plot to kill Caesar."

He fell silent. Was he puzzled or angry or too shrewd to answer? At last he spoke. "What are you talking about?"

"Surely your people won't let your death go unavenged.

Are the Gauls not bitter? Are they not proud? Can they allow the great Vercingetorix to die and do nothing to avenge his death?"

Again, there was silence; it went on so long that I became unnerved, imagining that he had slipped from his chains somehow and was drawing toward me. I braced myself and stood upright, letting the lamp's steady glow illuminate my face.

"I have no people," he finally said. "The best of the Gauls died at Alesia. The survivors were sold into slavery. The traitors who sided with Caesar received their reward." This was true; all over Gaul, Caesar had placed the native chieftains who had supported him in positions of authority over the rest. Some he had even elevated to the Roman Senate.

"But the Gauls have other ways to inflict harm on a man," I whispered. "Druid magic! How you must long for Caesar's death. Have you placed a curse on him?"

He laughed bitterly. "If the Druids possessed true magic, would Gaul be a Roman province? There's nothing I can do to cause Caesar's death. But he'll die soon enough."

"How do you know that?"

"Every man dies, even Caesar. If not this year, then the next, or the year after. Vercingetorix dies. Caesar dies. The same fate awaits us all. Strange, that I should have to remind Pluto of that fact."

He began to weep. I moved the lamp so that I could see him. He shivered and trembled. He hid his face in his hands. Insects and glistening slugs crept amid the strands of his matted, filthy hair. A rat skittered between us. My stomach churned with nausea.

I tugged on the rope and called to the warder above. The

winch gave a squeal. The rope pulled taut. I sat on the wooden plank and began to rise slowly. I turned my face up toward the opening, longing for light, desperate to fill my lungs with fresh, clean air.

VII

I hurried across the Forum with Rupa beside me, thankful for the simple freedom to gaze at the blue sky above and to run my fingertips over the smooth, sun-heated stone wall of a temple. From a food vendor near the Temple of Castor and Pollux I paused to buy a little pastry stuffed with fig paste and slathered with fish-pickle sauce. Rupa, who had never acquired a taste for Roman garum, waved his hand to signal that he wanted a pastry with fig paste only.

Together, eating as we walked, we passed the House of the Vestals and trudged up the Ramp to the crest of the Palatine. At the top, we turned down the winding lane that would take us to the house of Cicero, not far from my own.

As we rounded the crest of the hill, I had a clear view of the top of the Capitoline Hill across the way. The Temple of Jupiter, rebuilt after its destruction by fire during the days of Sulla, was as imposing as ever. In a prominent place before the temple, obscured by a canopy of sailcloth pending its unveiling, stood the bronze statue that would be dedicated the next day.

What pose had Caesar struck for his grand image on the Capitoline? That of a mortal supplicant, a man more than other men but still obeisant to the king of the gods? Or something more grand, the upright, unbowed image of a descendant of Venus, a demigod and junior partner to the Olympians?

We arrived at Cicero's door. Rupa gave a polite knock with his foot. To the slave who perused us through the peephole I stated my name and the desire to see his master on personal business. A few moments later, we were admitted to the vestibule, then conducted down a hallway to Cicero's library.

He was balder and fatter than I remembered. He rose from his chair, laid aside the scroll he had been reading, and gave me a beaming smile.

"Gordianus! How long has it been? I thought—"

"I know. You thought I was dead." I sighed.

"Why, no. I knew you were back in Rome. I probably knew it the day you arrived. I walk by your house almost every day, you know. And neighbors talk. No, I was going to say, I thought you'd never come to see me."

"I've been keeping to myself."

He nodded. "So have I. A lot of that going around these days. Best to stay at home, with a stout fellow to guard the door. Dare to stick your head up, and you're liable to get it whacked off." He made a vivid gesture, slashing one hand across his throat.

Like the orator he was, he exaggerated. "Caesar isn't Sulla," I said. "I haven't seen the heads of his enemies on spikes down in the Forum."

"No, not yet . . . not yet . . ." His voice trailed off. "But can I offer refreshment to you and . . . your companion?"

"This is Rupa. I adopted him before I left for Egypt. He doesn't speak."

Cicero smiled. "You and your extended family! Isn't this your third adopted son? He's certainly the biggest of the lot. But silent, eh? Well, there's been an addition—and a subtraction—to my own household, as you may already know. But my new family member most certainly speaks—oh, how that girl can speak! Hopefully she'll return from her shopping before you leave, and you can meet her. But what can I offer you? Are you hungry?"

"We just had a bite, actually. Perhaps some liberally watered wine to wash it down?"

Cicero clapped his hands and sent a slave to fetch the refreshment. He cleared away some scrolls that were stacked on chairs and the three of us sat.

"Well, Gordianus, tell me your news, and then I'll tell you mine." From the look on his face, I saw he could hardly wait to talk about his new wife.

"My news is not happy, I'm afraid. While I was away, I think you made the acquaintance of a good friend of mine, Hieronymus of Massilia."

"Ah, yes! I heard the bad news. I sent a message of condolence to your house just this morning. I'd have come myself, but as I said, I don't go out much."

"You know about his death already?"

Cicero nodded. "I send a man every day to check the new entries in the death registry. These days, one must keep abreast, or else fall hopelessly behind. There's nothing more embarrassing than to meet an old friend, or someone I once defended in court, and not to know that the fellow's brother or son or father

is dead. It makes one look uncaring, not to mention unin-
formed. Yes, I was sorry to learn of Hieronymus's death. How
did it happen?"

"He was stabbed, here on the Palatine."

"Stabbed? In the street?"

"More or less."

"But this is terrible! Do we know who did it?"

"Not yet."

"Ha! Caesar claims to have made the city safe again, but
there's more lawlessness than ever. Another reason I hardly budge
from my house. So, Gordianus, are you on the trail of the killer?
Slipping into your old role, playing the Finder to seek justice for
poor Hieronymus? Venturing hither and yon, uncovering scan-
dal and skullduggery and whatnot?"

"Something like that."

"Like the good old days, eh, when we were young, you and
I, when there was a point to seeking out the truth and striving
for justice. Will our grandchildren even know what a republic
was? Or how the law courts operated? If we're to have a king, I
suppose the king will mete out justice. No more juries, eh?
There won't be much use for an old advocate like myself." His
tone was more wistful than bitter.

I nodded sympathetically. "Speaking of Hieronymus, I was
wondering how well you came to know him."

"Oh, I had him here to my house a few times. He greatly
admired my library. He was a very scholarly fellow, you know.
Awfully well-read. And what a memory! I had an old scroll of
Homer that had suffered some water damage—needed to be
patched where a few lines had been lost. Can you believe that
Hieronymus was able to recite the missing lines by heart? He

dictated them to Tiro, and we restored the missing text on the spot. Yes, he was the model of the well-versed Greek, proof that the Massilian academies are every bit as good as they're reputed to be."

I nodded. Would Cicero speak as glowingly if he could read the parts about himself in Hieronymus's journal? Those passages were especially full of pedantic wordplay, as if Hieronymus enjoyed making fun of Cicero by using overwrought rhetoric.

The old satyr seems completely unaware of how ridiculous he looks to everyone except the fellow he sees in the mirror; if he would pause to reflect, he would die of blushing. The little queen with bee-stung lips he calls "my honey" will sting him sooner or later. (Some say he married her for money, not honey.) A bad case of the hives is likely to kill an old satyr like Cicero. . . .

"Publilia!" Cicero abruptly exclaimed, and rose from his chair.

Rupa and I did likewise, for Cicero's young bride had entered the room.

"My honey! I didn't hear you come in." Cicero hurried toward her. He took a plump little arm in one hand and stroked her honey-blond hair with the other. "You flit like a butterfly. You come and go without a sound. Your dainty little feet barely touch the earth!"

Rupa shot me a look and rolled his eyes. I tried not to laugh.

"Publilia, this is Gordianus, an old friend. And this is his son Rupa."

The petite, round-faced girl gave me a polite nod, then turned her attention to Rupa, who, I have noticed, seems to be just the sort of fellow most fifteen-year-old girls enjoy looking at. Publilia perused him openly for a moment, then tittered and averted her eyes. Cicero appeared not to understand the cause of her chagrin, but he delighted in her childish laughter and joined in with a cackle of his own.

"She's a shy thing, really."

"No, I am not!" the girl protested, pulling her arm free. She pouted for a moment, then shot another glance at Rupa and smiled.

"Ah, I think all that shopping has tired out my little honey, hasn't it?" crooned Cicero. "Or is this heat making her cranky? Perhaps you should take a nap, my dear."

"I suppose I could go . . . lie down . . . for a bit." She looked Rupa up and down, and sighed. "Especially if you men are talking about boring old books."

"Actually, we were talking about death and murder," I said.

"Oh!" The girl gave an exaggerated shudder, causing her breasts to quiver. They were surprisingly large for a fifteen-year-old.

"Gordianus, you've frightened her!" protested Cicero. "You should be more careful what you say. Publilia is hardly more than a child."

"Indeed!" I said under my breath.

"Run along, my honey. Have a drink. Cool yourself; call one of the slaves to come fan you. I'll join you a bit later. You can show me that cloth you bought for your new gown."

"Red gossamer from Cos," she said, "so light and gauzy, you can see right through it!"

The lump protruding from Cicero's throat bobbed up and down as he swallowed. He blinked. "Yes, well, run along, my honey."

"Your bride is utterly charming," I said, after Publilia had gone. "Did she bring a large dowry?" In the social circles to which Cicero aspired, this was not a rude question.

"Enormous!" he said. "But that is *not* why I married her."

"Oh, I can believe that," I assured him. "Still, it must have been painful, after so many years together, to end your marriage with Terentia."

Cicero smiled wryly. "I'm a strong man, Gordianus. I survived Sulla. I've survived Caesar—so far. And, by Hercules, I survived thirty years with Terentia!"

"Still, the divorce must have been painful for her, if not for you."

His smile vanished. "Terentia is a rock." The way he said it, the word was not a compliment. "She's indestructible. She'll live to be a hundred, mark my words. Don't worry yourself about Terentia."

If I were to worry, I thought, *it would be about you, Cicero. What do the Etruscans say? "There is no fool like an old fool!"* I bit my tongue.

"I'm happy, don't you see?" Cicero crossed the room with a swagger. I had never seen him so cocky, not even in court, and Cicero orating before a jury could be very cocky indeed. "Despite the dismal state of the world, despite the end of everything I've fought for all my life, about my personal life I have no complaints. In that sphere—after so many reverses, disappointments, outright disasters—at last, everything is going my way. My debts are all paid. Terentia is finally out of my life. And I have a wonderful new bride who adores me. Oh!" His eyebrows lifted. "And at long last, my dear little Tullia is expecting a child. Soon my daughter shall make me a grandfather!"

"Congratulations," I said. "But I heard that her marriage to Dolabella—"

"Is finally over," he said. "And Tullia is well rid of the beast. He caused her nothing but heartbreak. He shall come to a bad end."

Under normal circumstances, a respectable public figure like Cicero would hardly boast that his daughter was about to give birth out of wedlock. But circumstances were no longer normal—not in a world where Calpurnia consulted a sooth-sayer and Cicero was married to a vapid teenager.

In such a world turned utterly askew, could the vacillating, timorous, stay-at-home Cicero pose a genuine threat to Caesar? It occurred to me that his new marriage might be both symp-tom and cause of a major shift in Cicero's behavior. Might the old goat be thinking like a young goat—stamping the ground and getting ready to take a reckless run at Caesar with horns lowered? With a new bride—and a grandchild—to impress, did the husband of Publilia feel sufficiently virile to take a stand as savior of the republic?

And if that were the case, could Cicero have been behind the killing of Hieronymus? When I spoke of the murder, his re-sponse had seemed entirely innocent. But Cicero was an orator—Rome's greatest—and what was an orator but an actor? I had heard him boast of throwing dust in a jury's eyes. Was he throwing dust in my eyes even now?

If I could stay a bit longer, conversing and drawing him out, he might yet let something slip. I nodded to Rupa, who reached into the shoulder bag he carried and pulled out some documents.

"I was wondering, Cicero, if you might take a look at something I found among Hieronymus's private papers."

"A literary work?" Cicero raised an eyebrow. "Was our friend secretly composing a tragedy? An epic poem?"

"No, this is something more in a scientific vein, I think, though I'm not really sure. That's why I want to show it to you. With your vast knowledge, drawn from your wide reading, perhaps you can make sense of it."

Cicero smiled broadly. Did Publilia find it this easy to lead him by flattery?

I handed him the documents. He pursed his lips, squinted, clucked his tongue, and hummed as he perused them. He was stalling, I thought; he could no more decipher the arcane symbols and calculations than could I.

But at last he nodded and slapped the documents with the back of his hand, as if to indicate he had cracked the code. "Well, I can't make it all out—I'm hardly an astronomical expert—but clearly this has something to do with the calendar."

"The Roman calendar?"

"The Roman, yes, but also the calendars of the Greeks and the Egyptians and perhaps of others as well. There are many calendars, Gordianus. Every civilization has come up with its own way of reckoning the passage of time, dividing years into seasons, seasons into months, months into days. It was King Numa who devised the Roman calendar and established the priesthoods to maintain it. Numa was both a holy man and a king. The whole point of his calendar was to make sure that religious rites were remembered and performed on time.

"But as you must know, no one has yet devised a perfect calendar—that is to say, a reckoning of days that works equally well for every year. Irregularities inevitably creep into the process, and no one quite knows why. You'd think the movements of the stars in the heavens would be as precise and predictable as the measurements of a water clock, but it's more complicated than that. Which is why Numa's calendar has become such a mess. For most of my lifetime and yours, it's been at least slightly out of step with the seasons, and nowadays it's worse than ever."

"But aren't there priests who fix the calendar as we go along?" I said. "Every year they decide whether to introduce an extra month, and the month is as long as they wish—they add however many days they deem necessary to bring the calendar back into alignment with the planets."

"That's correct, Gordianus," said Cicero in a patronizing tone, as if he were surprised that a fellow like myself could grasp such an abstract concept. "You may remember, in the year that Clodius was killed on the Appian Way, we had an intercalary month between Februarius and Martius; twenty-seven days, as I recall." He hummed thoughtfully and looked toward the doorway. "I wonder if I should invite Publilia to join us. She could learn a great deal from this discussion. It's good for a female to stretch her mind occasionally."

Cicero was in pedagogic mode, craving a worthy audience. It struck me that few topics were more likely to bore Cicero's honey than this one.

"Ah, but she's probably napping." Cicero sighed and shrugged. "Where was I? Oh, yes—even with the addition of intercalary months, the Roman calendar has grown more and more out of step, so that nowadays the harvest festivals of our ancestors occur during the summer, which makes no sense, and the holidays that are supposed to relieve the tedium of midwinter arrive in the autumn, when everyone is busy with the harvest. And so on. This is the middle of September, yet the weather is sweltering and the days are long."

I nodded to show I understood. Cicero continued.

"Which is why our esteemed dictator for life is planning to introduce a new calendar, the first real advance on King Numa's ever attempted. Apparently, when Caesar was trapped for all those months in Alexandria, under siege in the palace complex, he had rather a lot of time to kill."

"I know. Rupa and I were there as well. I passed the time by borrowing books from the famous library of the Ptolemies. I read them aloud to Rupa and the slave boys. I think I must have read every book ever written about Alexander the Great."

"Caesar also took advantage of his access to the library. When he wasn't diddling that dreadful queen, he consulted with her astronomers—the library boasts an impressive faculty of scientists and stargazers—and it occurred to him that he might use his spare time to devise a more accurate and durable calendar. Now Caesar is back in Rome, and so is the Egyptian queen, along with her retinue, including scholars from the library. Even now, Caesar is said to be putting the final touches to his calendar, intending to unveil it on the final day of his triumphs, when he dedicates his temple to Venus. We shall have a new calendar for the new age." Cicero scowled, as the dispassionate pedagogue gave way to the thwarted republican.

"But surely that's a good thing," I said. "Whatever you may

think of Caesar's other accomplishments, if he can repair the Roman calendar, we shall all benefit."

"That is true. And if he can truly pull it off, it's only fitting that a Roman should be the man to give the world an accurate accounting of the movement of the heavens. I only regret that the man should be Caesar!"

This was as candid as I could wish. Throughout our conversation, not once had Cicero appeared to speak disingenuously. His guard seemed to be entirely down; he spoke to me as to a confidant. I was finding it hard to believe he could in any way be responsible for Hieronymus's death.

"All these notations and scribblings," I said, indicating the documents. "What do they mean, and why did Hieronymus possess them?"

Cicero pursed his lips thoughtfully. "Do you know what I think? I think Hieronymus made these calculations as a kind of mental exercise, a challenge to himself. He must have heard about Caesar's plan for a new calendar. Wouldn't it have been just like him to think, *if Caesar can do it, then so can I?* Or perhaps he somehow got hold of the proposed calendar and was attempting to find flaws. He was a very competitive sort of fellow. He had a high estimation of his talents and considerable cheek. Once, he told me that he thought he could quite easily become a finer orator than I. Can you believe that!"

I nodded. "I can believe it, indeed." It was easy enough to imagine Hieronymus obtaining information about the calendar from Calpurnia, or someone in her household, or perhaps from the household of Cleopatra, whom he had visited and whose scholars were working with Caesar on the project. But if Hieronymus had hoped to show up Caesar's calendar with one of his own, that dream, like all his others, had come to an abrupt end.

Cicero looked past me. The slave who had admitted me stood in the doorway.

"Speak," said Cicero.

"You have another visitor, Master."

"Who is it?"

"Marcus Junius Brutus."

Cicero smiled broadly and clapped his hands. "Ah, Brutus! He must have just arrived in the city. Show him in at once! And bring more wine and a basin of water and some food. Brutus will be hungry after his journey."

The slave hurried to obey.

"Thank you for the hospitality," I said, "and for your thoughts about Hieronymus." I began to rise from my chair, but Cicero gestured for me to sit.

"Please, Gordianus, stay for a while. I've shared your sadness for the loss of one friend; now you can share my joy at being re-united with another. By Hercules, not only is Brutus still breathing—a miracle!—but Caesar appointed him governor of Cisalpine Gaul. You do know Brutus, don't you?"

"Only by name," I said. "I don't think our paths have ever crossed."

Cicero nodded thoughtfully. "I always assume you know everyone, but that's not true, is it? You never did have any ties to Cato and his circle, did you? You were always too busy fetching and finding for Pompey or for Caesar. Well, then, you must stay, so that I can introduce you."

Brutus stepped into the room. His tunic and his shoes were still dusty from traveling. He and Cicero greeted each other and embraced. Rupa and I rose while Cicero introduced us, then we all sat. Brutus washed his face and hands in a basin of water held by a slave, then enthusiastically accepted a cup of wine.

He was a handsome man with a long face and keen eyes, not quite forty years old. Throughout his adult life, Brutus's family connections and political affiliations had repeatedly put him at odds with Caesar. Brutus had been the protégé of his uncle Cato, who was the champion of the most hidebound conservative clique and one of Caesar's most relentless enemies. When the civil war erupted, Brutus did not hesitate to side with Pompey. But on the eve of the battle of Pharsalus, Caesar explicitly ordered his officers to spare Brutus and take him alive. After the battle, he not only pardoned Brutus but took him into his entourage as an honored companion.

Why did Caesar show such special favor to Brutus? For a number of years, Brutus's widowed mother, Servilia, had carried on a torrid love affair with Caesar (despite the consternation of her brother, Cato). Brutus was only a boy when the affair began, and came of age with Caesar coming and going in his house. The bond that formed between Caesar and Brutus survived the eventual cooling of Caesar's passion for Servilia and also survived their political differences.

When Caesar sailed off to Africa to deal with the last defiant survivors of Pharsalus—including Cato—he sent Brutus in the opposite direction. The appointment to govern Cisalpine Gaul not only rewarded Brutus but also got him out of Rome and away from the battlefront. Caesar could hardly expect Brutus to be in at the kill of his beloved uncle.

Caesar had no son, unless he intended to acknowledge Cleopatra's child. Perhaps he thought of Brutus as a surrogate son. Perhaps, as some people speculated, he even intended to make Brutus his heir.

"How was the journey?" asked Cicero.

"Long, hot, and dusty! Thanks for asking and thanks for the wine. Awfully good of you." Even in casual conversation, Brutus spoke with a clipped, cultured accent. His family claimed to be descended from the famous Brutus who led the revolt against King Tarquin the Proud and helped to found the republic. I found myself comparing him to Antony, who was every bit as aristocratic but seemed far less pretentious.

"So, how are things in the hinterland?" said Cicero.

Brutus snorted. "Cisalpine Gaul is practically Italy, you know. The Rubicon isn't the Styx. We *do* have the rudiments of civilization—books, brothels, and garum. On a fast horse, Rome is only a few days away."

"You made it just in time for the triumphs."

"Yes, for better or worse. Caesar didn't exactly demand my attendance, but he made his desire clear enough in his last letter. I suppose I shan't mind watching him parade the spoils of Egypt and Asia and further Gaul, but if he uses the African Triumph to crow about his victory over Uncle Cato, I'm not sure I can stomach that. Oh, dear, have I just made the most awful pun?"

Brutus flashed a lopsided smile. In Africa, after a crushing defeat, Cato first tried to commit suicide by cutting open his belly.

"It's my understanding," said Cicero, "that the African Triumph will chiefly celebrate the victory of Roman arms over King Juba of Numidia."

"Who went down fighting the good fight along with Uncle

Cato." Brutus sighed. "Well, whatever else we may say of Caesar, the old boy won the war fair and square, didn't he? And saw fit to let you and me keep our heads, eh, Cicero? What about you, Gordianus? Not a military man, are you?"

"Gordianus has a son who's been serving under Caesar for quite some time," said Cicero. "You may have heard of him: Meto Gordianus."

"Numa's balls, not the fellow who wrote those memoirs for Caesar?"

"My son took Caesar's dictation, yes," I said.

Brutus snorted. "Dictation, eh? Caesar probably wasn't even in the tent while your boy was scribbling away. Give credit where it's due, old man. Everybody knows those memoirs were written by a shadow. And, by Hades, they certainly did their job! From the way those memoirs tell it, the poor Gauls didn't stand a chance. Quite a tale, all blood and thunder and beat my Roman chest. Pumped up Caesar's prestige with the common folk, eh? Made him look invincible. Scared the piss out of Cato, I can tell you. 'Wouldn't want to go up against that bloodthirsty madman,' quoth my doomed uncle. Well, bugger me! The father of great Caesar's ghost, sitting right here. This is quite the literary gathering, isn't it? Cicero's written his latest book especially for me, did you know? Been sending me chapters. *A History of Famous Orators,* dedicated to yours truly. Celebrating a dead art, I suppose. Who needs orators when the courts are closed and the Senate's a shadow? Nonetheless, my name shall enjoy immortality on the dedication page of Cicero's great opus."

Cicero smiled. "I have no doubt that you shall achieve immortality by your own actions, Brutus."

"Really? I don't see how. A hundred years from now, I

doubt that anyone's likely to remember who was governor of Cisalpine Gaul in the year of Caesar's quadruple triumphs."

"You're still a young man, Brutus. And Caesar—" Cicero glanced at me, then looked back to Brutus. "Caesar won't live forever."

"Ah, yes, and what will come *after* Caesar?" said Brutus. "People are already speculating about that. What does that tell you? We've begun to think just the way people think when they live under a king. We're not worrying about the next election or who's liable to get himself exiled for corruption or how to keep a foot in a game. We're wondering, 'How long will the old fellow live, and who will be his heir?' For shame!" Brutus tossed back his wine and held out his cup for the slave to refill it.

Wine, soothing the weariness of the journey, had loosened his tongue. He turned to Rupa and smiled. "It was my ancestor, also named Brutus, who founded this little thing we call a republic. Did you know that, big fellow?" He paused, as if expecting Rupa to answer, though he had been told when introduced that Rupa was mute. "Republic—comes from two fine old words, *res* and *publica:* the people's state. You're a fellow citizen, I suppose, being Gordianus's son by adoption?"

"That's correct," I said.

"Where were you born, big fellow? Somewhere quite exotic, I'll wager."

"Rupa is Sarmatian."

"Indeed, you come from the very ends of the earth, from the mountains where the sun rises! What's that line from Ennius? You know, Cicero, his epitaph for Scipio?"

Cicero raised his voice to a ringing orator's pitch. " 'The

sun that rises above the eastern-most marshes of Lake Maeotis illumines no man my equal in deeds!'" Far from being chagrined by his friend's loose tongue, he seemed to be as intoxicated as Brutus. This was not the Cicero I knew.

"That's right," said Brutus. "And you, you big Sarmatian fellow, you must have actually *seen* Lake Maeotis, though I'll wager you haven't a clue who Scipio was. No matter! That's the point, really. What a remarkable thing is this republic, eh? It grows and grows, spreading across the whole world, from the Pillars of Hercules to Lake Maeotis, laying down roads and building cities, establishing courts of law, securing the sea lanes, and rewarding its best and brightest with the greatest prize on earth, Roman citizenship."

"And enslaving a vast multitude in the process," I commented. Rupa had been enslaved, before he gained his freedom.

"I shall not debate the natural necessity of slavery, at least not here and now," said Brutus. "That's a book for Cicero to write; one of many, now that he's retired. The law court's loss will be the reader's gain! My point, if I may return to it, is the end of our republic, and everything it stands for. As I said, it was my ancestor who founded this thing." This was an exaggeration—the Brutus of ancient times hardly drove the Tarquins out of Rome single-handedly—but I let it go. "Over four hundred and fifty years ago! The republic has served us for many, many generations. The republic has made us masters of ourselves and masters of the world. As Brutus knew it would. How he loved the republic! No effort was too Herculean, no sacrifice too great to ensure its survival. Do you know what he did, Sarmatian, in the very first year of the republic, when he got wind of a conspiracy to bring back the king?"

Rupa shook his head.

"Brutus declared that any man involved in such a plot must die. Then a slave brought him proof that his own two sons were involved in the plot. Did he make an exception for them? Did he spirit them out of the city or destroy the evidence or pardon them? No, he did not. He had every royalist conspirator arrested. The guilty were lined up and forced to kneel, and the lictors chopped their heads off, one by one. Chop, chop, chop! Brutus watched the beheading of his own two sons, and the historians tell us he never flinched. And afterward, he rewarded the slave who had informed on them by granting the man citizenship—making him the first slave ever to become a Roman citizen. A precedent that has worked to *your* advantage, my Sarmatian friend!"

Brutus sat back, held out his cup for another refill, and drank it down. Talking had made him thirsty. "And that, fellow citizens, is a tale of true republican virtue. What man today could claim to be as brave, as resolute, as decisive as my forefather?"

"Perhaps his descendant," suggested Cicero, in a voice that was barely more than a whisper.

Brutus the founder had killed his own sons for the sake of the republic. Might another Brutus dare to kill his surrogate father for sake of the same *res publica*? And might Cicero, Rome's greatest advocate and orator, be just the man to persuade Brutus to do it?

"But what's this?" Brutus tossed his empty cup to a slave and picked up the astronomical documents Cicero had laid aside upon his arrival. He perused the notations, a bit bleary-eyed. "Symbols for Capricorn and Cancer, Virgo and Libra . . .

those are clear enough. But what are these extraordinary non-sense words? Egyptian months? Mesore, Phamenoth, Phar-mouthi, Thoth, Phaopi, Tybi, Hathyr, Mecheir, Epiphi, Choiak, Pachon, Payni. Quite a mouthful! And all these columns of numbers . . ." He squeezed his eyes shut for a moment and laid the documents aside. "What are you up to, Cicero, helping our dictator with calculations for his new calendar? I do hope he's not intending to saddle us with Egyptian months, along with an Egyptian queen. Really, that *would* be the last straw! 'Shall we dine on the Ides of Tybi?' 'Meet me in the Forum two days before the Kalends of Thoth.'"

He threw back his head and laughed.

"Actually, Gordianus brought these," said Cicero. "They appear to be the pet project of a mutual friend. A friend who no longer has need of a calendar, alas."

The time seemed right to depart. I rolled up the documents and handed them to Rupa. I asked Cicero to convey my farewell to his napping bride. I wished Brutus a good stay in Rome, and I took my leave.

V I I I

"Tomorrow!" said Bethesda, standing in the front doorway with her arms crossed. Her tone was adamant, her posture imperious. Hand her a flail and a crook, I thought, and put a nemes crown with a rearing cobra on her head, and she could pass for Egyptian royalty.

"You're right," I said. Even standing outside the house, I caught a whiff of the odor of putrefaction that was beginning to emanate from the body in my vestibule. "I shall organize a procession for tomorrow. We'll have him cremated outside the Esquiline Gate."

Bethesda nodded, satisfied that her point had been taken, and stepped aside to allow me to enter.

The odor was stronger in the vestibule, but not overpowering. Nonetheless, I could see how my wife, being at home all day, had reached her limit.

"Did anyone come to pay their respects while I was out?"

"No visitors."

"Ah, well, I'm not surprised. With all these preparations for

Caesar's triumphs beginning tomorrow, I suppose everyone's too busy. Only Fulvia came, then, and she didn't even know Hieronymus; her condolences were merely a pretext to question me. Ah, Hieronymus." I gazed down at his face. "You amused them, seduced them with your charm, spied upon them . . . and now, it seems, they've forgotten about you."

"No visitors," Bethesda repeated, "but some messengers did come. They brought these." She bent down to fetch a few pieces of parchment that had been tossed haphazardly in the corner near the door, as if they were bits of refuse. Bethesda had little respect for the written word. There was also a wax writing tablet among the messages.

"Bethesda, these are notes of condolence. They were brought for Hieronymus. You should have laid them upon his bier."

She raised a skeptical eyebrow and shrugged.

"I suppose I'm lucky you didn't burn them."

"Won't they be burned tomorrow, along with Hieronymus?"

"Yes, but only *after* I've read them."

"Who are they from, then?"

"This one's from Cicero. He told me he'd sent a message. 'The laughter and erudition of our learned friend from Massilia will be sorely missed in these trying times,' and so on."

"And the others?"

"Here's one from Antony. Cytheris added a note. She says she wants to provide the singers and mimes for the funeral procession; friends of hers, I imagine. And these others . . .'"

I scanned the names of the senders. They were all persons whose names appeared in Hieronymus's reports. These were the people he had visited, whose trust he had sought to cultivate with an eye toward uncovering any threat they might pose to Caesar. Did the fact that these people had sent condolences make them any more or less suspicious? Surely the person responsible for Hieronymus's death would have sent condolences along with everyone else.

Here was a note from Caesar's young grandnephew, Octavius, who was about to turn seventeen; he included an epigram in Greek, probably from a play, though I didn't recognize it. Here was a note from the sculptor Arcesilaus, with whom many years ago I had shared cherries from the garden of Lucullus; it was his statue of Venus that was to adorn the new temple built by Caesar. Here was a note from a new playwright in town, Publilius Syrus, who paraphrased the last lines of Ennius's epitaph for Scipio, from which Cicero had recited earlier: "If any mortal may ascend to the heaven of immortals, for you let the gods' gate stand open."

And here, upon a very heavy piece of parchment rimmed with an embossed border of a repeating lotus leaf pattern, was a note from the queen of Egypt:

To Gordianus, with fond remembrance of our meeting in Alexandria. I have discovered that the late Hieronymus of Massilia was a member of your household, and it is to you I should send a message of condolence. Now you are here in Rome, and so am I. We live in a very small world. But the realm of the afterlife, where I shall reign as Isis in splendor, is vast and eternal. May our mutual friend be guided there swiftly to enjoy his reward.

I laid the notes amid the flowers piled upon the bier. Still in my hand was the wax writing tablet.

I untied the strings of the wooden cover panel. The reusable wax surface contained not a message of condolence, but two questions, below each of which space had been left to scratch a reply. I felt a bit like a pupil being handed a test by his tutor. The name of the sender was not included, but the tablet obviously came from Calpurnia. The first question read:

To whom have you spoken? Reply using initials only.

That was done easily enough. The second question read:

Have you discovered anything to indicate that he *should not take part in tomorrow's event? Send your reply at once.*

In other words, had I discovered anything to indicate an immediate danger to Caesar? I considered how to answer. If something untoward occurred, Calpurnia might hold me accountable, even if Caesar was unharmed. But I had discovered no clear and present danger to Caesar. "No," I wrote. The word looked small and inadequate amid the blank space she had left for my reply.

I rose before daybreak the next morning. The family, appropriately garbed in our darkest clothing, gathered to share a simple meal of mourning, consisting of black bread with black beans.

Had it been entirely up to me, I would have given Hieronymus the simplest possible ceremony. But since Cytheris, with her connections in the performing world, had volunteered to provide the traditional mourners, musicians, and mimes, as well as some sturdy young slaves to carry the bier, it would have been churlish to refuse her offer. Amazingly, the entire troupe showed up on time. It was a good thing Bethesda had prepared extra food, since they all expected to be fed.

An hour after daybreak, our little procession set out. We took a roundabout route, walking up and down the streets of the Palatine so as to pass by various houses where Hieronymus had been an invited guest. If the inhabitants were not awake before we passed by, the screeching mourners and the musicians with their rattles, flutes, horns, and bells surely roused them from bed. Pedestrians paused and curious onlookers peered from windows to watch the mime, trying to guess whom he was impersonating. The fellow had met Hieronymus only once at one of Cytheris's parties, but he was remarkably gifted; wearing one of Hieronymus's favorite tunics, he produced an uncanny simulation of my friend's posture, gait, hand gestures, facial expressions, and even his laugh.

One passerby, after watching the mime for a moment, made a typical comment: "Hieronymus the Scapegoat? Is that him on the bier? Didn't know he was dead!" Such recognition was a testament to the mime's talent and to the impression Hieronymus had made on a surprising number of people. I was amazed at how many men and women seemed to have known him. Walking at a slow gait with the rest of the family behind the musicians and the funeral bier, I found myself staring at every stranger who paused to watch the procession, wondering if Hieronymus's murderer was among them.

Eventually we descended the western slope of the Palatine and crossed the Sacred Way at a point well away from the Forum. Had Hieronymus been a Roman man of affairs, a pass through the Forum would have been mandatory, but I decided to forego the area, where huge crowds were already gathering for the Gallic Triumph. We avoided the narrow, noisome streets of the Subura as well, and instead ascended the slope of the Esquiline through the Carinae district. Cytheris had requested that the funeral cortege pass before the House of the Beaks.

The performers knew who was paying them; as we approached the house, the moaning and shrieking and the drumming and fluting rose to an earsplitting crescendo. At the same time, the passable portion of the street narrowed considerably. True to his word, Antony was holding an auction in front of the house to sell off some of Pompey's possessions. The auction had not yet begun, but numerous objects had already been laid out for preview on makeshift tables.

There were odds and ends from silver table settings, many of the pieces dented or black with tarnish. A few items of jewelry, presumably from the collection of Pompey's wife, Cornelia, had been put on display. These included single earrings that had lost their mates, necklaces that needed repair, rings that had lost their stones, and stones that had lost their rings. There were piles of clothing, pieces of furniture, and a few bookcases stuffed with tattered scrolls.

Behind me I heard whispering. I turned to see that Bethesda and Diana were looking sidelong at the goods for auction and holding a hushed conference. I shushed them, but they seemed not to hear. "Respect!" I finally said, and they tore their eyes from the items on display, looking a bit chagrined.

"We can come back later and see what's left," I heard Diana whisper to her mother. I had to admit that I myself was tempted to rummage through the shelves and see which of Pompey's books were on offer.

"See anything you like, Finder? I can put it aside for you."

I turned to see Antony nearby, leaning nonchalantly against one of the display tables. He reached for a voluminous green tunic with silver embroidery and held it up by the shoulders. "Can this huge sack have been Pompey's? 'The Great One,' indeed! The old fellow had gotten as big as an elephant."

A hand snatched the tunic from him. Cytheris replaced it on the table and gave him a chiding look. Antony crossed his arms and pouted.

"Can't you see that Hieronymus is passing by?" she said.

"Ah, yes." Antony raised his arm in a mock salute. "Hail and farewell, Scapegoat! In Elysium there shall be endless parties for you to crash."

The day was just beginning, yet Antony was already drunk. Or had he stayed up all night drinking and not yet gone to bed? This was how he chose to mark the day of Caesar's Gallic Triumph, in which he should have played an honored role.

As we passed beyond the constricted area of the auction and into the open street beyond, I noticed a man leaning against a fig tree. Before he could step behind the tree, I saw his face clearly and recognized him as Thraso, one of Fulvia's slaves. Realizing I had seen him, he made no further effort to conceal himself and even gave me a slight smile and a nod. Something told me he was the man who had followed me after my meeting with Cytheris. Did Fulvia keep a watcher posted on the House of the Beaks every hour of every day?

At length we passed though the Esquiline Gate. Beyond the old city walls, sprawling over the gently sloping hillsides, was the public necropolis, the city of the dead. The unmarked graves of slaves and the modest tombs of common citizens were crowded close together. On a normal day, there would have been other funerals taking place, their flaming pyres scenting the necropolis with the smells of burning wood and flesh. But on that day, ours was the only one.

A little way off the road, atop a small hill, the pyre had been prepared. It was in the very same location where two years ago we burned the body of Rupa's sister, Cassandra. Hieronymus was laid upon the pyre. The keepers of the flame set about stoking the fire.

A few people had sent their condolences, but only my family saw fit to actually attend the ceremony. Granted, it was still early in the morning, and on that day much else was happening. But I wondered at the fickleness of those whom Hieronymus had supposedly befriended after I left Rome. Of course, when all was said and done, he had been a foreigner and an outsider, with no blood connection to the city.

It was incumbent on me to say a few words, even though only the family was present. I recalled my first meeting with Hieronymus in Massilia, when his intervention alone saved me from arrest; his hospitality to me and to Davus in that desperate, besieged city; his narrow escape from the fate that awaited him as the Scapegoat; and his journey with me to Rome. I reflected on the oscillating fortunes of his life; he had been born a child of privilege in the highest echelon of Massilian society, but his father's financial ruin and suicide had reduced the family to poverty and made them social outcasts. His selection to act as the Scapegoat promised him a brief period of the utmost luxury, followed by a sacrificial death. But it had not been so, and the doomed man became a guest in my home, and then, curiously enough, a sought-after dinner companion to the elite of the city. Then came a reversal as ironic as all the other reversals in his peculiar life, and with it, the end.

While I spoke, Davus began to weep, and Diana hugged him. Mopsus, Androcles, and Rupa seemed distracted by the work of the fire starters; they stared past me at the pyre, awaiting the first tongues of flame. Bethesda stood stiff and unbending; was she thinking of that other funeral, for Cassandra, which she had been too ill to attend? Eco was still in Syracuse, but his wife, Menenia, was here, along with their golden-haired twins, Titus and Titania.

"What can we learn from his death?" I looked from face to face amid the small gathering of those dearest to me. "Only what we already know: that fortune is changeable, that the love of the gods is no more steadfast than the love of mortals, that all who live must die. But the words and acts of the living carry on after them. The story of Hieronymus is not yet over, not while any one of us who remembers him still lives."

And not while at least one man continues to search for his killer and the true cause of his death, I thought.

I bowed my head. A little later I heard the crackling of wood, smelled the odor of burning, and felt the heat of the flames against my back.

"Farewell, Hieronymus!" I whispered.

I X

What does one do for the rest of the day, when the day begins with a funeral? Such days seem to take place outside normal time. A dull gloom settles over the world. After being made to confront mortality at its starkest, one is left to face the ensuing hours stripped of the simple comforts of a workday routine. Normal thought is impossible. A carefree laugh or an idle day-dream are out of the question. We have looked into the abyss, then have stepped back from the precipice still alive, yes, but touched at our core by the chill of death. For the rest of the day, one must simply endure the gloom and wait for the setting of the sun and the eventual escape into sleep that will bring the day after.

But this was not a normal day for anyone in Rome. This was the day of the first of Caesar's four triumphs.

Even before we reentered the city by the Esquiline Gate, I could hear a dull roar from within the walls. When every man, woman, and child in Rome has cause to be out of doors at the same time, all talking to one another at once, the whole city hums like beehive. Such a buzzing seemed to emanate from every quarter of the city, but it grew noticeably louder as we drew near the Forum.

Everyone was in the streets, wearing their brightest holiday attire. (How my family stood out, all garbed in black!) Everyone was headed for the same place, drawn toward the heart of the hubbub. Amid the contagious excitement, Bethesda and Diana completely forgot their intention to return to the auction at the House of the Beaks. Impatient to witness the spectacle, Mopsus and Androcles repeatedly ran ahead and then circled back, entreating the rest of us to hurry.

We reached the Forum. The doors of every temple stood open, inviting the people to visit the gods, and the gods to witness the day's events. Garlands of flowers decorated every shrine and statue. Incense burned on every altar, filling the air with sweet fragrance.

Historians say that King Romulus celebrated the first triumphal procession in Rome after he slew Acron, king of the Caeninenses, in single combat. While Acron's body was still warm, Romulus cut down an oak tree and carved the trunk into the shape of a torso; then he stripped the armor from Acron's corpse and fastened it onto the effigy. Carrying the trophy over his shoulder and wearing a laurel crown, he walked through the streets of Rome while the citizens looked on in awe. He ascended the Capitoline. At the Temple of Jupiter, he made a solemn offering of Acron's armor to the god, in gratitude for Rome's triumph.

Romulus's victory march was the origin and model for all subsequent triumphs. Over the centuries, the pomp and ceremony of these celebrations grew ever more elaborate. King

Tarquin the Elder was the first to ride a chariot instead of walk, and for the occasion he wore a gold-embroidered robe. In his day, only kings could celebrate a triumph, but with the coming of the republic, the Senate continued the tradition by granting triumphs to generals in recognition of a great military victory. Camillus, who liberated the city when it was occupied by the Gauls, was the first to harness four white horses to his chariot, in emulation of the quadriga statue atop Jupiter's temple, with its white horses pulling the king of the gods. In those days, the face and arms of a triumphant general were painted red to match the statue of Jupiter, which was dyed with cinnabar on holidays. What a strange sight that must have been!

I had witnessed a number of triumphs in my lifetime. The first I could remember was when I was six years old, and Caesar's uncle Marius paraded the captured Numidian king Jugurtha through the streets before executing him. A few years later, after repelling an invasion by Germanic tribes, Marius celebrated another triumph. In the year before I met Cicero, I saw Sulla the Dictator celebrate his victory over King Mithradates of Pontus. Cicero himself had been voted a triumph by the Senate, for the dubious achievement of putting down a band of brigands during his year as governor of Cilicia, but the civil war had postponed that event, probably forever.

Pompey had celebrated three triumphs in his career, beginning at the age of twenty-four. The last and most lavish of these was some fifteen years ago, to mark his conquests in the East and his eradication of piracy in the Mediterranean. That triumph had been spread over two days of unprecedented pomp and largesse, featuring not only processions but also huge public banquets and a distribution of money to the citizens; and in a move that surprised everyone, Pompey had spared the intended victims, proving that mercy could be exercised by a victorious Roman general.

But of all the triumphs I had seen, the celebration put on by Caesar that day, and in the days to come, eclipsed them all.

When a man has lived in a place as long as I have lived in Rome, he learns a few of the city's secrets. I happened to know the best vantage point for watching a triumph. While other latecomers pressed toward the front of the crowd, stood on tip-toes, or gazed enviously at those who had arrived early to find seats among the stands, I led the family to the Temple of For-tuna built by Lucullus. At the side of the temple, an easy climb along the branch of an olive tree allowed access to a recessed marble shelf along one wall, just deep enough and wide enough for my entire family to sit, if we huddled close together. Even an old fellow like me could make the ascent with no trouble, and my reward was a comfortable perch above the heads of the crowd below, with a perfect view of the procession along the Sacred Way. Dressed as we were, we must have looked like a flock of ravens roosting on the little outcrop of marble.

A roar erupted as Bethesda was settling herself beside me. We were just in time to see the beginning of the parade.

Following tradition, the procession began with the senators. They were usually three hundred in number. The body had been greatly depleted by the civil war, but new appointments by Caesar had replenished their ranks. Dressed in their togas with red borders, the senators flowed down the Sacred Way like a river of white flecked with crimson. For many of the newcom-ers, this occasion marked their first public appearance. I could pick out the new senators by how stiffly they adopted the politician's standard pose—one hand clutching the folds of the toga, the other raised to wave to the crowd. These included, either appropriately or ironically considering the occasion, a number of Gallic chieftains who had allied themselves with Caesar. Not one of them sported long hair or a giant mustache; they were as well-groomed as their Roman colleagues. Still, keeping together in a group, they were easy to spot by their stature. The Gauls towered above the sea of white.

Cicero and Brutus, who were usually the type to put themselves out front, marched near the back of the contingent. They strode with their heads close together, conversing, as if more interested in each other's company than in what was happening around them. Their attitude seemed almost deliberately disrespectful of the occasion. What were those two talking about?

Next in the procession came the white oxen that would be sacrificed on the altar before the Temple of Jupiter on the Capitoline, attended by the priests who would slaughter them, bearing their ceremonial knives. The oxen had gilded horns, brightly colored fillets of twisted wool on their heads, and garlands of flowers around their necks. Following were the camilli, the specially chosen boys and girls who would attend the priests, carrying the shallow libation bowls in which they would receive the blood and the organs of the sacrificed oxen.

Other members of the priesthoods followed, wearing long robes and mantles over their heads. These included the keepers of the Sibylline Books, the augurs responsible for divination, the flamens devoted to various deities, and the priests who maintained the calendar and reckoned sacred dates. Among this last group I saw a familiar face, the white-haired uncle of Calpurnia, Gnaeus Calpurnius, whom I had seen briefly in the garden at her house. Clearly, Uncle Gnaeus was in his element on this day, a priest among priests taking part in a great occasion. His expression was at once solemn and joyous; he had that smug look one often sees on priests, of knowing a little more than ordinary people and rather enjoying this superior knowledge. Now that I realized the priesthood to which he was attached, it occurred to me that it might have been Uncle Gnaeus who piqued Hieronymus's interest in the calendar, and perhaps even assisted him with astronomical calculations—if, indeed, he had deigned to have anything to do with Hieronymus. I made a mental note to ask him about it, if the opportunity arose.

Next came a band of trumpeters, blaring the ancient summons to arms, as if a hostile enemy approached. In fact, behind the trumpeters, an enemy did approach—the captive chiefs of the conquered Gauls. There were a great many of these prisoners; the Gauls were divided into scores of tribes, and Caesar had subdued them all. These once-proud warriors were dressed in rags. They shambled forward with their heads bowed, chained to one another. The crowed laughed and jeered and pelted them with rotten fruit.

At their head was Vercingetorix. He was as I had seen him in the Tullianum, nearly naked and covered with filth, but his appearance was even more appalling under bright sunlight. His eyes were hollow. His lips were dry and cracked. His hair and his beard were as tangled as a bird's nest. His fingernails were like claws, so long they had begun to curl. His shoes had disintegrated while he walked; bits of shredded leather trailed from his ankles, and each step left a bloody footprint on the paving stones.

Confused and exhausted, he suddenly came to a halt. A

soldier pacing alongside the prisoners, like a herd dog, ran up and struck him with a whip. The crowd roared.

"Fight back, Gaul!" someone yelled.

"Show us what you're made of!"

"King of the Gauls? King of the cowards!"

Vercingetorix lurched forward and almost fell. One of the other chieftains reached out to steady him. The soldier struck the man across the face and sent him reeling back. Spectators jeered and clapped and jumped up and down with excitement.

The chastened prisoners quickened their pace. A moment later, they passed beyond my sight. Bethesda touched my arm and gave me a sympathetic look. I realized I was gripping the edge of the shelf so firmly that my knuckles had turned white.

So this was the end of Vercingetorix. For him, the day would end where it began, back at the Tullianum, where he would be lowered into the pit and strangled. In quick succession, the other chieftains would meet the same fate. There would be no last-minute rescue. There would not be even a final show of defiance or pride or anger, only submission and silence. He had been broken to the ultimate degree that could still leave him breathing and able to walk. Caesar's torturers were exquisitely skilled at obtaining exactly what they wanted from a victim, and Vercingetorix had proved to be no exception.

Next came musicians and a troupe of mincing mimes who mocked the chieftains who had just passed. The tension aroused in the crowd by the sight of their enemies melted into screams of laughter. The mime who played Vercingetorix—recognizable by a ludicrously oversized version of the warrior's famous winged helmet, which almost swallowed his head—confronted a mime meant to be Caesar, to judge by his glittering armor and red cape. Their mock swordfight, attended by a great deal of buffoonery, excited squeals of laughter from the children watching and ended when the Caesar mime appeared to plunge his sword up the fundament of the Vercingetorix mime, who first gave a high-pitched scream, then cocked his head to one side and started rolling his hips, as if he enjoyed the penetration. The crowd loved this.

Dancers, musicians, and a chorus of singers followed. People clapped their hands and sang along to marching songs they had learned from their grandparents. "Onward Roman soldiers, for Jupiter you fight! The way of Rome is forward, the cause of Rome is right. . . ."

Next came the spoils of war. Specially made wagons, festooned with garlands, were loaded with the captured armor of the enemy. Superbly crafted breastplates, helmets, and shields were mounted for display, as were the most impressive weapons of the enemy, including gleaming swords with elaborately decorated pommels, fearsome axes, and iron-tipped spears hewn from solid oak and carved with strange runes.

The grandest wagon was reserved for the armor and weapons of Vercingetorix. The crowd applauded the sight of his famous bronze helmet with massive feathered wings on either side. There was also a display of his personal belongings, including his signet ring for sealing documents, his private drinking cup of silver and horn, a fur cloak made from a bear he himself had killed, and even a pair of his boots, crafted of fine leather and tooled with intricate Celtic designs.

More wagons rolled by, carrying captured booty from every corner of Gaul, artfully displayed so that the crowd could take in each object as it slowly passed by. There were silver goblets and pitchers and vases, richly embroidered fabrics, woven goods with patterns never before seen in Rome, magnificent garments made of fur, elaborately wrought bronze lamps, copper bracelets, torques and armbands made of gold, and clasps and pins and brooches set with gemstones of remarkable size and color. There were bronze and stone statues, crude by Greek or Roman standards, depicting the strange gods who had failed to protect the Gauls.

More wagons passed, stuffed with coffers overflowing with gold and silver coins and bullion. At the sight of so much lucre, people gasped with excitement and their eyes glittered with greed. Word had spread that Caesar intended to distribute a considerable portion of the captured wealth of Gaul to the people of Rome. Every citizen could expect to receive at least three hundred sesterces. We would all profit from the pillaging of Gaul.

As impressive as were these displays of bullion and jewels and metalwork, the human booty of Gaul far exceeded its other plundered wealth. Caesar had gone to war on borrowed money, but from the sale of humans he had become phenomenally wealthy. His enslavement of the population had taken place on a vast scale; in his memoirs, he boasted of selling over fifty thousand of the Aduatuci tribe alone. In celebration of this achievement, a small sampling of the most striking of Caesar's captives was presented. By the hundreds, with hands chained behind their backs and constrained by the shackles on their ankles to take baby steps, giant warriors with long red mustaches and naked youths with flowing locks shuffled past, their heads hung in shame. Looking even more miserable, a seemingly endless succession of beautiful girls draped in sheer veils were made to prance and twirl for the amusement of the crowd. These slaves would be sold at a special auction the next day. Their display in the triumph was a preview for interested buyers. Those who could not afford such exquisite merchandise could at least stare at them with amazement and be proud that Caesar had made slaves of such outstanding human specimens.

Having satisfied the crowd's prurient interest in death, greed, and lust—showing off the doomed and humiliated leaders, then the magnificent spoils of war, then an assortment of the flesh made available for purchase, thanks to Caesar—the procession continued with its educational component.

The crowd was shown a series of painted placards made of cloth stretched across wooden frames. Some of these placards, mounted on poles, were small enough to be held aloft by a single man, but others were quite large and required several men to carry them. Placards proclaimed the name of every vanquished tribe and captured city; accompanying these were models of the most famous cities and forts of the Gauls, crafted from wood and ivory. More placards depicted notable features of the Gallic landscape—its rivers and mountains, forests and bays. Other placards were painted with vivid scenes of the war, in which Caesar was usually at the center, mounted atop his white charger and wearing his red cape.

Speakers recited vivid episodes from Caesar's memoirs extolling his own ingenuity and the bravery of the Romans legions. Large models of siege towers rolled by, along with actual battering rams, catapults, ballistae, and other machines of conquest, with signs identifying the battles in which they had been used. In his campaign against the Gauls, Caesar and his engineers had greatly advanced the science of war; the many battles and sieges had allowed them to perfect new methods of inflicting mayhem and death, and here were the artifacts of the unstoppable war machine that had crushed not only the Gauls but also every one of Caesar's rivals.

Next, marching in single file, came Caesar's private bodyguard. As the multitude of armed lictors went by, their numbers seemingly endless, the crowd gradually ceased its raucous cheering and grew quiet.

Long ago, Romulus had surrounded himself with lictors, each bearing an ax to protect the person of the king and a bundle of rods to scourge anyone who defied him. When the monarchy gave way to the republic, the Senate assigned lictors to the consuls and other magistrates to protect them during their term of office. Despite their perpetually grim expressions and the fearsome weapons they carried, there was nothing alarming about the mere sight of a band of lictors; one saw them every day, crossing the Forum. What made the crowd uneasy that day, I think, was the sheer number of lictors. Never had I seen so many at one time. Not even the ancient kings had given themselves such a vast bodyguard. Even the most oblivious citizen was made to realize, by the sight of so many lictors, the unprecedented status that Caesar had claimed for himself.

Sobered by the parade of lictors, the crowd broke into a deafening roar when Caesar appeared. I saw the four snow-white horses first, tossing their proud heads and splendid manes, then caught a first glimpse of the golden ceremonial chariot. Caesar was wearing the traditional costume: a tunic embroidered with palm leaves, over which was draped a gold-embroidered toga. A wreath of laurel leaves covered his receding hairline. In his right hand he held a laurel bough, and in his left, a scepter. A slave stood behind him, holding above Caesar's head a golden crown ornamented with jewels.

While I watched, the slave leaned forward and whispered in Caesar's ear. No doubt he was reciting the ancient formula, "Remember, you are mortal!" The reminder was not meant to humble the triumphant general but to avert the so-called evil eye, the damage that could be inflicted by the gaze of the envious. Other talismans attached to the chariot served the same purpose—a tinkling bell; a scourge; and, placed in a hidden spot underneath by the Vestal virgins, the phallic amulet called a fascinum. The higher a man rose, the more protection he required against the evil eye.

Behind Caesar I saw the troops that followed, the foremost on horseback, and behind them, carrying military standards and spears adorned with laurel leaves, a great multitude of the legionaries who had served in Gaul.

Just as Caesar was passing before us, I heard a cracking noise, so sharp and loud that Mopsus and Androcles covered their ears. The ceremonial chariot lurched to a halt. Caesar was thrown violently forward. The slave holding the crown tumbled against him. The white horses clattered their hooves against the paving stones, tossed their heads, and whinnied.

My heart pounded in my chest. I felt an icy trickle down my spine. What was happening?

The nearest lictors turned and ran back to the chariot. Some of the officers on horseback sharply reined their mounts, but others bolted forward to see what was happening, with looks of alarm. Caesar was hidden from sight by the bodyguards and officers swarming around him. Confusion spread among the spectators.

I felt a sinking sensation. *Calpurnia was right, after all,* I thought. *There was a plot on Caesar's life—and now it's playing out right before my eyes. . . .*

The hubbub around the chariot continued. There were murmurs and cries of panic from the crowd.

At last an officer on horseback broke from the group. He raised his arm and addressed the crowd.

"Be calm! There's nothing to worry about. Caesar is unharmed. The axle of the chariot broke, that's all. The triumph will continue as soon as another chariot can be brought." The officer rode off to address another part of the crowd.

" 'That's all,' the man says?" muttered someone in the crowd below me. "An evil omen, for sure!"

The crowd around Caesar thinned. He was standing near the stalled chariot. I could see now that the carriage had collapsed and the wheels were askew. Aware that all eyes were on him, Caesar did his best to adopt a nonchalant expression, but he looked a bit shaken nonetheless. He tapped one foot fretfully. It must be hard to maintain one's dignity after very nearly being thrown from a chariot.

The wait stretched on. To pass the time, the idle soldiers sang a marching song, then shouted cheers for Caesar. As the waiting continued and the mood became more relaxed, some of the rowdier soldiers took up a rude chant about their commander:

Lock up your money,
Roman bankers!
He took it all,
To spend in Gaul!

Lock up your women,
quivering Gauls!
Here Caesar comes,
So bold, so bald!

Lock up your law books,
Senators, consuls!
Hail, Dictator!
Crown you later!

There were many more verses, some of them mildly obscene. The crowd responded with gales of laughter. Roman troops are famous for making fun of their commanders, and the commanders are famous for enduring it. Caesar managed a crooked smile.

As the mood grew even more relaxed, the chants grew more ribald, including one about Caesar's youthful dalliance with King Nicomedes of Bithynia:

All the Gauls did Caesar conquer,
But Nicomedes conquered him.
In Gaul did Caesar find his glory,
In Caesar, Nico found a quim!

The crowd laughed even harder. Caesar's face turned as red as if he had stained it with cinnabar, like the triumphant generals of old. He stepped onto the broken chariot, faced the soldiers, and raised his hands, still clutching the laurel bough and scepter. The men stopped chanting, though they continued to chuckle and grin while Caesar addressed them.

"Soldiers of Rome, I must protest! These songs are amusing, to be sure, and your bravery has earned you the right to indulge in a bit of levity on this day, even at Caesar's expense. But these verses about the king of Bithynia are unfair and unsubstantiated—"

"But not untrue!" shouted someone from the ranks farther back, to a burst of laughter.

"*And* untrue!" insisted Caesar. "Most assuredly, untrue. On my honor as a Roman—"

"Swear by Numa's balls!" shouted someone.

"No, swear by Nicomedes' staff!" shouted someone else.

The laughter was deafening. Caesar's face turned even redder. Did he realize how absurd he looked at that moment, a fifty-two-year-old man resplendent in his laurel crown and toga, perched on a broken chariot, attempting in vain to convince his soldiers that he had not been another man's catamite some thirty years ago?

The soldiers did not believe him. Nor, for that matter, did I. During one of our conversations in Alexandria, Caesar had spoken quite wistfully of his youthful relationship with the older king, despite the fact that his enemies had needled him about it many times over the years. It was not so much the affair itself that caused him embarrassment but the assumption that Caesar had played the receptive role, an unbecoming position for a Roman male, who is required always to dominate and penetrate. Whatever the true details of Caesar's intimacy with the king, the story had acquired a life of its own. The more Caesar denied it, the more it dogged him.

He was at last rescued from further ridicule by the arrival of the replacement chariot. As he climbed from the broken carriage, I could see the relief on his face.

The new chariot was an identical ceremonial model, with the same distinctive round shape, but not quite as splendidly gilded. A group of priests and Vestal virgins arrived to transfer the talismans for averting the evil eye. Among them I saw Calpurnia's uncle Gnaeus, who chanted under his breath and tinkled the bell as he fixed it to the new chariot. His expression of solemn joy was gone, replaced by a stern frown; perhaps he was peeved at having to perform this sacred duty a second time.

Meanwhile, another priest attached the scourge to the chariot, after flicking it in the air a few times. Then, under the supervision of the Virgo Maxima, a young camillus crawled under the broken carriage and removed the fascinum. Before it was placed under the new chariot, some in the crowd caught a glimpse of the phallic amulet, which is usually never seen, and uttered cries of religious awe.

The broken carriage was removed from the roadway. The white horses were attached to the new chariot. The procession recommenced. Caesar disappeared from view, and following him the multitude of soldiers marched by. The men were in high spirits, laughing and smiling.

The collapse of the axle had been a simple accident, it seemed. The outcome had been not only harmless but amusing, as the disruption allowed for some flashes of candor amid the orchestrated pomp and ceremony. The chants had been spontaneous, and Caesar's blustering reaction to them had certainly been unrehearsed.

But I kept thinking of what the man below me had said about the breaking of the axle: "An evil omen, for sure!"

There would be more days of celebration to come, and many more opportunities for the enemies of Caesar to act.

X

At the end of the long procession, Caesar left his chariot and ascended the Capitoline Hill on foot. The winding path, visible to those of us who remained below in the Forum, was flanked by forty elephants in bright regalia stationed on either side.

Before the Temple of Jupiter, he awaited word that Vercingetorix and the other prisoners had been executed in the Tullianum. When a crier arrived bearing the news, a cheer went up, and the sacrifice of the white oxen to Jupiter commenced. Various spoils of war were offered to the god. Caesar himself removed his laurel crown and placed it in the lap of Jupiter's statue inside the temple.

The new bronze statue of Caesar opposite the temple was officially dedicated. It depicted him in a victorious pose standing atop a map of the world. The inscription bearing the long list of his titles and attributes—"Conqueror of Gaul, Arbiter of the Pharaohs, Victor of the Nile," and so forth—ended with the declaration, "Descendant of Venus, Demigod."

A public banquet followed. The entire Forum became an

open-air dining room for the people of Rome, who brought their own plates or ate from skewers, standing or leaning against walls or sitting on temple steps.

As darkness fell, Caesar descended from the Capitoline. His way was lit by the elephants that flanked the path, holding aloft bronze torches attached to their trunks. Seen from the Forum below, the vision of those elephants and their flaming lamps, with Caesar in his gold-embroidered toga threading his way between them, was like a strange dream, utterly unexpected, awesome, unforgettable. This final flourish of the Gallic Triumph elicited cries of delight, rapturous applause, and sighs of wonder.

That night, when I finally returned home, a messenger was waiting at my door.

I allowed the man to follow me to my study, where I opened and read the wax tablet he handed me. It was unsigned but obviously from Calpurnia:

Egypt is next, the day after tomorrow. You must question the queen. How you manage an audience with her is up to you, but be quick! As for the queen's sister, I have arranged for you to see her, as I did with the Gaul. No need to reply now to this message, but I will want to know what you discover tomorrow. Wipe these words from the wax after you read them.

I smoothed the wax with the edge of my hand and returned the blank tablet to the messenger. He handed me a small wooden disk with the seal of Calpurnia's ring impressed in green wax—

the same sort of pass that had gained my admittance to the Tullianum—and told me when and where I could visit the captive Egyptian princess, Arsinoë, the next day.

For an hour before I slept, I perused Hieronymus's scribblings about Cleopatra and her less fortunate sister. And so my thoughts that day began and ended with Hieronymus, no matter that Caesar dominated the hours between.

The visiting queen of Egypt had been installed in one of Caesar's villas outside the city, located on a slope of the Janiculum Hill above the Tiber. The morning was so hot that I hired a litter in the Forum Boarium to carry me across the bridge and down the river road; I did not want to appear before a living goddess red faced and covered with sweat. The bearers balked at carrying Rupa, and Rupa balked at the idea of being carried, so he walked alongside the litter, flexing his muscles, thrusting out his jaw, and peering this way and that, trying to look like a bodyguard, I imagine, but appearing (to me, at least) more like an inquisitive, overgrown boy.

Was there a possibility, as Calpurnia seemed to think, that Cleopatra was involved in Hieronymus's murder and therefore in some plot against Caesar? To me, it seemed more likely that Calpurnia was confusing her dislike of the queen with a genuine cause for suspicion. And yet, Cleopatra was among those whom Hieronymus had visited. Also, the normal scruples against killing another human being that restrain most people, most of the time, could not be presumed to apply to Cleopatra. What did death, or murder, mean to a woman who believed herself to be the future monarch of the afterlife? To Cleopatra, the killing of a mere mortal like Hieronymus would count for nothing. Even the murder of a demigod—such as Caesar, since he claimed to be descended from Venus—might be contemplated with equanimity, if his death served to advance the interests of Isis's incarnation on earth.

At any rate, I was far from certain that Cleopatra would grant me an audience. Despite the pretty words of her note of condolence, my relationship with the queen in Alexandria had not exactly been friendly.

But, as she had done on previous occasions, Cleopatra surprised me. After giving my name to the guard at the gate, within a very short time a slave arrived to escort me into the queen's presence. Rupa was instructed to stay behind.

The slave did not enter the house but instead conducted me through the terraced gardens. Roses were blooming, scenting the warm air. Exquisite pieces of statuary were placed amid the flowers and shrubs. We came upon the queen taking breakfast beneath the shade of a fig tree, seated on a stone bench facing a spectacular view of the sparkling river and the city skyline beyond.

Cleopatra wore a sleeveless gown of thin, pleated linen, suitable for the hot weather. The line of the gown was simple, but even the plainest garments of the very rich betray their exquisite workmanship to the observant eye. Her supple leather slippers were likewise unostentatious but very finely made. Her jewelry was a matching set of bracelets and a necklace and earrings all made of hammered silver with settings of smoky topaz and black chalcedony. Her dark hair was pulled back into a bun, so that my first glimpse was of the profile, as seen on her coins, of a young woman with a very prominent nose and chin.

Her two-year-old son was seated on the grass nearby, dressed in a purple tunic and attended by cooing nursemaids. A bodyguard was leaning against the trunk of the fig tree. Handsome and long-limbed, he bore an uncanny resemblance to the deceased Apollodorus, the man who had delivered the queen to Caesar rolled up in a carpet. The bodyguard perused me through narrowed eyes.

The queen put aside a shallow dish piled with shelled almonds and dates. "Gordianus-called-Finder! I never thought to see you again."

I bowed deeply but did not prostrate myself. We were on Roman soil, after all. "I hope the surprise is a welcome one, Your Majesty."

For an answer, she gave me only a thin smile, then popped a date into her mouth.

To an old survivor like myself, the queen still seemed hardly more than a girl—twenty-three, I calculated—but since I had first seen her, emerging from that carpet to confront Caesar, she had matured considerably. She had been voluptuous before; motherhood had made her even more buxom. Her supreme self-confidence no longer seemed quite so precocious; the attribute seemed earned, not merely inborn. Cleopatra was a full-fledged queen now, the survivor of a bloody civil war, the ruler of the oldest kingdom on earth, and the living inheritor of Alexander the Great, since her distant ancestor Ptolemy had been Alexander's general and successor. She had also given birth to the son of a demigod, if the boy Caesarion was indeed Caesar's child.

It occurred to me that a triumphing general is traditionally accompanied by his sons on the joyous occasion; grown sons ride behind him, while sons in swaddling are carried in the chariot. Yet Caesarion had not accompanied Caesar during the Gallic Triumph. But was it still possible the Egyptian child would take part in Caesar's Egyptian Triumph?

"You found your wife, after all," said Cleopatra, referring to the end of my stay in Egypt.

"Yes, Your Majesty, I did. We're both back in Rome now."

"So she didn't drown in the Nile, as you feared?"

"Apparently not."

Cleopatra laughed. "Are you being ironic, Gordianus? Or do you perhaps have a trace of the mystic in you? Your answer leaves open the possibility that she *did* drown—yet still walks. And why not? The Nile is a god. It takes life, but it also gives life. Perhaps the Nile took both your wife and your life, Gordianus-called-Finder—and then gave them both back to you."

In truth, I had never been quite sure what happened that day I found Bethesda after our long separation. I had waded into the water seeking her, or seeking oblivion, if I could not find her. I entered the Nile, and the Nile entered me, through my open mouth. The water turned black. Then a woman emerged from the darkness and placed her mouth upon mine in a kiss. And then I was lying on the sandy riverbank beside Bethesda, beneath a purple sky shot with streaks of aquamarine and vermilion. . . .

I shivered at the memory, then strove to shake it off. The Nile was far away. The river below us was the Tiber, and this was Rome.

A slight breeze stirred the fig tree. Dappled sunlight played across the queen. Her silver jewelry glittered. Flashes of light reflected off the baubles of topaz and chalcedony. "Did you receive my message of condolence, regarding your friend Hieronymus?"

"I did, Your Majesty."

"Is that why you've come?"

She was making my task easy. I merely needed to nod. There was no need to explain that I had come as the spy of the wife of the man who had fathered her child.

"I'm surprised that my friend Hieronymus was able to make Your Majesty's acquaintance, let alone merit your condolences in death."

"But why not? Your friend Hieronymus and I had more in common than you may realize. He was an outcast; so was I during those wretched months that my brother held the throne and forced me to flee into the desert and hide among camel drivers and nomads. Hieronymus also spoke lovely Greek and was very well-read—qualities not easy to find in this city, despite the Romans' claim to be the guardians of Greek culture. Honestly, when that pompous fool Cicero tried to quote a bit of Aeschylus to me, I had to laugh out loud. His accent is so uncouth!"

No wonder Cicero detests you, I thought.

"Your friend also had a wonderful sense of humor," she said. "Hieronymus made me laugh, the way Caesar used to do."

"Does Caesar no longer make you laugh?"

She frowned and ignored the question. "Yes, I was sorry to learn of Hieronymus's demise. He was murdered, was he not?"

"That is correct. But that detail was not entered into the death registry."

She snorted. "I don't rely on public records for my information, Gordianus-called-Finder. And neither do you. What have you learned about your friend's death?"

"The killer remains unknown."

"But not for long, I'm sure. You're such a clever fellow. Have you come to seek my help? Or do you perhaps think I'm responsible? By Horus, there seems to be no crime too great or too small, but some Roman will accuse me of it."

"Actually, there is a question you might help me to answer, Your Majesty."

"Ask."

The previous day, it had occurred to me that Hieronymus's apparent interest in calendars might have been fostered by Calpurnia's uncle Gnaeus, in his capacity as a priest. But because Hieronymus had visited Cleopatra, and her scholars were assisting Caesar with his new calendar, it also occurred to me that someone in the queen's household might have instructed Hieronymus in astronomical matters.

I had brought his notes with me. I pulled them from my satchel and began to hand them to Cleopatra, but the bodyguard intervened. He stepped forward and snatched the scraps of parchment from me. He sniffed them and ran his hands over them systematically, front and back, as if testing them for poison. Toxins which can kill through contact with the skin have existed at least since the time of Medea. Satisfied that the notes were harmless, he passed them to the queen, who perused them with a curious expression.

"I was wondering if Your Majesty might recognize these."

"No. I've never seen them before. But clearly these computations have something to do with the movements of the moon and stars and the reckoning of days. Did these come from Hieronymus?"

"They were among his personal papers, Your Majesty."

She handed the documents back to me. "What a clever fellow he was!"

"I was wondering, Your Majesty, if Hieronymus might have consulted with your scholars about the new calendar Caesar plans to introduce."

"Absolutely not!"

"You seem very certain."

"At Caesar's request, I have instructed all those involved in devising the new calendar to speak to no one. Caesar is very insistent that there should be no public knowledge of the details before he makes his official announcement."

"Then Hieronymus must have made these calculations with instruction from someone else."

"Yes. He certainly had no precise knowledge about my new calendar."

"*Your* calendar? I thought the revised calendar was Caesar's brainchild."

She raised an eyebrow and nodded. "So it is. To be sure, it's my scholars who've performed the necessary computations, but if it pleases him, let Caesar take credit for the calendar. Caesar should take credit for all his creations." She looked at the little boy on the grass.

I followed her gaze. "Such a handsome lad!" I said, though to me the child looked no different from any other.

"He looks like his father," said Cleopatra. "Everyone says so."

The child had a fuller head of hair than Caesar, but perhaps I could see a resemblance around the cheekbones and the chin. "He has his mother's eyes," I said. And then, feeling daring, I asked, "Will he be taking part in the triumph tomorrow?"

She looked at me for a long moment before she answered. "That's a delicate question. The whole matter of the Egyptian Triumph is . . . delicate. The role that should be played by myself, and by our son, has been discussed at some length." Discussed by herself and Caesar, she surely meant, despite her careful passive construction. Those discussions had not been pleasant, to judge by the way the bodyguard rolled his eyes, not realizing I was watching him.

"In the end—so it has been explained to me—a Roman triumph is a purely indigenous celebration," she said. "A Roman triumph has everything to do with military conquest and nothing to do with diplomacy . . . or dynasty. The Egyptian Triumph will celebrate Caesar's victory over my renegade brother, Ptolemy, who refused to make peace with me and who died in the Nile for his treachery. The Egyptian Triumph is about Roman arms, not about Caesar's . . . personal connection . . . to Egypt."

"But you were his ally in the war. He fought on your behalf."

She smiled without mirth. "He fought to make peace in Egypt, because our civil strife was disrupting the supply of Egyptian grain to Rome."

"So Your Majesty will *not* be appearing in the triumph?"

"According to Caesar, a triumph is performed by Romans, for Romans. Even the most distinguished persons of foreign birth can have no place in the procession . . . except as captives."

I nodded. "They say your sister Arsinoë will be paraded in chains. I don't think any female of royal blood has ever been marched as a captive in a triumph before."

"So *some* innovation is possible in a triumph, after all," Cleopatra said drily. "Arsinoë dared to raise troops against me. She deserves her fate."

"But she's can't be more than nineteen. She was even younger, then."

"Nonetheless, she and her confederate, Ganymedes, will both be paraded as captives and put to death."

"Ganymedes?"

"Her tutor."

"A eunuch?" Most household attendants of the Ptolemies were castrated.

"Of course. After Arsinoë put to death her general Achillas, Ganymedes took over command of her troops, such as they were."

I shook my head. "Caesar's grand captives will be a teenaged girl and a eunuch? I'm not sure what the Roman people will make of that. I suspect they would have been far more impressed by the sight of you, Your Majesty, perhaps riding in state atop a giant sphinx."

She smiled, pleased by the suggestion. "What an imagination you have, Gordianus-called-Finder! Alas, Caesar did not possess such a vision. The triumph will celebrate *his* victories in Egypt. Although I was his collaborator and the beneficiary of those victories, I shall not take part."

"And neither shall Caesar's son?"

The bodyguard shuddered and shook his head reflexively. I had broached a topic that must have caused much heated debate between Caesar and the queen, perhaps in this very spot in the garden.

Cleopatra scrutinized me for a long moment. She was

displeased that I had brought up the subject, yet she was pleased that I had called the boy Caesar's son, without equivocation. "It has been decided that Caesarion will *not* ride in the chariot with his father tomorrow," she finally said.

Cleopatra was doing her best to hide her disappointment, but it seemed clear that one of the purposes of her diplomatic visit to Rome—perhaps the main purpose—had been to persuade Caesar to acknowledge her son. She had hoped to make the Egyptian Triumph a celebration of herself and Caesarion. It was easy enough to follow her reasoning. Why shouldn't the Romans be pleased that the heir to the Egyptian throne was a boy of Roman blood, the son of their own ruler? Should they not be impressed that Caesar had coupled with a woman who was the living heir of Alexander the Great, the latest representative of the world's most venerable dynasty, and the incarnation of a goddess?

I could also imagine why Caesar had balked at the idea. An open declaration of dynastic intentions was still too radical for the Roman people to accept, and an Egyptian queen of Greek blood, however regal, was still a foreigner, and an unsuitable mother for the children of a Roman noble. It might also be that Caesar had other plans for the future, and intended for someone other than Caesarion to be his heir.

For whatever reason, Caesar had refused to acknowledge Caesarion. Despite the opportunity presented by his Egyptian Triumph, Cleopatra had been thwarted. What now were her feelings toward Caesar?

It occurred to me that Caesar dead might now be more valuable to her than Caesar alive. The assassination of Caesar would plunge Rome into confusion, perhaps even another civil war. Amid the wreckage and the chaos, might Egypt drive out the Roman garrisons and cast off the Roman yoke?

Weighed against demands of state and her own ambition, any personal feelings she still harbored for Caesar might count for nothing. Cleopatra came from a long line of cold-blooded crocodiles who were notorious for devouring their own. Her older sister, Berenice, had usurped their father; when he regained the upper hand, their father put Berenice to death. Cleopatra had not shed a tear when her brother perished in their civil war. She now seemed to be looking forward to the impending humiliation and execution of her younger sister with grim satisfaction.

Was Cleopatra capable of plotting Caesar's death? Did she have sufficient motive to do so? I looked into her eyes and shivered, despite the stifling heat of the day.

X I

Unlike Vercingetorix, Arsinoë and Ganymedes were not being held in the Tullianum, but if all went according to plan, they would both end up there tomorrow, to be dispatched by the executioner.

Their quarters were located in the vast new complex housing Pompey's Theater on the Field of Mars. Calpurnia's messenger had given me instructions on how to find the place, but, wending our way among the shops and arcades and meeting halls, Rupa and I became completely turned around and found ourselves in the theater itself, with its countless semicircular tiers of seats surmounted by a temple to Venus. On the stage, a play was being rehearsed, no doubt one of the many scheduled to be performed as part of the ongoing festival that would follow Caesar's fourth and final triumph. Dramas, comedies, athletic competitions, chariot races in the newly expanded Circus Maximus, and mock battles on the training grounds of the Field of Mars—all this and much more had been announced. After so many months of deprivation and dread, Caesar intended to give the people of Rome a prolonged series of holidays full of feasting and every kind of public entertainment.

I regained my bearings and found the dedicated stairwell that led up, up, up to the topmost floor of the theater. Rupa and I came to a heavily guarded door, where I showed my pass. I expected Rupa to be kept behind, but, perhaps carelessly, the guards allowed us both to enter.

I never knew such a place existed—a private suite located behind the highest tier of seats and just beneath the Temple of Venus. Perhaps Pompey had built this aerie to be his personal hideaway, but its seclusion and limited access made it an ideal place to lock someone away. Its proximity to the Field of Mars, where Caesar's troops would muster for the triumph, would allow quick and secure delivery of the prisoners to their place in the procession.

The spacious room was sparsely but tastefully appointed, lit by windows along one wall. There was even a balcony with an expansive view of rooftops below and the winding Tiber and rolling hills beyond. The balcony was much too high to offer any means of escape.

Apparently, the princess had been allowed at least one servant while in captivity. An unusually tall, plain-faced lady-in-waiting appeared, wearing a shimmering robe with wide sleeves and a khat headdress that gathered her hair into a kind of pillow behind her head. She wore no makeup except for a few lines of kohl around her eyes.

"Who are you?" she said sharply, eyeing me with disdain and Rupa with something closer to alarm. Perhaps I looked sufficiently resolute and Rupa sufficiently brawny to pass for public executioners.

"You've nothing to fear from us," I said.

"Are you Romans?"

"Yes."

"Then my princess can expect nothing good from you."

"I assure you, we wish her no harm. My name is Gordianus. This is my son Rupa, who does not speak."

"I presume you come from Caesar? No one gets past those guards, unless they're sent by the king-killer himself." Obviously, her view of Caesar differed from that of Cleopatra; he was not the peacemaker who restored the throne to its rightful occupant but the man who had murdered one monarch, young Ptolemy, and was about to murder another.

"But that's not quite true, is it?" I said. "You've had at least one visitor who was not sent by Caesar, who gained admittance on his own initiative, to satisfy his curiosity and to show his sympathy, I imagine. I speak of my friend Hieronymus."

Her whole bearing changed. The stiff shoulders relaxed. The deep wrinkles of her face recombined into a smile. Her eyes sparkled. She clapped her bony hands together.

"Ah, Hieronymus! Your friend, you say? Then tell me, how is that charming fellow?"

I was struck by two things: the household of Arsinoë was ignorant of Hieronymus's death, and the lady before me was infatuated with him. Why not? She looked to be about the same age as Hieronymus. Indeed, with her long neck and narrow, homely features, she might have been his female counterpart.

"I'm afraid that's why I've come. I have some bad news for your mistress."

She responded with a guttural, very unladylike laugh. "Bad news? On this of all days, the day before— What news could possibly qualify as 'bad,' considering the fate that hangs over the princess?" She shook her head and glowered at me—setting the wrinkles into a new configuration—then suddenly raised her eyebrows and gasped. "Oh, no! You don't mean that something has happened to Hieronymus? Not dear Hieronymus, of all people?"

"I'm afraid so. But I would prefer to deliver the news directly to your mistress. Or perhaps to her minister, Ganymedes—"

Even as I said the name, so did someone else who had just entered the room. Over the lady's shoulder, stepping toward us through a doorway, I saw the princess Arsinoë.

"Ganymedes!" She was saying. "Ganymedes, who's that at the door? What do they want?"

I stared at the lady-in-waiting. I blinked. In an instant, the illusion created by my own assumptions melted away. I looked at the bony hands; the flesh was soft and had never known physical labor, but they were not a woman's hands. I looked at the throat and detected the telltale bump, like a tiny apple. I looked at the plain, wrinkled face and wondered how I could have been mistaken. The lady was no lady. It was Ganymedes the eunuch who stood before me.

Arsinoë was allowed no servants, after all. She and her minister were the only inhabitants of the suite. No wonder the princess was so simply attired, since there was no one to dress her. Her long, shimmering robe was not much more elaborate than that worn by Ganymedes. Having no one to wash and set her hair, she concealed it inside a striped nemes headdress made of stiff cloth, which covered her brow and hung in lappets on either side, framing her plump, round face. Short and voluptuously built like her sister, Arsinoë had put on weight in captivity.

Ganymedes did not look starved either. A potbelly inter-rupted the otherwise straight line of his robe. Except for the nervous glint in their eyes, they looked like two bored house-guests who had nothing to do but eat all day.

Perhaps because neither was truly a warrior, it had not been thought necessary to reduce them by torture and starvation to a wretched state of near collapse. Or perhaps the lack of ill-treatment was on account of their genders. No princess had ever been paraded to her death in Rome before, and I do not think a eunuch had ever been paraded in a triumph, either. The organiz-er of the triumph (perhaps Caesar himself) may have considered the two of them sufficiently unmanly to begin with, so that no further degradation was deemed necessary to make them ready to be displayed for the scorn and contempt of the Roman people.

"Ganymedes, who are these men?" Arsinoë drew alongside the much taller eunuch and stared up at me.

Ganymedes delicately wiped a tear from one eye, careful not to smear the kohl. "Friends of Hieronymus," he whispered, his voice choked with emotion. "Dear Hieronymus!"

"My name is Gordianus. My son, who does not speak, is Rupa," I said. "Your Majesty," I added, and even made a slight bow, elbowing Rupa to do the same.

I could see she appreciated the gesture, however perfunc-tory. "You may be the last mortals on earth to call me that and acknowledge me with a bow," she said wistfully.

"Not true, Your Majesty," said Ganymedes, overcoming his tears. "I shall address you by your title and bow before you un-til the very end."

"Of course you will, Ganymedes," said the princess. "Not counting you, I mean. What's this about Hieronymus, then?"

"I'm very sorry to tell you that he's dead."

She drew a breath. "How?"

"He was murdered; stabbed to death."

"When?"

"Five nights ago, on the Palatine Hill."

She shook her head. "Is there no end to the wickedness of this world? Poor Hieronymus."

I decided that her plumpness was not unbecoming. She was prettier than her older sister, and the softness of her features made it more difficult to imagine her as a rapacious crocodile. Behind me, I heard Ganymedes weeping.

"I understand that Hieronymus managed to visit you here, Your Majesty, on more than one occasion."

"Yes, he was one of the very few visitors we've received, other than our jailors. He sent a message first, explaining where he came from and who he was, and saying he was curious to meet me. The curiosity was mutual."

"How so, Your Majesty?"

She walked toward the balcony and stepped up to the parapet. I followed at a respectful distance. "Massilia and Alexandria both were founded by Greeks near the mouth of a great river," she said. "Both became centers of culture, learning, and commerce. Alexandria is by far the greater city, of course, but Massilia is older. Hieronymus was chosen to serve as Scapegoat for Massilia, a sacrificial victim to bear away the suffering that might otherwise consume the whole city—suffering inflicted by Caesar. Am I not the Scapegoat of Alexandria? Caesar came. Caesar imposed his will upon us by brute force. The city surrendered. And now there must be a victim to display to the bloodthirsty people of Rome. I am that victim."

She gazed at the city below. "Vile place! Vile people! And to think that a Ptolemy should be paraded before them like a criminal, and put to death like a dog. The gods will have much to answer for when I join them in Elysium!"

She turned around and transfixed me with a smoldering gaze. She seemed much older than her nineteen years, and projected a presence beyond her stature. "But Hieronymus eluded the Fates. He was the Scapegoat who escaped! We were hoping that some of his good fortune would rub off on us—eh, Ganymedes? Alas, his luck must have rubbed off on something, if he was murdered, as you say. How well did you know him?"

I briefly explained my relationship with Hieronymus, and gave a reason for coming. "Since his death, I've been reading his personal papers. He said very kind things about you." In truth, he had written very little about Arsinoë. Yet he had visited her more than once. Why had he come back to see her, if there was nothing of interest to report? Hieronymus had not even mentioned Ganymedes, which seemed odd, given the eunuch's obvious infatuation with him.

Had Hieronymus been so embarrassed by Ganymedes' attentions that he kept silent about them, even in his private journal? I thought not. Hieronymus was not easily flustered, and not easily silenced. If he had considered the eunuch's infatuation absurd, he would have said so; it was not like Hieronymus to miss a chance to ridicule someone. But such was not the case.

This left a curious possibility: that the attraction had been mutual. I tended to think of Hieronymus as a voluptuary with an appetite for beautiful boys or girls; such were the pleasures that had been offered to him when he was the pampered Scapegoat. Plain-faced Ganymedes hardly seemed a likely recipient for his passions. But there is nothing as unpredictable as the attraction of one mortal for another.

What did I know about Hieronymus's most secret longings, or about Ganymedes, for that matter? No doubt there was more to the eunuch than met the eye, I thought—and winced at the cutting pun Hieronymus could have extracted from that observation. Ganymedes had risen to a position of power in one of the most competitive royal courts in the world, amid the most elegant and sophisticated surroundings imaginable. His learning and wit had served him well; he had lived the sort of life that Hieronymus should have lived, had Fortune not turned against him when he was young. Then Fortune turned against Ganymedes, at a time when Hieronymus seemed to be living a charmed existence. Each might have served as a mirror image to the other. Could that have been the root of a mutual attraction?

If Hieronymus had indeed felt drawn to the eunuch, it was perhaps not surprising that no mention of the fact appeared in his papers. He would not have told Calpurnia, considering it none of her business, and I suspected he would have kept such feelings out of his personal journal, which was more a repository for scathing observations and witty wordplay than for heartfelt confessions.

I turned to the tearful Ganymedes. I looked long and hard into his glittering eyes, and knew that my supposition was right. *Hieronymus, Hieronymus! Will you never cease to surprise me? Even in death, you throw up new puzzles.*

Had Arsinoë known? Had she allowed the two of them privacy, when Hieronymus came to visit? His visits could not have lasted long; the guards would not have allowed it. It might be that the intimacy of the Scapegoat and the eunuch extended to no more than a touch or a fleeting kiss. Some relationships are all the more intense for being limited by tragic circumstance.

"Wait a moment!" Arsinoë walked up to me and stared at my face. "I *knew* you looked familiar, and now I know why. You were with Caesar in Alexandria! Do you deny it?"

"It's true, Your Majesty. I was in the royal palace when Caesar was there. But I don't recall that you and I ever met—"

"I remember you, nonetheless. I recognize your face. You were among the Romans in the grand reception hall that day—the morning after Cleopatra smuggled herself into Caesar's presence and into his bed. Caesar gathered all the royal siblings and proceeded to apportion our father's kingdom among us. Cleopatra and Ptolemy were to share the throne in Alexandria. I was to be given Cyprus. Of course, that arrangement lasted as long as a drop of water in the Egyptian desert." She looked me up and down. "Who are you? One of Caesar's officers?"

"Certainly not."

"One of his political advisers? Or one of those merchants who came to Egypt with Caesar to pillage our grain supply?"

"I didn't arrive in Alexandria with Caesar, Your Majesty. I traveled to Egypt on personal business. I happened to find myself in the royal palace only because—"

"How well do you know my sister?"

I came to a halt in mid-speech, my mouth open.

Arsinoë locked her eyes on mine. "No ready answer for that question, eh? When did you last see Cleopatra?"

The crocodile had stirred within her. The menacing edge in her voice sent a chill up my spine, never mind that it came from a plump, teenaged girl who at that moment was a helpless captive. This was the conquered enemy whom Caesar considered formidable enough to be paraded in his triumph, and dangerous enough to be put to death.

If I lied, she would know. "I saw your sister this morning, Your Majesty. I've just come from visiting her, as a matter of fact."

"Did she send you to spy on me? Is she afraid I might yet escape? I would if I could! And then I'd go straight to the villa where Caesar is keeping her, like his personal whore, and strangle her with my bare hands!"

She clutched the air with her plump little fingers. The illusion of the crocodile vanished. She was a furious, very frightened child. She bolted toward me. I grabbed her wrists.

"Unhand me, you filthy Roman!" she shouted.

Ganymedes started toward us, but Rupa blocked his way.

"By the ka of my own father, I swear that I am not your sister's spy," I said. The oath seemed to calm her, but I kept a firm grip on her wrists.

"Then what business did you have with her?"

"We talked about Hieronymus."

"Hieronymus visited Cleopatra as well?"

"Yes. But he was not your enemy, and neither am I."

Arsinoë tore herself from my grip and turned her face away. She trembled and heaved, then steadied herself. "Tell Caesar, or my sister, or whatever person sent you, that the rightful queen of Egypt is ready to confront her fate. She shall do so with her head held high and her shoulders back. She will not weep, she will not tremble, she will not tear her hair and beg for mercy from the Roman mob. Nor will she throw herself from this balcony—though I suspect that was Caesar's hope when he placed us in these quarters, that I would kill myself and save him the shame of executing a woman."

She turned to face me, sufficiently composed to stare into my eyes again. "My fate is in the hands of the gods. But so is Caesar's, whether he knows it or not. His crimes against me are an offense to the gods, who never forget and seldom forgive. Caesar will not escape their judgment. When the time comes, his punishment will be terrible. Mark my words!"

The door flew open. One of the guards stepped into the room. "What's the shouting about?"

"My visitors will leave now." Arsinoë turned her back on me and returned to the balcony. Ganymedes, with his nose in the air, strode past me to join her.

As we made our way down the many flights of steps, I pondered the threat posed to Caesar, and to Cleopatra, by Arsinoë. She would certainly kill them both, if she could. The death of Cleopatra would clear the way for Arsinoë to seize control in Alexandria, presuming she could return there alive. The death of Caesar could lead to chaos in Rome and to full independence for Egypt. Yet what means did Arsinoë possess to bring about anyone's death or to engineer her own escape? Did she have confederates in the city, ready to act on her behalf? Might there be individuals in the entourage of Cleopatra who were secretly loyal to Arsinoë?

These were idle speculations. I had no reason to think that Arsinoë could possibly devise a double assassination and a last-minute escape. And yet, Hieronymus had asserted that the threat to Caesar came from an unforeseen quarter. . . .

Skipping ahead of me down the steps, Rupa kept turning back, attempting to tell me something by using his personal system of gestures and facial expressions. I frowned, unable to understand him.

"What are you trying to say, Rupa? Here, stop for a moment, so that I can see you clearly."

He was fairly bursting with emotion. He made a shapely gesture to indicate Arsinoë; that was clear enough. But the feeling he was trying to express was so grand it defeated his vocabulary.

I smiled sadly. "Yes, Rupa, I agree. In her own way, Arsinoë *is* magnificent."

He nodded vigorously. I saw a bemused look on his face and tears in his eyes.

Oh, Rupa! I thought. *It's no good for a fellow like you to have such feelings for a princess—especially a princess who'll be dead tomorrow.*

X I I

"So, you managed to endure them both in one day," said Calpurnia. "Which sister struck you as the more wicked?"

The last rays of sunlight from the windows illuminated the room with a soft glow; it was not quite the hour of lighting lamps. Caesar's wife and her haruspex sat side by side while Rupa and I remained standing. Porsenna's yellow costume was the brightest thing in the room; it seemed to absorb all the ambient light and cast it back again.

" '*Wicked*' is not necessarily a word I would use to describe either of them," I said. "They're not as simple as that."

"Nonsense! Don't tell me you've been taken in by the so-called Ptolemaic mystique, Finder—this absurd notion they put about regarding their supposed divinity."

I raised an eyebrow. "The new statue of Caesar on the Capitoline declares him to be a demigod, I believe."

"Descending from a goddess and incarnating a goddess are two different things," she said.

"I'll have to take your word for that."

Calpurnia ignored my sardonic tone. "All this fuss they make about the many generations of their royal line, going back to the first Ptolemy. When did he reign? Two hundred and fifty years ago? My own family descends from King Numa, and he lived more than six hundred years ago. The Ptolemies are mere upstarts compared to the Calpurnii. Isn't that right, Uncle Gnaeus?"

She nodded to the white-haired priest, who had just stepped into the room.

Gnaeus Calpurnius gave his niece a kiss on the forehead. He snapped his fingers. A slave brought a chair.

Uncle Gnaeus sat down with a grunt. "That is correct, my dear; our line is far more ancient than that of the Ptolemies. And what did any Ptolemy ever achieve, compared to the ac- complishments of our ancestor Numa? Numa established the order of the Vestal virgins. He set the dates for the holy festivals and sacrifices, prescribed the rituals for venerating the gods, and established the priesthoods for performing these sacred duties. Through the mediation of his beloved, the nymph Egeria, he communed with great Jupiter himself. What did any Ptolemy ever do, except build a lighthouse?"

Which you obviously have never seen, you pompous fool! I thought. The Pharos lighthouse was the tallest building on earth, with a beacon visible across a vast expanse of land and sea, a true wonder of the world. It was likely to still be standing long after Numa's decrepit reckoning of days was long forgot- ten, supplanted by Caesar's new calendar—which had been de- vised by scholars from the library established by the Ptolemies.

I refrained from saying any of this. Uncle Gnaeus's boasting was merely a distraction. Calpurnia wanted to know whether

Cleopatra or Arsinoë posed any threat to her husband. Hieronymus's notes on his visits were worthless in this regard. I had to rely on my own observations and instincts.

"It's my belief that the Queen of Egypt came to Rome with one goal in mind: to persuade Caesar to acknowledge her son as his offspring."

"Something he will never do!" said Calpurnia. "For one thing, the child isn't Caesar's. Porsenna has studied the matter."

"Is that right?" I said.

The haruspex smiled. "I managed to obtain a few strands of the boy's hair, never mind how. I performed a sacrifice. When the hair and the entrails of the sacrificial beast were burned, the pattern of the smoke clearly indicated that the child has no Roman blood whatsoever. The science of haruspicy is never wrong in such matters."

"It's probably the whelp of that lackey of hers, the one who toted her about inside a carpet," said Uncle Gnaeus. "Any woman who would resort to such an indignity would probably allow even a servant to have his way with her."

I doubted this. If there was anything Cleopatra took seriously, it was the dignity of her person. For a woman who considered herself a goddess, copulation was a serious and sacred matter. "Is Caesar aware of the results of this divination?"

Calpurnia made a face. "Caesar does not always accord sufficient importance to the ancient ways of knowing."

"He observes the rituals, but he lacks true understanding." Uncle Gnaeus shook his head.

"Enough, Uncle!" said Calpurnia sharply. "Now is not the time to discuss Caesar's deficiencies in matters of religious insight. Let the Finder finish his report."

"As I said, the queen came to Rome hoping to establish her son's legitimacy. She hoped tomorrow's triumph might celebrate that event. Her intentions have been thwarted. I think she misunderstood how the Roman people might react to such an announcement. I think she misunderstood the true nature of a Roman triumph. Caesar corrected her mistaken viewpoints."

"What does she intend to do now?" said Calpurnia.

"Cleopatra is a pragmatic woman—pragmatic enough to hide in a carpet if it serves her purpose. But she's also tremendously willful. I wouldn't want to disappoint her. I certainly wouldn't want to be her enemy."

"And is Caesar, having disappointed her, now her enemy?"

"I don't know. Perhaps you should ask Caesar what he thinks. I'm much more certain about the feelings of Princess Arsinoë. I have no doubt that she would do away with both Caesar and Cleopatra, if she possibly could."

"But how could she do such a thing?"

"Does Arsinoë have allies in the city? With your network of agents, you're more likely to know that than I am, Calpurnia."

"But what is your *feeling* about these Egyptians, Finder? What does your *instinct* tell you?"

What a question, from the once hardheaded Calpurnia! Had she entirely abandoned cold logic and deduction in favor of divination and intuition?

I sighed. "Here is what I think. Cleopatra almost certainly could kill Caesar if she wanted to, but she probably doesn't. Arsinoë would kill him without hesitation if she could, but she almost certainly can't."

"Then Caesar will survive tomorrow's triumph?" Calpurnia

looked at her uncle, then at the haruspex, and finally at me. She was demanding reassurance.

"I have no reason to think otherwise," I said, and prayed to Fortuna that I was right.

Rupa and I crossed the Palatine at twilight. The streets were almost deserted. For many people, this had been a day to recover from the festivities of the Gallic Triumph and to rest up for the next day's Egyptian Triumph. The only people stirring were slaves on ladders outside houses, setting torches in sconces to light the doorways and illuminate patches of the street.

We rounded a corner. My house came into sight, a little way down the winding street. A small company of armed lictors was standing outside my door. Rupa gripped my arm to alert me.

"Yes, I see them, Rupa. Lictors at the door—never a good sign." I tried to keep my tone light, but my heart was pounding.

The nearer we drew, the bigger the lictors appeared. Every one of them was half a head taller than Rupa and considerably broader. Veritable giants, they were; quite possibly Gauls, I thought, next to whom the Romans are a little people. Gallic senators, Gallic lictors—one of the chief complaints one heard against Caesar nowadays was that he had infested the city with Gauls. He had exterminated the Gauls who opposed him— Vercingetorix was presumably the last—and those who remained were loyal only to Caesar. Or were they? Everywhere I looked now, I sought threats to Caesar. Could even his own lictors be trusted?

But more to the point: what were the dictator's bodyguards doing outside my house?

As I approached the door, never breaking my stride, one of the men stepped forward to block my way.

"Remove yourself," I said, trying to keep my voice from quavering. "My name is Gordianus. I am a citizen. This is my house."

The man nodded. He looked at Rupa warily, but stepped aside.

Even as I reached toward the door, it swung open. There before me, framed by the doorway, stood Caesar himself.

I had not seen him face-to-face since our time together in Alexandria, where he had grown sleek and tan beneath the Egyptian sun. Now he looked thin and pale, almost as pale as his toga, and there was more gray than I remembered amid the scant hair on his head. For just an instant, I saw his face unguarded. The mouth was turned down, the eyes slightly vacant, the brow furrowed; he looked like a man with many worries. In the next instant he saw me, and his face was transformed by a beaming smile.

"Gordianus! Just the man I've come to see. They told me you were out and didn't know when to expect you. I waited for a while anyway. How blessedly peaceful it is in your quaint little garden. I was about to leave—but here you are!"

"Yes. Here I am."

"And who's that, behind you? Ah, yes, Rupa. I remember him from Alexandria."

"Those were memorable days, Dictator."

Caesar laughed. "No need to address me formally, Gordianus. We've been through too much together."

"Nonetheless, I am a Roman citizen, and you are my dictator. The office is a venerable one, is it not? Our ancestors created the dictatorship so that strong men could save the state in times of peril. The short list of citizens who have held the office is most distinguished."

His smile twisted at one corner. "The dictatorship was tarnished by Sulla, to be sure. Hopefully, I can burnish it to its former luster in the hearts of the Roman people. Well, now that you're here, perhaps you might invite me to rest a bit longer in your garden."

"Of course, Dictator. If your lictors will allow me to pass."

In fact, no one was really blocking my way, but at a nod from Caesar, the lictors all drew back. Caesar himself stepped aside to make way for me.

Bethesda, Diana, and Davus were standing in the vestibule. Mopsus and Androcles lurked behind them. Everyone looked stiff and uncomfortable; apparently they had just bade Caesar a formal farewell. As I passed, allowing Caesar to precede me, Diana whispered in my ear, "What in Hades does he want with you, Papa?"

I answered her with a shrug, since I had no idea. Unless, of course, he was aware of his wife's activities and was about to tell me what he thought of my investigations on Calpurnia's behalf.

Lamps had been lit in the house, but the garden was growing dark. I told Rupa to fetch some lights, but Caesar shook his head.

"No need for that, Gordianus. I don't mind the darkness, if you don't. It's rather pleasant like this, smelling the jasmine and the roses in the warm twilight."

We sat in chairs facing each other. In the gloaming, I found it difficult to make out his expression. Perhaps he liked it that way. It occurred to me that he must grow weary of being constantly scrutinized by others eager to read his thoughts and intentions.

And then my heart gave a lurch and my mouth turned dry, for it suddenly struck me that Caesar might have come with news of Meto. Had something occurred in Spain, where the scattered remnants of Caesar's enemies were said to be gathering in hopes of mounting yet another challenge to his supremacy? I pressed my hand to my chest, as if I could still my racing heart. Surely Caesar would not have greeted me with such a beaming smile if he had come to deliver bad news. . . .

I must have muttered Meto's name aloud, for Caesar smiled again—I could see that, even in the gloaming—and said the name back to me. "Meto—ah, yes, dear Meto. How I miss that boy! And so must you. Of course, he's hardly a boy anymore, is he?"

"He turned thirty-three in Quinctilis," I said, my mouth dry.

"That's right! Do you know, I think I forgot to send him a greeting. A bit late to do so now, even belatedly. I wish he could be here now, but his service in Spain is too important. I need men there I can trust, and your son's devotion to me is truly a gift from the gods."

I relaxed. He had not come with bad news, after all. "I'm surprised you can spare a thought for such trivialities as birthdays. You must have so many things on your mind."

"Indeed I do. Which is why I completely forgot about you yesterday, Gordianus."

"But why should you have thought of me at all, Dictator?"

He clucked his tongue, to chide me for my insistent formality. "Because of Meto, of course. Your son should have been with me yesterday, to celebrate the Gallic Triumph. He was with me everywhere in Gaul, at practically every moment. He was always there, always ready and eager to receive my dictation, sometimes in the middle of the night."

I cleared my throat. Meto and I had never explicitly discussed his relationship with Caesar, but I had long assumed that my son had been receptive to more than Caesar's dictation. Their intimacy was none of my business, of course, and at any rate it seemed to have cooled with the passing years, as such affairs almost invariably do. As for their relationship as author and amanuensis, according to Meto, he himself had written a large part of Caesar's memoirs of the Gallic campaign, taking his imperator's raw notes and fleshing them into prose, with Caesar merely amending and approving a final version before it was copied and disseminated.

Caesar's expression became impossible to read in the darkness, but the politician's bluffness fell away from his voice. His tone was wistful. "Can I speak to you candidly, Gordianus? To call Meto my loyal secretary is to make light of what he's meant to me over the years. Meto has fought for me, spied for me, even risked his life for me, not once but many times. He was there with me in Gaul, and at Pharsalus, and in Alexandria; he was with me in Asia and Africa. He should have been here for all my triumphs. Instead, he's on a vital mission in Spain, which is only further testament to his unflagging loyalty."

Caesar sighed. "Meto has seen me at my best—and at my worst. Over the years, I've learned to trust him, to take off my armor in his presence, so to speak—not an easy thing for an old warrior to do. He's as close to me as a son—yet in no way have I ever presumed that I could take the place of his father."

"Meto is not of my blood. I adopted him."

"And yet you are as surely Meto's father as if you had made him yourself. I envy you that, Gordianus—having a son, especially a son like Meto."

"Does Caesar have no son?" I thought of Cleopatra.

He was silent for a long moment. "That . . . is a complicated question. Ironic, isn't it? One man produces a son—at long last!—yet hesitates to call himself the boy's father, while another man adopts a boy not of his blood and becomes a father in every way that matters to gods and mortals."

Caesarion was his son, then—or so he believed. Caesar breathed deeply. "Do you know, this is the first time I've come to a complete halt in . . . well, I have no idea how long it's been! I can't relax like this in my own garden. Servants are always hovering, supplicants are in the vestibule, senators are at the door, my wife is forever fussing and fretting over me. . . ."

"Your wife?" Did he know of Calpurnia's fears and the divinations of her haruspex?

"Calpurnia, the old dear. No man could have asked for a better wife in wartime. While I was away from the city, Calpurnia did everything necessary to see that my home was well run. She watched the other women of Rome with a careful eye; she made sure that any conspiracies against me came to nothing. There is the world of the bloody battlefield, and there is the world of the hearth and the loom, and any war—especially a civil war—must be waged in both arenas. Calpurnia was my commander for the home front, and she conducted herself brilliantly.

"But now that the peace has been won . . ." He shook his head. "She's become a different woman. She fills her head with

superstitious nonsense. She pesters me with dreams and por-
tents. I wonder if it's not the influence of that crazy uncle of
hers. Gnaeus Calpurnius is always in the house these days. The
old fellow's a priest, and takes himself very seriously—so proud
of his descent from King Numa!"

I nodded, and considered the irony that the master of the
world should be so unaware of events in his own household.
From what I had observed, Uncle Gnaeus disapproved of his
niece's obsession with the "superstitious nonsense" fostered by
the haruspex Porsenna, of whom Caesar appeared to know
nothing.

He laughed softly. "But why am I telling you all this? It
must be that gift you possess."

"Gift?"

"Your special gift—the power to compel the truth from
others. Cicero warned me about it a long time ago. Catilina said
the same thing—do you remember him?—and Meto confirmed it. The gift of Gordianus—that must be what's loosened
my tongue. Or perhaps . . . perhaps I'm just tired."

The moon had risen above the roofline. Its blue light
gleamed on Caesar's bald pate. He turned his face upward into
the moonbeam, and I saw that his eyes were closed. He fell
silent and breathed so deeply that I thought he might have
fallen asleep, until he sighed and spoke again.

"Ah, but I've strayed from the point of my visit. I wanted to
give you this."

He produced a thin, square token carved from bone. I took
it from him. Squinting under the moonlight, I saw there was a
letter and a number painted on it.

"What's this, Dictator? What does 'F XII' refer to?"

"It's the section reserved for you and your family in the viewing stands. I'm told the seats are quite good. They're rather high up, but that's what you want for a spectacle, isn't it? A bit of distance? You wouldn't want to be too close; you're not the sort to make a rush at the captives as they pass or to bait the exotic animals. Just show that token to the usher, and he'll lead you and your family to your seats. They're reserved for tomorrow's triumph, and for the next two triumphs as well."

"This is for Meto's sake?"

"Because Meto cannot be here, yes, I'll honor Meto's father and family in his stead. But you deserve a seat on your own merits, Gordianus, at least for tomorrow's Egyptian Triumph. You were there in Alexandria, after all. You witnessed history in the making. Now you can witness the celebration."

I began to object, but Caesar silenced me with a gesture. "No, don't thank me! You've earned this favor, Gordianus. It's the least I can do." He stood and straightened his toga. "I meant to ask: did you manage to find good seats for the Gallic Triumph on your own?"

"As a matter of fact, yes. There's a little ledge at Lucullus's Temple of Fortuna that affords a good view of the route."

"Ah, yes." He nodded, then his face grew long. "If you were at the Temple of Fortuna, then you must have seen the . . . unexpected interruption."

"When the axle of the chariot broke? Yes. But I thought you handled it very well. The episode provided a bit of relief from all that grandiose formality. Your soldiers must love you very much indeed to think they can tease you so mercilessly."

"Yes," he said, his tone a bit cool. "A funny thing, that—the axle breaking. When we examined it later, it appeared almost as if someone had tampered with it."

"Tampered?"

"Caused it to break intentionally. It looked to me as if the wood had been partially sawed through. But it was impossible to be sure, the way the wood had splintered."

"Sabotage? But who would have done such a thing?"

He shook his head. "It was probably a simple accident, after all. And now I really must be going. Calpurnia becomes especially worried if I'm not home after dark."

I accompanied him through the house and into the vestibule, where the family still gathered, suspending their normal activities as long as the dictator was among us. Diana nudged Davus, who nudged Mopsus, who gave his little brother a kick. Androcles rushed to open the door, and Caesar, his thoughts now elsewhere, departed without another word.

The family gathered around me. While they peppered me with questions, I peered at the token in the palm of my hand. I would have preferred to stay at home the next day, avoiding the Egyptian Triumph altogether, but now that Caesar himself had gone to the effort to present this gift to me, I could hardly be absent. On the morrow, I would have an excellent view of the princess Arsinoë and her minister Ganymedes as they took their final walk on this earth.

XIII

Bethesda was quite pleased when I showed her the token Caesar had given me and explained what it was good for. Such signs of favor from a social superior always seemed to matter to her far more than they did to me, perhaps because of her origins. She had been born a foreigner and a slave; now she was a Roman matron and proud of it, despite clinging to certain foreign ways.

My own attitude toward the elite and the favors they could bestow was more problematical. Though born a Roman, I had realized from an early age that I would never become one of the so-called *nobilitas,* "those who are known" for having won public office; I never expected even to be allowed into the homes of such people. Now, after a lifetime of serving them, I was still not the sort of person they cared to invite to dinner. Rome's noble families are few in number and they closely guard their privileges, though outsiders of exceptional ability and ambition can occasionally join their ranks; Cicero was the prime example of such a New Man, the first of the Tullius family to be elected to office and set upon the Course of Honor in the quest to become consul for a year.

Many of those nobles, who had thought me barely worthy to serve them and certainly unworthy of their friendship, were dead now, while I, a humble citizen of no distinction, was still alive. For those aristocrats who had survived, what did the Course of Honor or nobility itself mean now, with one man installed in a permanent position at the apex of power?

And what did this token of favor from the dictator mean to me? I pondered this question as I examined the little piece of carved bone in my hand by the soft morning light in my vestibule. I was already dressed in a toga, with a simple breakfast of farina and stewed fruit in my belly. Menenia had just arrived with the twins. Bethesda insisted that the family set out early to claim our seats, even though I tried to explain to her that the whole point of possessing such a token was to allow us to show up whenever we wanted, since the seats were reserved for us. I think she wanted us to be seated early so that we might be conspicuously visible to the arriving throng, ensconced in our place of privilege.

With my family surrounding me, including Mopsus and Androcles ("We'll need them to fetch food and drinks," Bethesda had insisted), I set out, descending from the Palatine directly to the Forum, which was already more crowded than I would have expected at such an early hour. The stands with our seats were located near the end of the route, facing the foot of the Capitoline Hill and high enough to afford a panoramic view. Directly across from us were the most prestigious of the viewing stands, upon which curtained boxes with plush appointments had been erected for the comfort of important dignitaries. Those seats were still empty.

Beyond and between the dignitaries' boxes, I could clearly see the trail that led up the slope of the Capitoline to the Carcer. Later, if I cared to, I could probably watch Arsinoë and Ganymedes being led to the very door of the prison, behind which they would meet their deaths in the pit of the Tullianum.

While we waited for the procession to begin, I thought about what Caesar had said regarding his accident during the Gallic Triumph. If someone had deliberately severed the axle of his chariot, did the sabotage support Calpurnia's suspicions of a plot against Caesar? It was hard to see how; such an accident could hardly have been counted on to injure Caesar, much less kill him. Perhaps it had been devised merely to embarrass him, but by whom and for what reason? Renegade Gauls in the city might have wished to mar his victory over Vercingetorix, but how could they have obtained access to the sacred chariot? Caesar's veterans had felt free to tease him with lewd verses; might some of them have been so bold as to sever the axle to play a practical joke on him?

Had Caesar only imagined signs of tampering, and, if so, what did such imaginings indicate about his state of mind? Or was Caesar's speculation about sabotage a ruse? He had seemed to reveal this concern in a genuinely unguarded moment, but did such a man ever speak without premeditation? It might be that Caesar was disseminating this rumor of sabotage with the intent of dispelling any notion that the accident was an evil omen, the result of divine displeasure rather than human intervention.

"Husband!"

My thoughts were interrupted by Bethesda. Her voice was hushed, her tone excited.

"Husband, is that *her*?"

I blinked and looked about. While I had been staring abstractedly into empty space, the stands around me had filled up. Below us, every spot along the route was taken. The Forum was a sea of spectators bisected by the broad path left open for the triumph.

"Over there," Bethesda said insistently, "in the special seats. Is that really *her*?"

I gazed across the way. The boxes for dignitaries had also filled up. Amid the gaudily attired ambassadors and emissaries and visiting heads of states sat a lone female, resplendent in a purple gown and a golden diadem. The walls and high parapet of the box kept her from being seen by the crowd around and below her, but because our seats were directly across from the box, we had a clear view of her.

"Yes," I said. "That is Cleopatra."

The queen had arrived without fanfare. No one in the crowd seemed to be aware of her presence. Barred by Caesar from taking part in the triumph, she was merely another spectator amid the thousands present that day.

Bethesda squinted, tilted her head to one side, and frowned. "She's not as pretty as I had imagined."

I looked sidelong at my wife and smiled. "She's certainly no rival to you."

It was the right thing to say; Bethesda could not suppress a smile of triumph. And it was true. In her heyday, Bethesda had been much more beautiful than Cleopatra, and when I looked at Bethesda now, did I not still see the girl she had been?

A deafening cheer rang out. The procession had begun.

First came the senators and magistrates. Again I saw Cicero

and Brutus strolling side by side, talking to each other and ignoring the crowd, as if nothing of importance was taking place.

The trumpeters followed. Their fanfare had a distinctly
Egyptian flourish to it, and charged the air with anticipation.
What wonders from the distant Nile would Caesar present to
the people of Rome?

The spoils of Gaul had been vast and impressive, but the
items from Egypt were of another order of magnificence. They
were not booty, strictly speaking, since Caesar had not conquered the country; his role had been to end the civil war between the royal siblings and install one of them on the throne.
Many of the items displayed that day were gifts from Queen
Cleopatra to demonstrate her gratitude to Caesar and to the
people of Rome for taking her side in the war with her siblings.

There was a towering black obelisk etched with hieroglyphs
and decorated with gold bosses in the shape of lotus blossoms.
There were bronze statues of various gods, including an incarnation of the Nile represented as an old man surrounded by
river nymphs, with creatures of the deep entwined in his flowing beard. There was a grand procession of magnificent sphinxes,
one after another, carved from granite and marble.

The wagons bearing these massive objects were pulled not
by beasts but by exotic-looking slaves from the teeming markets
of Alexandria. These slaves came from far-off lands whose very
names excited wonder—Nubia, Arabia, Ethiopia—and the sight
of their dark, gleaming bodies excited almost as much comment as the treasures they were pulling.

The crowd gasped with amazement at the appearance of the
final sphinx. It was being pulled by the longest train of slaves,
and at a distance appeared to loom far larger than the other

sphinxes. This was a trick of the eye. It was not the sphinx but the slaves who were out of scale; these were the miniature people called Pygmies who were said to dwell in a land of dense forests near the source of the Nile. The incongruity of the sight appealed to the Roman sense of humor and prompted gales of laughter.

A replica of the sarcophagus of Alexander was presented, along with several statues of the conqueror. The founding of Alexandria had been his most enduring accomplishment, and his burial place was one of the principle shrines of the city.

There followed a visual catalog of the municipal achievements of Alexander's successors, the Ptolemies. A remarkably detailed model of Alexandria carved from ivory depicted the walls of the city, the great library and museum, the royal palace and the theater, the broad avenues decorated with ancient monuments, and the jetties embracing the great harbor. (Caesar had very nearly met his death in that harbor, when his ship was sunk in a naval engagement and he was forced to swim ashore).

A towering model of the Pharos lighthouse rolled by, complete with a fiery beacon at the summit. This was followed by a model of the gigantic Temple of Serapis and a statue of the god whom the Greek Ptolemies had established as the chief deity of Egypt; Serapis resembled bearded Zeus, or Jupiter, sitting on a throne and wielding a scepter, but on his head he wore a grain basket for a crown and at his feet crouched a three-headed dog meant to be Cerberus but rendered in a style more akin to the jackal-headed Egyptian god, Anubis.

An exotic bestiary followed, featuring the fabled creatures of the Nile and of regions even more remote. Muzzled crocodiles were paraded, fitted with harnesses attached to leashes held by teams of beastmasters: the creatures were so strong and unpredictable, it seemed to take all the keepers' strength to prevent them from lurching into the crowd. Images were displayed of the *híppos potámios,* the famous Nile river-horse, and of the *rhinókeros,* which looks like a leathery, overgrown boar brandishing a single monstrous tusk.

The beast show ended with a genuine crowd-pleaser: a troupe of Pygmies rode by, mounted on the gigantic, flightless birds the Greeks call *strouthokamelos,* "camel-sparrows," famed for their magnificent feathers and absurdly long necks. They are said to hide their heads in the sand when frightened.

There followed an exhibit celebrating the various crops grown along the Nile, the great granary of the Mediterranean, thanks to its yearly inundation. The pretty Egyptian maidens in pleated linen gowns carrying sheaves of grain were not as exciting as crocodiles on leashes, but they nonetheless garnered the crowd's applause, and cheers rang out for Caesar when a crier announced that a distribution of free grain to the citizenry would follow the triumph.

The tone of the procession grew more martial as placards were exhibited showing incidents of the war. (Caesar had promised to tell the full story in his continuing memoirs, but that volume had not yet been published.) There were scenes of the battles in the harbor of Alexandria, in which the skies were filled with flaming missiles hurled from shipboard ballistae. Other scenes illustrated the long siege of the royal palace by the Egyptians, who attempted for months to penetrate Caesar's defenses or else to cut off his water supply, and failed at every turn. There were several scenes of the final, decisive battle on the banks of the Nile, where young King Ptolemy's royal barge was capsized by fleeing Egyptian soldiers. The king's remains were never found; nonetheless, a number of his personal effects had been retrieved from the Nile, including some of his ceremonial weapons and armor, and these magnificent pieces were displayed as trophies.

Other scenes depicted the deaths of Caesar's chief enemies in Egypt. King Ptolemy's lord chamberlain, the eunuch Pothinus, had been forced by Caesar to drink poison for conspiring against him; the man had died before my eyes, cursing both Cleopatra and her brother. The placard illustrating his death portrayed him with exaggerated breasts and hips, which he had not possessed, and feminine makeup, which he had not worn; Pothinus was reduced to a Roman caricature of a eunuch. The crowd laughed and cheered as they were shown the picture of him writhing in agony at Caesar's feet, the death cup still clutched in his hand.

Another placard showed the death of Achillas, the Egyptian general who had mounted the siege against Caesar; it was Arsinoë who eventually executed him for treachery. Achillas was a name of infamy in Rome, for he had been among the murderers of Pompey, delivering the blow that struck the Great One's head from his shoulders even before he could step ashore in Egypt.

Curiously, there was no placard to illustrate Pompey's demise, or the subsequent presentation of Pompey's head as a gift from King Ptolemy to Caesar. Pompey's defeat at Pharsalus, his desperate flight to Egypt, and his ignominious death were not to figure in any of Caesar's triumphs. Whether for fear of hubris, or in deference to the lingering sentimental attachment many Romans felt for Pompey, Caesar did not seize the occasion to gloat over his rival's desecrated corpse.

Others besides me noticed this omission; and clearly not everyone felt sentimental about the Great One. A man called out, "Where is Pompey's head? Show us the head!"

Some joined in this call, but many others groaned, shushed their neighbors, and booed. A ripple of discord passed through the crowd, sparking restlessness and loosening tongues.

"And while you're at it, show us Cleopatra!" someone yelled.

"Yes, where's Cleopatra? Let's have a look at the little nymph who has Caesar so hot and bothered!"

"Show us the queen! Show us the queen!"

"There should at least be a picture of her . . ."

"Preferably naked!"

The wags in the crowd remained unaware that Cleopatra was among them, seated amid the dignitaries. I looked across the way, and saw that she had moved back from the parapet, as if to further conceal herself. Her face showed no expression.

The inevitable chants followed, speculating on the activities of Caesar and the Egyptian queen during their long boat trip up the Nile. Many in the crowd already knew these lewd ditties and joined in at once, clapping in unison as they recited one verse after another. Men share such bits of doggerel in the Forum; wives bring them home from the marketplace; soon, even children know them by heart. For all his earthly glory, Caesar was powerless to stop the spread of a rude joke or an awful pun at his expense.

I gazed at Cleopatra across the way. Her face remained impassive, but even at such a distance I could see that her cheeks had reddened a bit. The queen was not used to being mocked.

Then, abruptly, the ditties fell silent and the clapping

stopped. As if conjured by the will of the crowd, Cleopatra suddenly loomed before them—or rather, her image loomed, for approaching on the path, mounted on a platform and pulled by a team of Nubian slaves, was a breathtaking statue of her.

It was larger than life and appeared to be made of solid gold, though it was probably gilded bronze. The gilt shimmered brightly beneath the sun; flashes of golden light dazzled my eyes. The queen was portrayed not in the outlandish garb of the pharaohs, which the Ptolemies had appropriated when they assumed the rule of Egypt, but in elegant Greek dress, wearing a simple diadem on her brow. The statue's face had a stern, almost mannish quality; perhaps the sculptor made his subject look older and plainer than she was, so as to emphasize her qualities as a ruler of men rather than an object of male desire. The face, with its sparkling lapis eyes and elusive smile, nonetheless projected a powerful feminine allure; one could see why a man like Caesar had been captivated by such a woman.

I drew a sharp breath. Caesar's inclusion of the statue—a gift from the queen herself?—was a considerable gamble. Who could predict the crowd's reaction? Or did he brazenly parade the statue for just that reason, as a means to gauge the temper of the Roman mob? If the statue had been a piece of captured booty, and Cleopatra a vanquished enemy, there would have been no controversy; but Caesar's war in Egypt had affirmed Cleopatra's claim to the throne, so the appearance of the statue seemed to be a celebration of the queen herself. Here, for all to see, in golden splendor, was the exotic creature who claimed to have borne Caesar's son and whom many thought was encouraging Caesar's royal ambitions. If the crowd found the statue offensive, they might break into a full-scale riot.

I looked around me, wondering if our high seats would prove to be our salvation or our doom. Would we remain above the rampaging mob or be driven up and over the top, to fall to our deaths? There was also the possibility that the crowd might realize that Cleopatra was present and vent their fury against her.

I gazed at the queen in her box across the way. Our eyes met. Cleopatra nodded slightly, to show that she recognized me. She saw the alarm on my face, and her own expression grew apprehensive. She raised her eyebrows slightly. She frowned.

But the reaction of the crowd was far from violent. A hush fell over the throng. There were no jeers, no cries of outrage, not even any ribald jests. The golden statue seemed to cast a spell. People gazed up in wonder as it passed before them.

Across the way, I saw the queen of Egypt smile. She turned to confer with someone in her entourage. She turned back and began to stand. Did she intend to draw attention to herself, to make her presence known to the crowd?

Before that could happen, the moment passed. The mood of the crowd abruptly changed. The air rang with jeers, shouts, and taunts, for immediately following Cleopatra's statue came the procession of Egyptian prisoners. From the golden glory of the queen, the crowd's attention was drawn to the abject misery and wretchedness of her vanquished enemies.

Cleopatra sat. Her smile vanished.

The few surviving officers of Ptolemy's army were paraded before us in chains and rags and tattered Egyptian headdresses. A few of these were eunuchs, and the crowd peered at their near-naked bodies curiously, looking for distinguishing characteristics. To be sure, the eunuchs were not as hirsute as some of their compatriots, but their bodies had none of the voluptuousness of women; perhaps because they had been fed so poorly, all the prisoners looked gaunt and bony. Nor did the eunuchs express emotions differently from their fellows. The eunuchs and the other exhibited the same range of reactions: a few stared back defiantly at the crowd; some hid their faces; and many trembled and wept, broken by their humiliation and the approach of death.

The last but one of the prisoners was Ganymedes. I had last seen him in a shimmering, wide-sleeved gown and a khat headdress, with kohl outlining his eyes. Now he wore only a filthy loincloth, and his undressed hair hung in tendrils around his pale, wrinkled face. His chains robbed him of any pretense of dignity; the shackles on his ankles and wrists forced him to bow and take shambling steps. He was barefoot and his feet were bleeding.

Someone in the crowd hurled a piece of fruit—a green, unripe fig—and struck him between his legs. Ganymedes flinched but did not cry out. Others hurled more bits of fruit and even stones, always aiming for the same spot. They were mocking him with blows that would have made an intact man scream with agony but served only to humiliate the eunuch by drawing attention to the part of his anatomy that had been amputated.

Following Ganymedes, at a distance which clearly set her apart, was Arsinoë. The princess, too, was barefoot and dressed in rags, baring more of her arms and legs than was considered decent for a high-born woman in public, inviting the prurient inspection of the crowd. The manner in which she was chained seemed calculated to emphasize her debasement; her ankles were connected by a short chain and her hands were bound tightly behind her, forcing her to mince forward with her shoulders back and her breasts thrust forward. But the position also allowed her to hold her chin high. Her face was clearly visible, and her expression was surprisingly composed. She looked neither fearful nor defiant; there was neither hatred nor panic in her eyes. Her face was sphinxlike, without emotion, as if her thoughts were completely elsewhere, far removed from the degradation to which her body was being subjected.

As Arsinoë slowly drew nearer below us, I looked from her face to that of Cleopatra. They appeared to wear the same expression, despite the difference in their situations. Cleopatra watched her sister's march to oblivion without showing the least sign of regret or rejoicing. Arsinoë moved toward her fate with no more expression than if she were gazing at the slow, steady, unending flow of the Nile. Of what stuff were these Ptolemies made?

What had Caesar presumed would happen, when he decided to parade a helpless young woman in his triumph? He had presided over the rape of many cities; he had seen the merciless reaction of his soldiers to the sight of tender females stripped of all protection. Did he think the Roman mob would react in the same way at the sight of Arsinoë in chains, allowing a desire to revel in her debasement to overcome any impulse toward pity?

I would not have been surprised to see the onlookers pelt Arsinoë with fruit, cruelly aiming for her breasts, and taunt her with lascivious remarks and perhaps even reach out to strip the remaining rags from her body, forcing her to walk naked to her death.

But that was not what happened.

Instead, the crowd, which had been so eager to jeer at the captured military men and ministers of state, fell silent as Arsinoë passed by. Foulmouthed men became speechless.

In the sudden quiet, the soft clinking of Arsinoë's chains was the only sound. Then a murmur passed through the crowd. I could not make out any words, only a low grumbling, but its tone was clear. This was not right. What we were seeing was improper, indecent, wrong—perhaps an affront to the gods. The murmur grew louder, the crowd more uneasy.

It was Rupa who took action.

He was sitting next to me. When he stood, I thought he was getting up for some other reason—to go relieve himself or simply to stretch his legs. But something about the urgency of his movements caught my eye as he stepped over the spectators and made his way to the nearest aisle. Others saw him as well and took notice; there was a resoluteness about his demeanor that drew attention, especially amid that uncertain, suddenly anxious crowd.

He reached the bottom of the stands, and then, looming taller than everyone around him, he elbowed his way through the standing spectators. He stepped onto the triumphal path. He ran toward Arsinoë.

There were gasps of surprise and cries of apprehension. Rupa was so much larger than the princess, and his movements so determined, that some people must have thought he was about to attack her. Instead, before he reached Arsinoë, he turned and raised his hands, waving them in the air to catch the crowd's attention. At the same time, he opened his mouth and made a strange braying noise, a plaintive cry that echoed around the Forum.

His behavior excited cries from the crowd.

"Who is that big fellow?"

"Awfully good-looking—"

"And what does he want?"

"He's trying to say something—"

"Can't you see? He must be mute."

"Makes a loud noise, though."

"What's he up to?"

"Looks big enough to do whatever he wants with the little princess!"

Caesar's lictors, preceding the triumphal chariot, were not far behind Arsinoë. Seeing Rupa, the foremost among them broke from the processional file and rushed toward him. My heart lurched in my chest. Like everyone else in the stands, I jumped to my feet.

Amid the sudden tumult, a few voices rang out more clearly than the rest.

"The lictors will protect the princess!"

"From what? The mute won't hurt her. He means to escape with her!"

"Escape where? She's heading straight for the Tullianum, along with her pet eunuch!"

This last comment referred to Ganymedes. Realizing that something was transpiring behind him, he had turned. With a look of alarm on his wrinkled face, he was frantically shambling back toward Arsinoë, as if he could somehow protect her despite his shackles.

But Arsinoë was in no danger. With every eye fixed upon him, Rupa turned toward the princess. For a moment, he loomed over her. Then he dropped to his knees and bowed deeply. With a great flourish of his outspread arms, he touched his lips to one of her bare feet.

Throughout the entire episode, Arsinoë's expression, or lack of expression, had remained unchanged. But when Rupa's lips touched her big toe, a smile lit her face, transforming it completely. It was like the face of Alexandros's Venus of Milos—serene and aloof, sublime and majestic.

The reaction of the crowd was instantaneous and overwhelming, like a thunderbolt from Jupiter. People raised their hands in the air, giddy with excitement. They laughed, squealed, roared, shouted. Some of them mimicked the plaintive noise that Rupa had made, not mocking but paying homage.

I looked at Cleopatra across the way. Had she ever met Rupa? I thought not, and there was nothing to indicate that she realized who was kissing her sister's toe while all Rome watched. But on her face was a frown as dark as her sister's smile was dazzling.

Ganymedes, reaching Arsinoë and seeing that she was in no danger, fell to his knees beside Rupa. Awkwardly, because of his chains, he bowed deeply and kissed the princess's other foot.

The crowd became even more jubilant.

The lictors yanked Rupa to his feet. I held my breath, fearing the worst, but the lictors only threw him back into the crowd, where he sent spectators tumbling in all directions, like a boulder hurled from a catapult.

The lictors reached for Ganymedes. Flailing against his chains, the eunuch managed to thwart them and remained on his knees, abasing himself before Arsinoë.

"Spare the princess!" someone shouted.

"Yes, spare the princess!" cried others.

The cry quickly became a chant: "Spare the princess! Spare the princess! Spare the princess!"

"But what about the eunuch?" shouted someone.

"Kill the eunuch!" came the answer, followed by a roar of laughter.

This was added to the chant: "Spare the princess, kill the eunuch! Spare the princess, kill the eunuch!"

Ganymedes was finally pulled to his feet and shoved forward, with blows from the lictors' rods to speed him along. On his face was a look of both triumph and despair. Arsinoë, her head held high, the smile still lighting her face, resumed her mincing forward progress.

The princess passed from view, and the long file of lictors paraded before us, but still the chanting continued: "Spare the princess, kill the eunuch! Spare the princess, kill the eunuch!"

By some magic of group mentality, the crowd spontaneously split the chant between the two sides of the triumphal pathway. Those opposite the Capitoline Hill shouted, "Spare the princess!" Those on the other side responded, "Kill the eunuch!" The two sides competed to see which could yell the loudest. In the middle of this deafening crossfire came Caesar in his triumphal chariot. The chants roared back and forth, like volleys from rival catapults.

"Spare the princess!"

"Kill the eunuch!"

"Spare the princess!"

"Kill the eunuch!"

Caesar looked vexed and confused, and doing a poor job of trying not to show it, much as he had appeared in the Gallic Triumph when his soldiers teased him for his youthful liaison with Nicomedes. I saw him lift his gaze to the dignitaries' box and exchange a look of consternation with Cleopatra. These two should have been sharing the afterglow of the crowd's reaction to the golden statue of the queen; instead, they were being subjected to acclamations for Arsinoë.

Up in the stands, we were all on our feet, and my own family members had joined in the chant. Fortunately, we were on the side calling to spare the princess; I doubt that my wife, daughter, or daughter-in-law would have joined in calling for the death of Ganymedes, but Davus might have done so, and the bloodthirsty slave boys would not have hesitated. I myself remained silent.

As if trying to make sense of the crowd's fervor, Caesar ran his eyes slowly over the reviewing stands, looking from face to face. He saw my family, chanting with the rest; he saw me, standing silent. For an instant, his eyes met mine. He had no way of knowing that it was my adopted son who had set off the crowd's reaction.

The triumphal chariot eventually passed from view, followed by rank upon rank of veterans from the Egyptian campaign. Infected by the crowd's enthusiasm, even the soldiers took up the deafening chant: "Spare the princess, kill the eunuch! Spare the princess, kill the eunuch!"

"Oh, Rupa!" I whispered to myself. "What have you done?"

XIV

"Rupa, what were you thinking? You could be dead right now! The lictors could have dragged you up to the Carcer along with those wretched Egyptians and dropped you into the Tullianum, and we would never have seen you alive again!"

The sun had set. The moon had risen. Occasionally, here in my lamplit garden, I could hear snatches of music and revelry from the Forum, where the feast that followed the triumph still continued, with endless Egyptian delicacies on offer. But I was in no mood to eat and drink. Every time I thought of the terrible risk Rupa had taken that day, my blood ran cold.

"But, Papa," objected Diana, "what did Rupa do that was against the law?"

"I'm pretty sure that a citizen is not allowed to interrupt the progress of a triumph."

"He didn't interrupt it. He took part in it! People do that sort of thing all the time. They run onto the path to taunt the prisoners, or to get a closer look at some trophy, or to plant a kiss on a soldier's cheek. We've all seen such things. Unless Caesar has passed some law against kissing a girl's toe—"

"Rupa embarrassed the dictator!"

"I'm pretty sure that's not against the law, either, Papa. Caesar's not a king. We don't live and breathe at his pleasure."

"Not yet," I muttered.

"And nothing untoward happened. The lictors came running, they threw Rupa off the pathway, he disappeared back into the crowd, and that was the end of it. Apparently, Caesar doesn't even know it was Rupa who saved the princess."

"Saved the princess!" I uttered the statement incredulously, amazed at the enormity of it. Arsinoë had been spared, and Rupa was the man most responsible for saving her. "A foreign-born freedman does not go about thwarting the will of a Roman dictator and nullifying a death sentence ordered by the Roman state. Such things do not happen!"

"But apparently they *do*, Papa."

"It was a mad act."

"I think it was terribly heroic," insisted Diana.

"So do I," said Bethesda.

The two of them converged on Rupa and planted kisses on his cheeks. He had been frowning and staring at the ground while I lectured him, but now he smiled and hugged himself. All my admonishments were for nothing.

"Besides," said Diana, "Rupa acted purely on impulse. There was nothing deliberate about what he did. He couldn't possibly foresee the outcome of his actions."

I was not so sure about this. In earlier days, Rupa and his sister, Cassandra, had been street performers in Alexandria. He was not an actor, just a mime, playing burly silent parts; nevertheless, he must have learned how to anticipate and manipulate the reactions of an audience. Bowing before Arsinoë and kissing her foot had played adroitly upon the crowd's sentiment, and the result had been just what Rupa desired. At the conclusion of his triumph, Caesar had bowed to the will of the people; criers announced that the princess would be spared and sent into exile, while Ganymedes and the other captives were duly executed.

I gazed hard into Rupa's unblinking eyes. His wits were on the simple side of average, that was certain, but because he was a mute, and brawny as well, had I underestimated his native intelligence? He might not possess the verbal capabilities of a Cicero, able to sway a jury with well-chosen words, yet he had proven himself able to rouse a multitude with a single, bold, perfectly timed gesture.

"Besides, Papa, you wanted to see Arsinoë spared, just like everyone else. Admit it!"

"The poor girl!" Bethesda shook her head. "An Egyptian princess, at the mercy of those Roman brutes—terrible!" More than ever since our return from Egypt, my wife loved to play the part of the cosmopolitan Alexandrian appalled by Roman barbarity.

"Poor girl?" I threw up my hands. "Arsinoë is a conniving royal brat, responsible for hundreds, maybe thousands, of deaths back in Egypt. She put one of her own generals to death! She's a viper, no less than her sister."

"Even so, Caesar had no business threatening to execute the child, just to show off," insisted Bethesda. "It did him no credit. It made him look bad, parading that poor girl in chains."

I had to agree. And, when all was said and done, I was not sorry that Rupa had acted on his impulse.

"Let us speak no more of the matter," I said. "And let there be no boasting about this to the other women in the market, do you understand? You may praise Rupa all you like here in the privacy of our home, but you're not to whisper a word of this to anyone else. If Caesar were to find out . . ."

"Yes, Papa?" said Diana. "What might the big, bad dictator do?"

"Let's pray that we don't find out."

Caesar had survived his first two triumphs. The only damage he had sustained was to his dignity, and that was minor. The teasing from his soldiers only served to endear him to them all the more, while his clemency to Arsinoë made him appear not weak and vacillating but decisive and wise, and won him even greater favor with the crowd.

If not from the Gauls or the Egyptians, or from disaffected Antony or ambitious Fulvia, or from love-addled Cicero or glib Brutus, then from what quarter came the threat to Caesar that Hieronymus had hinted at? Rather than feeling relieved that the dictator had survived his first two triumphs unscathed, I felt more anxious than before. What danger might Caesar face in the next two triumphs?

First would come the celebration of his recent victory in Asia, where King Pharnaces of Pontus had taken advantage of the civil strife between Pompey and Caesar to reclaim the kingdom of his father, the great Mithradates. Pharnaces's ruthlessness had been shocking, at least to Roman sensibilities; in conquering city after city, he not only plundered the property of a great many Roman citizens but also made a practice of castrating all the youngest and best-looking males, including Roman citizens, before selling them into slavery. News of these atrocities caused outrage throughout the Roman world, but Pharnaces's successes had gone unchecked until Caesar himself, after settling affairs in Egypt, moved to reassert Roman rule in the region. Pharnaces was routed at the battle of Zela, fled for his life, and was eventually captured and killed by one of his own treacherous underlings.

With Pharnaces dead and largely unmourned, it was hard to imagine who might choose the Asian Triumph as a venue to try to kill Caesar. But hadn't Hieronymus speculated that danger would come from an unexpected quarter?

Late that night, looking through Hieronymus's writings for links to the upcoming Asian Triumph, I came across a passage in his private journal I had not read before:

And what of this speculation one hears about young Gaius Octavius, Caesar's grandnephew? Antony repeats the tale with great zest, and for all I know the rumor originated with him (if, indeed, it is only a rumor). I realize that Antony is piqued at Caesar, but why should he spread salacious gossip about Octavius, unless he thinks Caesar intends to make the boy his heir, and Antony imagines that he himself deserves that honor (even though he has no blood tie to the dictator). Or . . . could the tale be true? I decided to see the boy with my own eyes, to judge whether he might tempt a man like Caesar. The meeting was easy to arrange. Octavius is a bright lad, easily bored, always looking for distraction; he was quite fascinated by me.

Is he a match for Caesar? Well, I suppose he's pretty enough, though not to my taste; his face is too broad and his eyes are too sharp—I should think a man would more likely cut himself on those

eyes rather than become lost in them. But who knows what Caesar
may have gotten up to with the boy? Octavius is ambitious, and am-
bitious boys are pliable. Caesar bestrides the world like the Colossus
of Rhodes, but even giants long for lost youth, and I must admit the
boy has a certain engaging freshness to him. As Antony says, Caesar
gets to play Nicomedes, and Octavius gets to play Caesar.

Or is Antony making it all up? Antony loves to gossip more than
any man I've ever met, and Cytheris constantly eggs him on. . . .

This tale was new to me. Clearly, Hieronymus was of two
minds whether to give it credence. On its face, the idea that
Caesar might seek sexual favors from a younger man did not
strike me as unlikely. I believed that Caesar had sought such a
relationship with Meto, though I did not know and had never
asked to know the exact details. I had reason to believe that
Caesar had done the same with young King Ptolemy in Egypt,
with whom he shared a most intimate relationship before they
turned irrevocably against each other and Caesar finally chose
to side (and share his bed) with Ptolemy's sister Cleopatra. And,
for all I knew, Caesar might have shared such an intimacy with
Brutus; that might explain the enduring but strangely volatile
nature of their relationship.

I had never met Gaius Octavius. I tried to recall what I
knew about him.

He was Caesar's grandnephew, being the grandson of one of
Caesar's sisters. He had been born in the year that Cicero served
as consul (and put down the so-called conspiracy of Catilina);
that would make Octavius about sixteen now.

His father had been a New Man, like Cicero, the first of the
family to become a senator; the elder Gaius Octavius was a

banker and financier and began his political career by distributing bribes to gangs on election days. His chief claim to fame had been tracking down a band of runaway slaves made up of the last remnants of the long-destroyed armies of Spartacus and of Catilina. For as long as thirteen years some of these fugitives had remained at large, living by their wits and eluding capture. In the vicinity of Thurii, the elder Octavius managed to round up these ragged runaways and put them all to death. Thus he established his credentials as a serious proponent of law and order, and seemed destined for a particularly ruthless political career, but after a year as provincial governor of Macedonia he died of a sudden illness.

If I calculated correctly in my head, young Gaius Octavius was only four years old when his father died. Perhaps that explained his devotion to the women who raised him. When his grandmother died, Octavius, at the age of twelve, delivered a eulogy at her funeral that was said to have wrested tears from Caesar himself. Oratorical skills aside, the boy had never seen battle and was still too young to have made a mark on the world. But he must be very near the age of manhood, I thought, and when I began to read again, Hieronymus confirmed this:

On the other hand, Octavius is now sixteen, which is the very age that some older men find most appealing. Will Caesar turn fickle the day the calf becomes a bull? Octavius will turn seventeen and don his manly toga on the twenty-third day of September (or as the Romans calculate the date, eight days before the Kalends of October). Octavius boasted that his granduncle may allow him to appear in one of his triumphs, to celebrate his ascent to manhood. Never mind that the boy fought in none of the foreign campaigns (I doubt he has ever even picked up a sword), Caesar intends to parade him as a conqueror, presenting him formally to the Roman people—and that reinforces the idea that Caesar may be grooming young Octavius to become his heir. Because of the family tie? Because Caesar sees something extraordinary in the boy? Or because his catamite deserves a generous reward?

I whistled aloud at Hieronymus's boldness. At least he had confined such reckless speculations to his private journal, rather than putting them in his reports to Calpurnia, but I was surprised he had written them down at all. It suddenly occurred to me that Caesar himself might have had Hieronymus killed. But if that were the case, wouldn't Caesar have tracked down and destroyed this offending document? I shook my head. As far as I could tell, Caesar knew nothing about either his wife's Etruscan haruspex or about her Massilian spy.

If Hieronymus had the date correct, Octavius's birthday was tomorrow. Caesar's Asian Triumph would take place the next day, with the African Triumph to follow two days after that. Would Octavius be taking part in either one?

Hieronymus claimed that Octavius had been fascinated by him. What if Hieronymus had misread the boy's reactions? Hieronymus was not always tactful, and not always skilled in hiding his thoughts; had he given away to Octavius his suspicions about a relationship between the boy and Caesar? Had Octavius been embarrassed, offended, even outraged? Had he suspected that Hieronymus was maliciously spreading rumors about him? Antony was too powerful to be killed for such a thing, but

Hieronymus was not. Here was yet another possible motive for someone to murder Hieronymus.

Or, if the story was true, did it provide Octavius with a motive to plot the death of his granduncle? The notion that Caesar's sixteen-year-old grandnephew and possible heir might conspire to kill him seemed far-fetched—and thus perfectly matched Hieronymus's warning of a menace from a quarter no one expected. But was the idea so unlikely? Catamites have been known to turn against their older lovers for all sorts of reasons. Perhaps Octavius was of the insanely jealous sort. Or perhaps he resented submitting to the domination of an older man, considering it a form of degradation, and craved revenge, no matter that his personal fortunes depended on Caesar.

Until I knew more about Gaius Octavius, these ideas were no more than idle speculation. Like Hieronymus before me, I decided that I needed to meet the boy face-to-face, so as to form my own judgment of him.

X V

The house of the widow Atia, Octavius's mother, was not far from my own on a slope of the Palatine. The next morning I put on my best toga, called for Rupa, and went to pay a visit— and encountered a crowd outside the house of Atia so large it blocked the street.

Most of the men wore togas. Others were dressed in military regalia. In the sea of faces I recognized senators, magistrates, high-ranking officers, and wealthy bankers. There were also a number of foreigners, including diplomats, traders, and merchants. I seemed to have stumbled into a open-air gathering of the most elite men in Rome.

I had expected a crowd, though not quite this big. It was traditional for well-wishers to pay their respects to a young citizen and his family on the day he reached adulthood and put on his manly toga. Usually, such guests trickle in over the course of the day. But in this case, the young man happened to be the grandnephew of Julius Caesar, and the well-wishers were legion. Because the rather modest house of Atia was too small to accommodate more than a handful of guests at once, an officious-looking slave was keeping strict order at the door, allowing only one or two callers to enter at a time, as other guests departed.

"Well, Rupa," I said, "we shall never get in. Mentioning Hieronymus won't count for much in these circumstances."

The situation was even worse than I first thought. After watching awhile, I realized that callers were not being admitted by order of arrival; instead, the less important visitors were expected to give way to the more important. Even as I watched, Caesar's rabble-rousing favorite Dolabella showed up. With a swaggering gait, Marc Antony's young nemesis (and the erstwhile son-in-law of Cicero) strode through the throng. No elbowing was necessary; the crowd parted for him as if by instinct. He stepped past the officious doorkeeper and into the house without so much as a nod.

If admission was by order of influence, I would be the last man admitted, unless perhaps I could argue my way ahead of young Gaius Octavius's fuller or shoe mender.

"Come, Rupa," I said, "let's go home." I was about to leave when I felt a strong grip on my shoulder.

"Gordianus, isn't it? The father of Meto Gordianus?"

I turned around to see a man in his middle forties. He had a plump but handsome face, twinkling eyes, and touches of gray at his temples. A neatly trimmed beard strengthened his round jaw. The outlines of his toga suggested a robust physique with a touch of plumpness to match his face. The toga's purple border, and the fact that lictors attended him, indicated he was a praetor, one of Caesar's handpicked magistrates in charge of the city.

He looked vaguely familiar, but I couldn't place him. He saw the uncertainty on my face, slapped my shoulder, and laughed.

"Hirtius is the name. Not sure we've ever been properly introduced, but I know your son very well, and I've seen you before. Let me think; was it in Caesar's tent outside Brundisium, that day we ran Pompey out of Italy? No?" He tapped his forefinger against his lips. "Or maybe it was at one of Cicero's estates? You're thick with Cicero, aren't you? So am I. Very old friends, Cicero and I; we have adjoining properties down in Tusculum, see each other more there than we do here in the city. He gives me oratory lessons. In return, I share my favorite recipes with Cicero's cook—and beg Caesar not to cut the fool's head off when he will insist on picking the wrong side!"

His good humor was infectious. I smiled and nodded. "No, I don't think we've been introduced before, but of course I know of Aulus Hirtius." He had been one of Caesar's officers in Gaul and had fought with Caesar in Spain at the outset of the civil war. In the political arena, he had authored laws limiting the rights of Pompeians to serve in public office and legitimizing some of Caesar's more high-handed actions. Hirtius was a Caesar loyalist through and through.

"Here to pay respects to young Octavius, eh?" he said.

"Yes. One of the multitude, it seems."

"Know him, then? Octavius?"

"No," I admitted. "But I believe we had an acquaintance in common, a Massilian named Hieronymus."

"Ah, the Scapegoat. Yes, I heard about his death."

"Did you know Hieronymus, too?" I had not encountered Hirtius's name anywhere in Hieronymus's writings.

"I met the Scapegoat in this very house, as a matter of fact, that day he came to call on Octavius. I'm here rather a lot lately; spending time with the boy, at Caesar's request. Briefing him, you see, because I know my way around Spain, and Octavius will be heading there soon, now that he's old enough to serve. Your son is in Spain already, I believe."

"Yes, he is."

"Right. Meto is probably gathering intelligence, assessing the loyalty of the locals, judging the strength and resolve of the resistance, laying the groundwork for Caesar to sweep in and obliterate the enemy. Meto's good at that sort of thing. A Spanish campaign will give young Octavius a chance to gain valuable experience in the field—spill some blood, show his uncle what he's made of. I've been teaching the boy everything I know about the lay of the land and the local customs, reviewing basic strategy and tactics, drilling him in the use of different weapons. But there I go, still calling him a boy! Starting today, Gaius Octavius is a full-fledged citizen and the paterfamilias of his household."

Hirtius surveyed the crowd, which had grown even thicker since his arrival. He put his hands on his hips and shook his head. "Well, there's no way I'm waiting to take my turn. I have far too much to do today, getting ready for tomorrow's triumph. Lictors, clear a path to the front door. Easy does it. Gently but firmly!"

He stepped forward, looking over his shoulder to flash a parting smile. He saw my glum expression, leaned back, and grabbed my arm.

"Here, come along with me, Gordianus."

"Are you sure?" Even as I made a show of demurring, I

signaled to Rupa to stay behind, and moved alongside Hirtius. "This is most gracious of you, Praetor."

"My pleasure, Gordianus. It's the least I can do for Meto's father."

As we reached the door, Dolabella was just leaving. In his mid-twenties, with a boyish face, the radical firebrand didn't appear much past his own toga-donning day. He and Hirtius exchanged a brief but boisterous greeting, with much grinning and shoulder slapping, but as we stepped past him, Hirtius made a face and lowered his voice. "What does Caesar see in that young troublemaker?"

We were greeted in the vestibule by Octavius's mother, Atia, dressed in a sumptuous stola made of richly woven cloth and wearing a great deal of jewelry. She must have been greeting visitors since daybreak, but her smile for Hirtius appeared completely genuine. She planted a kiss on his cheek.

"Greetings, stranger!" she said.

Hirtius laughed. "No stranger than that fellow who just left, I hope."

Atia narrowed her eyes. "Young Dolabella—such a charmer!"

Hirtius clucked his tongue. "Just be sure to keep him away from Octavia. Now that Dolabella is free of Cicero's daughter, no young lady will be safe. Or do you have your eye on the rogue yourself?"

Atia laughed. "You know my reputation as a chaste widow. All the dictator's women must be above suspicion—Caesar's niece as well as Caesar's wife."

Hirtius nodded. "Where *is* your uncle? I thought Caesar would be here by now."

"He's supposed to be. Too busy with some crisis or other, I'm sure. He'll eventually show up. He'd better! I certainly can't be the one who takes Gaius for a walk across the Forum in his new toga, and then up to the Capitoline to take the auspices. They're planning to perform the ritual in front of Uncle's new statue. We couldn't ask for finer weather. But who is this fellow?"

Hirtius introduced me. Atia's demeanor at once became more formal, softened by a smile that was obviously synthetic. Perhaps her uncle had taught her how to put on a politician's face when called upon to greet a horde of strangers.

We were shown to a small garden. A short young man in a toga stood inconspicuously amid the shrubbery. His face in repose displayed a thoughtful, almost somber expression. His forehead was quite broad but covered by a very thick head of fair hair. His eyebrows nearly met. His mouth was finely shaped but almost too small in proportion to his long nose. When he saw Hirtius, his lips curved into a smile, but his eyes remained distant. The result was an ironic expression that seemed precocious for his years.

The two greeted each other warmly, gripping elbows in a near embrace. Impulsively, it seemed, Hirtius leaned forward and kissed Octavius on the lips, then gave his cheek a playful pinch.

"My boy, my boy! Or should I say, my good man—look at you in that toga! How proud your uncle will be when he sees you."

"Do you think so? All I know is, this thing is hotter than I expected. I shall faint if I have to stand under the full sun when they take the auspices."

"Nonsense! You'll conduct yourself with perfect grace, as you always do." Hirtius grabbed Octavius by the scruff of the neck. The young man submitted to this familiarity with neither embarrassment nor apparent pleasure. He turned his curiously distant gaze to me.

"This is Gordianus," said Hirtius, "the father of Meto Gordianus, your uncle's amanuensis."

Octavius raised an eyebrow. "I see."

"You know my son?"

"Only by reputation."

What did Octavius mean by that? His detached manner hinted at thoughts unspoken and judgments made in silence. Or was I merely imagining this?

"Greetings on this special day, citizen," I said.

"Thank you, Gordianus."

"You two know someone in common," said Hirtius. "Or *knew*."

"Hieronymus of Massilia," I said quickly, wanting to see Octavius's reaction.

For a long moment, Octavius showed no expression at all. Then he lifted both eyebrows. "Ah, the Scapegoat. Excuse me, but so many names have passed through my head today, I drew a blank."

"I understand that the poor fellow was found stabbed to death," said Hirtius. "Somewhere on the Palatine, wasn't it, Gordianus?"

"Yes."

"Sad news," said Octavius. "Such a terrible crime, in the heart of the city. His killer?"

"Unknown," I said.

"An outrage. Has my uncle been told? He must do something about it."

"I still have hope that the killer, or killers, may be exposed," I said. Octavius nodded. His expression had never altered. "But, forgive me, citizen, for marring the day with such tidings. This is a joyous occasion."

"It is, indeed!" Atia came striding into the garden. "And joy must be shared. We have many more visitors waiting to pay their respects."

Hirtius put on a wounded face. "Have we outstayed our welcome already?"

"You? Never! But right now, you're welcome to go find my uncle and bring him here, if you want to be useful." Atia smiled and left the garden.

"Farewell, then." Hirtius gazed wistfully at Octavius and cocked his head. "My boy, my boy, how very fine you look in that toga!" He took a step toward Octavius, and for a moment I thought he might kiss him again. But Octavius stiffened slightly and drew back, and there was something awkward and perfunctory about their parting embrace.

We left the garden and returned to the vestibule, where the next visitors were already being greeted by Atia.

Hirtius's lictors were waiting for him on the doorstep. As we headed back toward the place where I had left Rupa, with the lictors clearing a path, a murmur ran through the crowd. Heads turned in a single direction. In a hush, the name "Caesar" passed from tongue to tongue, then was shouted aloud: "Caesar! Hail, Caesar!"

Octavius's granduncle had finally arrived. He was attended by a considerable retinue and surrounded by lictors, but he broke away from his party to walk, alone and unprotected, into the gathering before Atia's house.

Everyone of importance in Rome appeared to know that this was the toga day of Caesar's grandnephew and that Caesar himself, sooner or later, would be in attendance. If anyone desired to harm Caesar in a public place, here was the perfect opportunity. How many knives might be hidden in that crowd? It would take only one to kill a man. How quickly could a determined assassin strike, before anyone could stop him?

I stood on tiptoes to watch Caesar's slow progress through the gathering. Men pressed forward to touch him, utter words of greeting, and speak their names in hopes that he would remember them. Every time Caesar turned or nodded, I flinched. By my heartbeats, I counted the number of times he escaped a possible death.

He saw Hirtius and moved toward us.

"Aulus Hirtius! How is our boy holding up on his special day?"

"Splendidly, Caesar. He was born to wear a toga."

"Good, good. And can this be Gordianus beside you? Tell me, Finder, did you enjoy your seats at yesterday's triumph?"

"We were able to see everything, Dictator."

He nodded and pursed his lips. "Including that business with Arsinoë and her anonymous admirer?"

My mouth went dry. Rupa was standing only a few feet away. I did my best not to look in his direction. "That was quite unexpected," I said.

"Yes. After a lifetime in politics, a man thinks he knows the Roman people, yet they continue to be full of surprises. But let's hope there'll be no more surprises in the triumphs to come."

I nodded. "Will your nephew be taking part?"

Caesar brightened. "He will, indeed. Not in tomorrow's triumph but in the one after, the final triumph, over Africa. Gaius Octavius shall receive military honors and ride at the head of my troops, and after the procession, he shall join me when I dedicate the new temple; Venus is his ancestress as well as mine. It's my hope that the people of Rome will love him as dearly as I do, and as does Hirtius here."

"They will, Caesar," said Hirtius. "How could they not embrace him?"

"I look to you, Hirtius, to see that the boy is properly outfitted and knows how to conduct himself in the triumph. We don't want him to look like a raw recruit by the way he handles his weapon or leaves a piece of armor unbuckled."

"I have every confidence that the boy—the young man—will satisfy your expectations," said Hirtius.

Caesar nodded and pressed on. A few moments later, he disappeared into Atia's house unharmed. I felt relieved.

I also experienced a nagging uncertainty. The rumors recounted by Hieronymus were stuck in my head; they had shaped my ideas about Octavius before I had a chance to meet him. I had found Hirtius's casual but insistent habit of touching the young man, and Octavius's passive but unemotional reaction to being touched, not innocent and endearing but oddly disturbing. What was the exact relationship between Caesar and Octavius, and between Octavius and Hirtius?

Was I allowing gossip and innuendo to color my observations? To be seduced into error by way of preconception—this was a common, often dangerous mistake made by amateurs such as Hieronymus when they set about uncovering secrets.

I reminded myself that Octavius was only seventeen, a sheltered youth without a father and hardly any practical experience of the world. He must be acutely self-conscious about living in his granduncle's shadow, and was probably a bit intimidated by the huge public reaction to his birthday. What I took to be aloofness was more likely the closely guarded expression of a young man who did not yet know himself and was quite uncertain of his place in the world.

When I arrived home, Calpurnia's messenger was waiting for me.

Again, she asked whom I had interviewed and what I had discovered. Despite her deliberately cryptic choice of words, I could sense her increasing anxiety.

Again I sent a reply saying I had nothing significant to report.

I spent the rest of the day in a strange state of mind, hardly stirring from my garden. The day was brutally hot. I thought of young Octavius sweltering in his toga while augurs watched the flight of birds from atop the Capitoline, no doubt assuring Caesar that all the auspices were good. I drank only water, abstaining from wine, and took a number of brief naps. From time to time I reached for Hieronymus's reports, but his handwriting seemed more indecipherable than ever and his prose more pointlessly prolix. There was still a great deal of material I had not yet read or had only scanned in a haphazard fashion.

Finally, shadows began to lengthen, but the heat of the day gave no indication of relenting.

My daughter joined me in the garden.

"Are you all right, Papa?" said Diana.

I considered the question. "I'm not unwell."

"It's this heat! Davus and I were just down at the riverside market. The whole city is in a kind of daze."

"Good. I thought it was only me."

She frowned. "Your work isn't going well, is it?"

I shrugged. "Who can say? A sudden revelation could come to me at any moment. That's happened before. But right now, I have no idea who killed Hieronymus or why."

"It will come to you. You know it will. But something else is bothering you."

I nodded. "You can see inside my head; you inherited that ability from your mother."

"Perhaps. From the look on your face, I can see that you're troubled."

I shaded my brow and squinted at the sun. It seemed to have caught on the edge of the roofline; I could have sworn it was just sitting there, not moving. "When I accepted this mission from Calpurnia, I told her I was doing so for only one purpose: to see justice done for Hieronymus. But that's no longer true, if it ever was. Somehow, I've become caught up in her zeal to safeguard Caesar. Today, outside the house of Gaius Octavius, there was a large gathering. Caesar walked through the crowd alone, without any lictors, without even friends to protect him. I found myself very nearly in a panic when I thought of the danger he was facing. My breath shortened. My pulse began to race. I was relieved beyond words when he passed safely through the crowd and disappeared into the house."

"Was he any safer inside?" said Diana. "Weren't all those

people going to follow him in, one or two at a time, to pay their respects to his kinsman? And might not this Gaius Octavius himself pose a threat to Caesar? You must have thought so, or you wouldn't have paid a call on him."

"You *can* see inside my head! I never discussed any of this with you."

She smiled. "I have my own ways of 'finding,' Papa. But the point is, neither you nor anyone else can protect Caesar all the time, especially if someone close to him is determined to harm him."

"True enough, Daughter. But you miss the point."

"Which is?"

"Why should I care whether Caesar lives or dies? I told Calpurnia I would study these documents and follow them wherever they led only so that I might discover who killed Hieronymus. Caesar means nothing to me."

"Not true. Caesar means something to all of us. For better or worse, he's brought an end to the civil war and all its suffering."

"Caesar himself inflicted a great deal of that suffering!"

"But now it's over, at least in Rome. People are beginning to live again—to hope, to plan, to think about the future. To think about life instead of death. No one wants a return to the bloodshed and sorrow of the last few years. If Caesar were to be murdered—especially before he names an heir—the killing would start all over again. You don't have to love Caesar to want him to keep breathing. You don't even have to like him. You can despise him—and still want him to stay alive, for the sake of peace, for the good of all of us."

"Has it come to that? Must a man submit to having a king,

and want him to live forever, because the alternative is too awful to consider?"

Diana cocked her head. "It must be terrible to be a man and to have to think about such things, even in this heat. For those of us who can't vote, or fight, or own property—or ever hope to do any of those manly things—it's all much simpler. How many more people have to die before the world can be at peace? If Caesar were to be killed, I don't know if any good would come of it, but I'm certain a great deal of evil would follow. That's what you dread, Papa. That's why you care about what happens to Caesar."

I looked up, and realized that the sun had slipped behind the roofline. Twilight would come after all, followed by night, and then another day.

I closed my eyes.

I must have slept, because I seemed to be in the Tullianum. The dank, cool darkness was almost pleasant compared to the brutal heat of the day. Amid the shadows, lemures were all around me—the lemures of Vercingetorix and Ganymedes and countless other Gauls and Egyptians, soon to be joined by more victims from Asia and Africa and unheard-of lands beyond. But the lemur of Hieronymus was not among them.

XVI

The next day, for the Asian Triumph, we arrived a bit late, and with our party incomplete. There was some minor crisis with little Beth, and after much discussion, Diana convinced her mother to come along while she stayed home. Our seats were waiting for us in the viewing stands. We missed the opening procession of senators and magistrates—small loss!—but managed to take our places just as the trumpets were sounding to mark the parade of trophies.

The rebellious King Pharnaces had overrun Cappadocia, Armenia, and Pontus. All these regions, which Caesar had subsequently reclaimed, were represented by precious objects donated by the grateful inhabitants. A golden crown and other treasures, with which Pharnaces had attempted to placate Caesar upon his arrival in Asia, were also displayed, along with a statue of the moon goddess Bellona, the principal deity of the Cappadocians, to whom Caesar had sacrificed before he began the campaign.

Among the captured weapons and machines of war,

Pharnaces's own chariot was wheeled before us. It was an impressive vehicle. The carriage was heavily plated, and fearsome-looking blades projected from the wheels.

A placard displayed the flight of Pharnaces at the battle of Zela. The king was shown in his chariot, his crown tumbling from his head, his face a mask of panic. On one side of him loomed a stern-looking Caesar, his hands on hips. On the other side loomed Pharnaces's treacherous henchman Asander, the man who would murder him, flashing a wicked grin. The crowd bust into laughter at the sight of these exaggerated but cleverly rendered caricatures.

I could see that a very large placard was approaching, as wide as the pathway would permit and twice as tall as the men carrying it. The sight of it elicited a tumultuous cheer as it passed. When it came into view, I saw why. In a single battle, within five days after his arrival and within four hours after sighting the enemy, Caesar had vanquished Pharnaces. The magnitude of his victory was impressive; its speed was astonishing. Rendered in huge golden letters upon the placard were the words *I CAME, I SAW, I CONQUERED.*

Always eager to take up a chant, the crowd began to repeat Caesar's terse boast. One side shouted, "Came!" The other side shouted, "Saw!" Then, all together, as loudly as possible: "Conquered!"

I had been feeling the call of nature ever since we sat and could wait no longer. "I think I shall go, stand, and relieve myself."

"Take Rupa with you," said Bethesda.

He rose to accompany me, but I waved him back. "No, Rupa, there are some things it is safe for me to do all by myself. Stay and watch—and don't get into any trouble!"

Bethesda gave me an exasperated look, but I ignored her. I made my way to the aisle, descended the steps, and threaded a path through the crowd. The nearest public latrines, built directly above the Cloaca Maxima, were not far away.

The chamber was one of the largest public facilities in the Forum, but when I stepped inside I found myself alone. The most exciting part of the triumph for many spectators—the procession of prisoners—was coming up, and probably no one wanted to miss it. I had my choice of whichever of the scores of holes I wanted. I followed my nose to the freshest-smelling part of the room and stood before the receptacle. The roar of the crowd outside echoed through the stone chamber, sounding strangely distant.

I was just beginning when someone entered the chamber.

From the corner of my eye, I saw that he wore priestly garments. I took a closer look and I saw that it was Calpurnia's uncle, Gnaeus Calpurnius. He must have left his place in the procession to come relieve himself. He gave me a grunt of recognition as he walked up to a nearby receptacle and made ready, hitching up his robes. He had interrupted me, and I was slow to start again. He was slow to begin at all, which was not surprising for a man his age. We stood in silence for a long moment.

"Hot today," he finally said, staring straight ahead.

"Yes," I said, a little surprised that he would deign to strike up a conversation with me, even about the weather. "Though not as hot as yesterday, I think."

He grunted. I kept my gaze politely averted, but from the corner of my eye I saw that Uncle Gnaeus appeared to be adjusting himself, yet to no avail, for still I heard no release.

"My niece has great faith in you," he said.

"Does she?"

"*Should* she?" He turned his head slightly and trained a single eye upon me. "Or are you no better than the other one, the one who got himself killed, wasting her time and filling her head with yet more nonsense?"

"Hieronymus was my friend," I said quietly. "I would prefer that you not speak ill of him in my presence." My flow began. "Tell me, did you ever discuss astronomy with him?"

"What?"

"Hieronymus made notations having to do with the movements of the stars and such. You're a keeper of the calendar, aren't you? I thought perhaps you gave him instruction."

He snorted. "Do you seriously think I would waste my time giving sacred instruction to one of my niece's minions, and a foreigner, at that? Now tell me, Finder, are you wasting Calpurnia's time? Have you discovered anything of interest? Are you at all close to doing so?"

"I'm doing my best," I said. *And in some ways doing much better than you,* I thought, for still there was no relief for Uncle Gnaeus. No wonder he was so irritable!

He snorted. "Just as I thought. You've found nothing, because there is nothing to find. This menace to Caesar that consumes my niece is entirely imaginary, created from thin air by that haruspex, Porsenna."

"If that's true, then why did someone murder Hieronymus?"

"Your friend was poking his nose into other people's business—powerful people, dangerous people. Who knows what embarrassing or incriminating information he may have uncovered, having nothing at all to do with Caesar? The Scape-goat surely offended someone, but his death is hardly proof of a plot against Caesar."

What he said made sense, yet I found myself recalling the cryptic "key" that Hieronymus had mentioned in his journal. I repeated the words aloud. " 'Look all around! The truth is not found in the words, but the words may be found in the truth.' "

"What in Hades is that supposed to mean?"

"I wish I knew," I said. Then, seemingly from nowhere, a memory came to me, and I felt a sudden chill.

"What's that look on your face?" said Uncle Gnaeus.

I shivered. "A long time ago, in a public latrine here in the Forum, I was very nearly murdered. By Hercules, I'd almost forgotten! It was thirty-five years ago, during the trial of Sextus Roscius, the first time I worked with Cicero. A hired killer fol-lowed me into a latrine near the Temple of Castor. We were alone. He pulled a knife—"

"All very interesting, I'm sure, but perhaps you could leave a man in peace!"

I turned and left at once, almost feeling sorry for Uncle Gnaeus. Judging by the silence, he still had not managed to be-gin relieving himself.

The crowd had grown even thicker than before. I looked in vain for a way to pass through. The din of the shouting and laughter was deafening.

I realized I had no desire to return to my seat in the stands. I had seen quite enough of doomed, humiliated prisoners, of

Caesar in his ceremonial chariot, and of lictors and cavalry officers and marching legionaries.

I suddenly longed to be anywhere else. I started walking, heading away from the triumph, fleeing the crush and the noise. At length, taking a roundabout path of least resistance, I found myself at the Flaminian Gate in the old city walls.

I kept walking. Once through the gate, I was outside the city proper, on the Field of Mars. When I was a boy, much of this area had still been literally a field, with vast parade grounds. Some areas of the Field of Mars remained undeveloped, but in my lifetime the greater part of it had been filled with new tenements and temples and public buildings. It had become one of the liveliest neighborhoods of Rome.

But on this day, the streets were almost deserted. From beyond the Capitoline Hill, which now loomed between me and the Forum, I could still hear the roar of the crowd but more and more faintly as I continued to walk toward the great bend of the Tiber. I felt a sense of freedom and escape—from haughty Uncle Gnaeus, from Caesar, from Calpurnia, from my fretful wife, and even from Rupa, my constant companion in recent days.

At length I came to the new neighborhood of shops and apartments that had sprung up around Pompey's Theater, where I had come to visit Arsinoë. Was she there still, returned to her high prison, but alone now, without Ganymedes to look after her?

I wandered past the empty porticos. All the shops were closed. I came to the entrance to the theater itself. The gate was open and unmanned. I wandered inside.

The tiers of seats were empty. I gazed up row after row, fascinated by the play of sunlight and shadow on the repeating semicircles, all the way to the top, where the Temple of Venus stood. Lost in thought, I slowly ascended the steps.

I remembered the enormous controversy that erupted when Pompey announced his plans to build the theater. For centuries, conservative priests and politicians had thwarted the construction of a permanent theater in Rome, arguing that such an extravagance would lead the Romans to become as decadent as the stagestruck Greeks. Pompey circumvented their objections by adding a temple to the complex, so that the whole structure could be consecrated as a religious building. The design was clever; the rows of theater seats also served as steps leading up to the sanctuary at the summit.

"Can you hear me?"

I was not alone. A lone figure with a white beard, dressed in a tunic of many colors, had stepped onto the stage.

"I said, can you hear me up there? Don't simply nod. Speak."

"Yes!" I shouted.

"No need to yell. That's the whole point: acoustics. I'm barely talking above normal volume now, and yet you can hear me perfectly well, can't you?"

"Yes."

"Good. La-la-la, la-la-la. Fo-di-da, fo-di-da." He continued to utter a series of nonsensical noises. I realized he was a performer limbering his throat, but I laughed aloud anyway.

"Well, I can see you're going to be an easy audience!" he said. "Sit. Listen. You can help me with my timing."

I did as I was told. I had come here seeking escape, after all. What better escape could I hope for, than a few moments in the theater?

He cleared his throat, then struck a dramatic pose. When he spoke again, his voice was utterly different. It had a rich, dark tone, full of curious inflections. It was an actor's voice, trained to fascinate.

"Friends and countrymen, welcome to the play. I am the playwright. This is the prologue—my chance to tell you what to think about the tale you're about to see. I could let you simply watch the play and make up your own minds—but being fickle Romans, I know better than to trust your judgment. Oh that's right, jeer and boo . . ." He broke from his pose. "Well? Jeer and boo!"

I obliged him with what I imagined would be a suitably obscene jeer, involving his mother.

"That's better," he said, and continued his soliloquy. "I know why you're all here: to celebrate a great man's good fortune. Not a good man's great fortune; that would be a different matter—and a different man."

I obligingly laughed at this witticism, which was clearly a jab at Caesar, the sponsor of the upcoming plays. My laughter may have sounded a bit forced, but Decimus Laberius—for now I recognized the man, one of the leading playwrights and performers of the Roman stage—seemed not to care if my reactions were sincere as long as I gave him a token response to help him with his timing.

"But why am *I* here?" he continued. "To be perfectly candid, I had rather be at home right now, with my feet up and my nose in a book. I've had enough of all this carrying-on and celebrating; it grates on an old man's nerves. Yet here I am, with a new play produced on demand, and why? Because I'm desperate

to beat that fool Publilius Syrus out of the prize? No! I don't
need a prize to tell me I'm a better playwright than that babbling freedman.

"No, I am here because the Goddess of Necessity compels
me. To what depths of indignity has she thrust me, here at the
end of my life? You see me at twice thirty years, a broken man.
When I was thirty—or better yet, half thirty—oh, how young
and proud I was! No power in heaven or on earth could bend
me to its will. Neither begging nor bribery, cajoling nor threatening could move me one iota. But now—look at me jump!"
Laberius executed a sudden leap and barely stopped himself
from tumbling head over heels; his awkwardness was so con-
vincing that I laughed out loud. He paused for a moment, as if
waiting for the laughter of a huge audience to subside. "A most
unbecoming activity for a man my age! So why do I jump? Because a certain man demands it.

"No, that's unfair. The fellow does not *demand* it. He asks.
He makes a polite request. He says, 'Laberius, dear friend, best
and boldest of playwrights, would you be so kind . . .' And
Laberius—jumps!" He executed an even more fitful leap with a
hair-raising recovery.

"And here's the rub: it matters not a fig that I should stand
here and complain; he merely takes my mutterings as a compliment. Look, he's laughing now!" Laberius pointed at the box of
honor in the midst of the seats, which was as empty as the rest
of the theater. He shook his head. "Bitter are the twists and
turns of Fortune. My own success has made me another's slave.
The dazzling jewel of Fame had turned me into another man's
ornament. My gift for words renders me . . . mute. But oh, can

I jump!" Again he took a leap, but something in the halting movement was more pathetic than absurd, more pitiful than funny. I did not laugh at all.

He cocked his head. "Do you remember that game we played when we were boys called king of the hill? Well, I imagined I was very nearly at the top of that hill for a while, but then I took a tumble, and now I find myself at the bottom—just like all of you—looking up at the winner, who's so high above me I have to squint to see him." In a quavering childlike voice, so strange it gave me gooseflesh, he quoted from the ditty boys sang when they played the game:

> *"You will be king*
> *if you can cling*
> *to the height.*
> *Do the thing*
> *to prove you're right,*
> *send 'em tumbling*
> *with all your might!"*

I sat forward in my seat, no longer pretending to be his attentive audience but genuinely riveted. In my mind, his voice conjured images of boys at play, so seemingly harmless in their rush to compete. But I also saw fields of dead bodies and heads on stakes, the terrible outcomes of those boyhood games carried into the world of men. I was reminded of how completely an actor could command the stage, controlling his audience's emotions with a change in the tone of his voice or a simple shrug of his shoulders.

"Ah, but I suppose I was getting too big for my toga anyway," said Laberius with a sigh. "I was due for a bit of taking down.

Weren't we all, O people of the toga? We forgot the way of the world. All cannot be first, and the highest rank is the hardest to hold on to. From the pinnacle of success, the only direction is down. A man has his day and falls; his successor will fall in turn, and his successor, and so on. Only the immortals hold fast to their place in this universe, while everything around them changes in the blink of a god's eye.

"We rightly fear the gods. We rightly fear certain men, but mark my words: the man who is feared the most has the most to fear—"

A shrill voice, coming from behind me, interrupted him. "Laberius, you old fraud! You will *never* dare to speak that line from the stage. Why are you even bothering to rehearse it?"

I looked over my shoulder and saw a striking figure, a man perhaps in his forties with touches of silver in his dark beard. He struck me as the type who's quite handsome in his youth but runs to fat in middle age. He was striding down the aisle toward the stage, followed by a troupe of actors.

"I'll rehearse the prologue just as I wrote it!" snapped Laberius. "Whether I deliver it that way . . . is another matter, and none of your business, Publilius Syrus. If the temper of the audience and the exigencies of performance call for a bit of spontaneous rewrite—"

"How about a spontaneous exit?" The newcomer had passed me and was fast approaching the stage. "You shouldn't even be here. This is the hour scheduled for *my* troupe to practice, and you know very well that we rehearse in secret. I can't have eavesdroppers plagiarizing my best lines."

"How dare you, Syrus? As if I would steal a single one of your tired platitudes. You—you *freedman!*"

"That's right, insult a man who's actually made his way in this profession by merit! Go on, Laberius, off with you! Disappear! Send a puff of smoke out of your rear end and vanish through a trapdoor."

"You're the one who resorts to such vulgar stage effects, Syrus. I rely on words and the instrument of my body—"

"Well, get your instrument out of here! And take your assistant with you."

I cleared my throat. "Actually, I am not this man's assistant. I only happened to be—"

"Whoever you are, get out! Or I'll have Ajax throw you out." Syrus gestured to one of his actors. Whether Ajax was his name or his role in the play, it suited the man's brawny build. I suddenly regretted having wandered off on my own without Rupa.

I had no desire to become involved in a brawl between rival playwrights, though I was curious about the men themselves. Both Laberius and Syrus were listed by Hieronymus as frequent guests at Marc Antony's parties. Syrus must have known Hieronymus; he had sent a message of condolence to my house.

I headed out the way I had come, and was walking down a long portico when I felt a hand on my shoulder. I turned to see Laberius.

"What did *you* think of my prologue, citizen?"

I shrugged. "Amusing. Provocative, I suppose. I'm not a great follower of the theater—"

"Yet you laughed in all the right places, and when I did the bit about the boys playing king of the hill, it gave you chills, didn't it? Admit it!"

"It did."

"Come with me, Citizen." He took my arm and steered me to a nearby doorway. The door was plain and unadorned, but the chamber into which it opened was quite grand. We had entered by a side door into the great meeting room in the theater complex. Pompey had built it expressly to accommodate gatherings of the Senate. The hall was an oval-shaped well, with seats on either side descending in tiers to the main floor. Marble was everywhere, in many colors and patterns. The design and workmanship of even the smallest detail was exquisite.

A common citizen like me is seldom allowed into such a place. I must have gawked like a tourist, for Laberius laughed and gave me a friendly pat on the back.

"Quite a room, isn't it? Come, see the man who built it."

We descended to the main floor. Laberius indulged in a bit of mummery, raising his arms and twirling like a speaker orating to his colleagues. He ended his little mime show by doing an about-face and bowing low before a statue placed conspicuously against the wall, where everyone in the hall could see it. I did not need to read the inscription on the pedestal to recognize Pompey, the man who had built this complex as a gift to the city and to serve as his crowning accomplishment.

The statue depicted Pompey in a toga, as a statesman rather than a soldier. On his blandly handsome face was an amiable, almost serene expression. My most enduring memory of Pompey's countenance was quite different. Once, in a rage, he tried to kill me with his bare hands, and the look on his face then had been anything but serene. I still had bad dreams, haunted by Pompey's face.

As depicted by this statue, the Great One looked harmless

enough, gazing with a smile at the grand assembly room he had provided for his colleagues.

"A great patron of the theater," said Laberius, with a sigh. "Though, to give him his due, Caesar promises to be even more generous. For the upcoming competition, he's offering the winning playwright a prize of a million sesterces. A million! That could go a long way to easing an old man's retirement."

"So your reason for taking part in the festival isn't entirely because a dictator compels it," I said.

"No? I don't see much difference, jumping because I fear the man who tells me to jump, or doing it because he owns all the world's gold and promises to throw a few coins my way."

"Strong words, playwright!"

"When politicians give up on liberty, it falls to poets to preserve it. Or to write its epitaph."

"I don't know what your play is about, but with a prologue like that, can you really expect Caesar to give you the prize?"

"Why not? It would prove that he allows dissent, loves freedom, and has excellent taste. What harm can I do to Caesar? At my worst, I'm no more than the buzzing of a gnat in his ear. All my ranting is mere flattery to such a man. I meant what I said: 'It matters not a fig that I should stand here and complain; he merely takes my mutterings as a compliment.'"

"Still, that last bit—how did it go? 'The man who is feared the most . . .'"

"'Has the most to fear.'"

"No tyrant likes to hear that sort of talk." Calpurnia certainly wouldn't like it, I thought.

"Better that such words be shouted in public than

whispered in private," said Laberius. "At least I'm no hypocrite, like that no-talent Pig's Paunch."

"Who?"

"Syrus. That's his nickname. Since he arrived in Rome, he eats it at every meal."

"Which makes him a voluptuary, perhaps, but not a hypocrite."

"No one speaks more scathingly about the dictator behind his back than Syrus. Yet his so-called play consists of nothing but insipid platitudes in praise of Caesar."

"A million sesterces could purchase an endless supply of pig's paunch. But how do you know this? Syrus rehearses in secret."

Laberius snorted. "I know every line of drivel in his new play. 'A gift worthily bestowed is a gift to the giver.' 'Too much wrangling and the truth is lost sight of.' 'A quick refusal is a kindness half done.' One cloying banality after another!"

"But how do you know this?"

He smiled. "That fellow Ajax? Looks the strong, silent type— but indulge his weakness for wine, and he sings like a lark!"

I shook my head. In Caesar's Rome, even playwrights employed spies against each other!

"Let me understand you, Laberius. You're saying that you speak harshly about Caesar but pose no threat to him. But a man like Syrus, who appears completely obsequious—"

"Is far more likely to be up to no good. But Caesar knows this. He's a shrewd judge of character. How else has he kept his head on his shoulders?"

"Are you seriously suggesting that Syrus might pose a threat?"

"A grave threat! The man who wrote the line, 'You never

defeat danger by refusing to face it,' could murder the theater outright!"

"I see. Tell me, who is this Publilius Syrus?"

"He was born a slave in Syria; thus the uncouth cognomen. Acquired the name Publilius from his master, when he was freed. How that came about, no one knows, but they say he was a beautiful boy; Syrus wouldn't be the first slave who rose in this world by trading on his looks. Made his way to Italy and presented himself as a playwright. He's had a bit of success in the hinterlands, doing the small-town festival circuit. Now he thinks he can make a name for himself in the big city. Ha! What passes for cleverness in Calabria won't make them chuckle in Rome. Of course, with an audience made up of Gallic senators and the like, who knows what passes for popular taste nowadays?"

I sighed. "Indeed, persons of true refinement are few and far between. And now there is one less such person in the world. I'm thinking of a friend of mine who was murdered recently. He was a very cultured fellow and a true lover of the theater. I think perhaps you might have met him: Hieronymus of Massilia."

Laberius looked at me blankly.

"Perhaps at one of those parties Marc Antony is famous for?" I suggested.

"Ugh! Not my crowd. For those affairs, I show up early, recite a few lines, eat and drink my fill, and then run home to an early bed."

"But you attend such parties nonetheless. A free meal is a free meal?"

"The playwright's credo!"

"But you never encountered my friend Hieronymus?"

He shrugged. "The name is vaguely familiar. But if the fellow was the type to arrive late and stay till dawn, Syrus would've been more likely to make his acquaintance. Syrus is frequently seen staggering downhill from the House of the Beaks at dawn." He frowned. "But you say your friend was murdered—"

"We need not speak of it, since you didn't know him."

Laberius nodded respectfully, then seized my arm. "Now, citizen, if you would be so kind, take a seat about midway up. I'll stay down here and finish reciting my prologue. The acoustics here aren't the same as in the theater, but I can still practice my movements and hone my timing—"

"I'm afraid I should leave now."

"Without hearing the rest?"

"I'll hear it when you perform it for Caesar, I suppose."

"Citizen! I'm offering you a rare opportunity to witness theatrical history in the making, to hear the unexpurgated version—"

"That's the problem, I fear! You see, Laberius, I left the triumph and wandered in this direction in search of escape. I thought that's what I was in for, when I paused to listen to you in the theater. Instead, what did I hear? Topical satire about the state of Rome, veiled references to the dictator—the very things from which I was fleeing! No, thank you, playwright. If there's no escape from the dictator anywhere in Rome, not even in the theater, then I might as well spend the day with my loved ones. Which reminds me, my wife will be desperately worried by now. Hercules protect me—I must face the wrath of Bethesda! Now there's a subject for a play."

With a final glance at Pompey, who gazed over our heads with a placid smile, I took my leave of Decimus Laberius.

XVII

When I returned to my seat at the triumph, Caesar had already passed, without incident. The legionaries who had served him in Asia were marching by.

I was a bit taken aback by Bethesda's reaction. She seemed hardly to have noticed my absence. Perversely, perhaps, I felt obliged to point out that I had been gone a rather long time.

"Have you?" she said. "When there's so much to watch, the time simply flies. You missed the Cappadocian acrobats. I swear, those boys and girls must have wings, to fly through the air like that!"

"And the Bithynian archers—they were impressive!" offered Davus.

"Archers?" I said.

"They shot hundreds of arrows high into the air," explained Bethesda, "from which multicolored pennants unfurled. The arrows fluttered down, as harmless as a rain of rose petals. It was really quite spectacular."

"You know, I could have been in danger," I said.

"Danger? When all Rome is watching a triumph? How?"

"I don't know. Someone might have tried to stab me in the public latrine. That happened once before—"

"Oh, that was a long time ago!" said Bethesda.

"Which doesn't mean it couldn't happen again. So, it never occurred to you to send Rupa or Davus to look for me?"

She shrugged. "I assumed you ran into someone and were chatting away. I should hate to interrupt when you're busy catching up on gossip with some lowlife from the Subura or some wharf rat from the docks—"

"Excuse me, Wife, but most of my chatting these days is done with people considerably higher up the social scale than that. I talk to senators and magistrates, and relatives of the dictator, and famous playwrights—"

"Yes, yes," she said. "Now shush. The soldiers have broken into one of those chants they love so much. By Bona Dea, it's not about Caesar and King Nicomedes *again,* is it? I suppose those archers from Bithynia reminded them. . . ."

If this was material for a play, it was decidedly a comedy, and at my expense. I sat through the remainder of the triumph in glum silence.

The feasting that followed the triumph left me torpid and drowsy. I meant to read more of Hieronymus's reports when I returned home, looking especially for anything to do with the playwrights Laberius and Syrus, but I could hardly stay awake long enough to tumble into bed. I slept like a stone. Bethesda complained of my snoring the next morning.

During breakfast, I received another message from Calpurnia.

Come at once! I am desperately fearful! My wise counselor assures me the danger increases as the time grows shorter. Have you discovered nothing? Rub the words from this wax as soon as you have read them and report to me in person.

Now there, I thought, is a woman who knows how to fret over her husband. Taking Rupa with me, I went to her house at once.

Porsenna the haruspex was with her, looking as self-important as ever. Uncle Gnaeus sat with his arms crossed, shaking his head from time to time to express his opinion that all this fuss was for no good reason. Calpurnia was in a highly agitated state.

"You realize there is only one more triumph remaining?" she said.

"Yes, tomorrow's African Triumph," I said, "ostensibly to celebrate the defeat and death of King Juba but also to mark Caesar's triumph over his Roman opponents who fled to Africa after the battle of Pharsalus. No Roman has ever before celebrated a triumph for killing other Romans—"

"Which makes this occasion all the more dangerous for Caesar," said Calpurnia. "How his enemies would love to pull him down even as he reaches the pinnacle of his glory!"

"Is that what your haruspex tells you?"

"Porsenna's warnings are dire. But it's also common sense."

"Then surely your husband will take every precaution. No

man has more common sense than Caesar. Why, only yesterday, someone was telling me what a good judge of character Caesar must be—"

"Enough prattling!" said Calpurnia. "Have you discovered anything that might be useful? Anything at all?"

I sighed. "I'm no closer to being able to tell you who killed Hieronymus, and why. As I told you from the outset, that is my real purpose for pursuing this matter."

"When will you know something?"

"It's impossible to say. And yet . . ."

All three of them leaned toward me.

"Go on!" said Porsenna.

"Over the years, I seem to have developed a certain instinct. As others can smell rain before it comes, so I can smell the truth approaching."

"And?"

"My nose has begun to twitch."

"What is that supposed to mean?" snapped Uncle Gnaeus.

"I sense that I'm drawing closer to the truth, though I don't yet have an inkling of what that truth is or where or how the revelation will come. It's like the first whiff of a scent. You know you recognize it, even though you can't put a name to it. At least, not yet. . . . but soon . . ."

"You sound as mystical as Porsenna!" said Calpurnia. "I thought you relied on logic and deduction, like a Greek philosopher."

"I do. But sometimes I seem to skip a step or two in the chain of reasoning. I arrive at the truth by a kind of shortcut. Does it matter how I get there?"

"It matters *when* you get there," she said. "In time to save Caesar!"

I took a deep breath. "I'll do what I can."

I returned home. Once again I set to studying Hieronymus's reports and his personal journal. Though the hour was early, the day was already hot. No breeze stirred the baking heat of the garden.

I found nothing new to pique my interest, but I did come across a passage I had not read before, concerning the doorkeeper at Hieronymus's building, the slave called Agapios. In passing, Hieronymus noted, "What a flirt the boy is! Today he actually winked at me. To be sure, Cytheris served wine of Chios last night, and that vintage is said to restore the allure of the drinker's lost youth."

"Hieronymus, Hieronymus!" I muttered. "What a vain old fellow you were, and how easily you were flattered." In fact, I felt a bit put out by the passage. Agapios had flirted with me as well, but obviously the young man did so promiscuously and without the least sincerity. Some slaves acquire a habit of flirting with their superiors; they ingratiate themselves by reflex.

Diana brought me a cup of water. She surveyed the scrolls and scattered bits of parchment all around me. She seemed to hesitate, then spoke.

"Papa, do you think you've given sufficient weight to the note Hieronymus left for whomever might find his private writings? I mean the part where he says, 'Look all around! The truth is not found in the words—' "

"Daughter! Have you been looking through these documents behind my back?"

"You never forbade me to read them, Papa."

"But I never asked you to do so." I scowled at her. The heat was making me irritable.

"Hieronymus was my friend, too," she said quietly.

"Yes. Of course he was." I sipped the water.

"I want to know what happened to him, just as you do," she added. "And since you think it unseemly that I should go about asking questions of strangers, as you do, what else can I do but read his reports and try to imagine which of those people wanted to kill him?"

"I'll grant that you have the advantage of younger, stronger eyes. How much have you read?"

"Only bits and pieces. Some of his Greek I can't follow, and sometimes his handwriting is very hard to make out."

"As I know only too well! But what were you saying earlier, about something I've overlooked?"

"I don't know that you've overlooked it, Papa. But it strikes me that it might be significant. It's this part here." She reached for a scrap of parchment and read aloud. "'I dare not write my supposition even here; what if this journal were to be discovered? Must keep it hidden. But what if I am silenced? To any seeker who finds these words and would unlock the truth, I shall leave a key. Look all around! The truth is not found in the words, but the words may be found in the truth.'"

I nodded. "Yes, yes, I noticed that passage at once when I discovered his private writings. There was no literal key, or at least none that I could find. As for looking all around, I did so. I scoured every corner of his rooms."

"Was Rupa with you?"

"No, this was before your mother issued her proclamation that I should never venture out alone. Why do you ask?"

"Another pair of eyes might have seen something you overlooked."

"Do you think I should go back and look again, and take Rupa with me?"

"No, I think you should take *me* with you."

"Diana, you know how I feel about your interest in this sort of—"

"But, Papa, you just admitted that my eyes are younger and stronger. Might I not see something that you overlooked? Four eyes are better than two."

"An aphorism worthy of Publilius Syrus!"

"So you *will* take me with you to Hieronymus's apartment?"

"I never said that!"

But that was what I did.

An hour later, three of us arrived at the building in the Subura: Rupa, Diana, and myself. Agapios the door slave was nowhere to be seen, but we did not need him; I had the key to Hieronymus's rooms. As we made our way up the stairs, Diana bounded ahead of me. I could see she was very excited to be accompanying her father in the performance of his work.

But her excitement gradually faded as we conducted our examination of the rooms. Together, we searched the furniture, looked for hidden compartments in the walls and the floor, and sorted though Hieronymus's few possessions. We looked through the various scrolls that remained in the bookcase, searching for any scraps of parchment with Hieronymus's handwriting. We circled the rooftop terrace, searching for hidden compartments in the exterior walls.

We discovered nothing of interest.

At length, Diana sighed. "I was so sure we'd find something."

I nodded. "I know that feeling."

"And yet, I was wrong."

"I know that feeling, too. There's a great deal of frustration and disappointment in this sort of work. But when there's nothing to see, four eyes are no better than two."

"I suppose you're right. But I'd be even more frustrated if I hadn't been able to take a look for myself. Thank you, Papa."

As we made our way down the stairs, I heard voices from the vestibule below. We came upon young Agapios in conversation with Gnaeus Calpurnius. The old priest looked surprised to see me, and even more surprised at the sight of Rupa and Diana.

"What are these people doing here?"

The usually cheerful Agapios seemed completely cowed by Uncle Gnaeus, who was no doubt immune to his powers of flirtation. "The one called Gordianus has the key to the rooftop apartment," he explained.

"How did he acquire that?"

"He took it from me. He showed me the mistress's seal—"

Uncle Gnaeus boxed his ear. "A fine job you've done, looking after this property. I should send you to the salt mines." No sooner had Agapios recovered himself than Gnaeus struck him again.

"Stop!" I said. "It's as the slave says. I took the key by Calpurnia's authority. What business is it of yours?"

"My niece delegated the running of this property to me months ago. She's much too busy to deal with evicting tenants or collecting rents. The slave should never have given you a key to this building without my authority."

"Gnaeus Calpurnius, I think you know the importance your niece attaches to my work, whether you respect it or not. Would you have denied me the key? I think not. For Numa's sake, leave the boy alone!"

"How dare you invoke the name of my ancestor on behalf of a slave, Finder!"

"Here, take back the key. I don't need it anymore." I tossed it at his feet, but it was Agapios who scrambled to retrieve it. The groveling slave offered it to Gnaeus Calpurnius, who gave him a kick.

I hurried out, with Diana and Rupa behind me.

"Now you've seen another side of my work, Daughter." I could see that Diana was shaken by the exchange. "It isn't all sipping wine with Cytheris or trading barbs with Cicero. Strip away their cultivated manners, and you'll find that our betters are a nasty lot."

"What an awful man!" Diana shuddered.

"I've encountered worse," I said, but at the moment I couldn't remember where or when.

After sharing a midday meal with the family, I was inclined to take a nap, but Diana insisted that we sit together in the garden and continue reading Hieronymus's notes. Having worn me down in her pursuit to share my work, she was eager to continue.

It was Diana who came across a passage that neither of us had read before:

Do I miss living in the household of Gordianus? I certainly miss Bethesda's cooking. I miss Gordianus's largesse and his conversation. But the two of them are gone, perhaps never to return. I miss the others, too, of course, but there is much to be said for striking out on one's own and not looking back. I am living my own adventure.

"His own adventure," I whispered, "which came to such a sad end."

Diana nodded. "There's also a bit about that haruspex Porsenna."

Part of the fun is seeing how far I can trick a fellow trickster like Porsenna into trusting me (and inducing Calpurnia to pay me). The fellow is probably a charlatan through and through, but I wonder if he hasn't convinced himself of his powers of precognition. If I validate his prediction of a plot against the dictator, his hold on Calpurnia can only increase. If I were to show him up as a fool or a fraud, even she could not protect me from his fury.

"Do you think he's exaggerating, Papa, about how dangerous Porsenna might be? You've met the man. I haven't."

"Hard to say."

"It's a thought, though, isn't it? Hieronymus might have been killed because he was close to proving that Caesar was *not* in danger from a plot on his life."

I gazed at her and shook my head. "You have your mother's looks, thank the gods, but I fear you've inherited your father's devious mind."

This made her smile.

"I was also wondering, Papa, if we shouldn't be thinking more about the dedication ceremony at the new Temple of Venus."

"What of it?"

"It's scheduled to take place shortly after the completion of tomorrow's triumph. Might that not be a more likely occasion for someone to gain access to Caesar, if they wanted to do him harm?"

"Perhaps. I presume work on the temple is finished, but I'm not sure about the surrounding area. There's a great deal of new construction taking place. I suppose there might be hiding places suitable for staging an ambush, traps that could be made to look like accidents, that sort of thing."

"Perhaps we should have a look."

"*We?*"

"It was my idea, Papa."

I sighed. "Very well. Go find Rupa. Let's take a look at Caesar's new temple."

X V I I I

With typical modesty, Caesar intended to call his new complex of buildings the Great Forum, to differentiate it from the ages-old Forum (officially, the Forum Romanum) created by our forefathers. As yet, only the outlines of the Great Forum could be discerned; except for the completed Temple of Venus, prominently situated at one end of the concourse, the area was a vast construction site, with its constituent parts in various stages of completion.

When it was finished, the Great Forum would become the legal center of Rome, with hearing rooms, judicial halls, offices for advocates, and legislative archives clustered around a large square bordered by a colonnaded portico. In its center would stand a monumental equestrian statue of Caesar (as yet, only the huge pedestal was in place), while the area in front of the Temple of Venus would be graced by an elaborate fountain (for which only the pipes had been laid down).

The site was swarming with workmen. For tomorrow's dedication ceremony, the space in front of the temple was being cleared of debris and tidied up so as to accommodate a great many spectators. Most would be expected to stand. For the more important personages, benches were being delivered and arranged in rows before the temple steps. At the foot of the steps, a marble altar for sacrifice was being set up.

The temple was a magnificent sight, made entirely of marble. It was built on a high podium accessed by a long flight of steps, with the columns set close together. Every detail of the facade—the cornices and capitals, the pediment and sculptural decorations—had been exquisitely crafted.

This was the temple Caesar had pledged to erect on the eve of the battle of Pharsalus, should he be victorious, in honor of his divine ancestress. Its full name was the Temple of Venus Genetrix. Pompey's temple atop his theater was officially consecrated to Venus Victrix, but the victory of Venus had been bestowed on Caesar.

I surveyed as much of the construction site as the workmen would allow us to enter, looking for potential places of ambush or traps. It seemed unlikely that anyone could engineer such a threat in secret, with so many men involved in clearing and cleaning the site.

"Let's have a look inside," said Diana.

"I'm not sure we can. The temple isn't open yet."

"Nonsense—the doors are standing wide open! Besides, you have Calpurnia's seal, don't you? And she's an in-law of Venus, isn't she?"

Without waiting for me, Diana headed up the long flight of steps. I dutifully followed and gestured for Rupa to come along. She paused on the porch for me to catch up, then together we stepped through the wide doorway.

The interior was even more sumptuous than the facade. The marble floors, walls, ceiling, and columns presented a staggering array of colors and patterns, and everything was newly finished, so that all the surfaces gleamed with a mirrorlike polish. To decorate the facing walls of the vestibule, Caesar had acquired two of the most famous paintings in the world, the Medea and the Ajax by the renowned artist Timomachus. A series of ornate cabinets exhibited an extraordinary collection of jewelry and gemstones acquired by Caesar in his travels. Not the most beautiful, but surely the most exotic, was a savage-looking breastplate strung with tiny pearls; a placard noted that it came from the island of Britannia, at the furthest end of the world.

From the sanctuary, I could hear the tapping noise of a sculptor's hammer and chisel. Diana heard it, too, and we exchanged a curious look.

"You don't think someone is still at work on the statue, on the very day before the dedication?" she said.

"Let's find out," I said. We entered the sanctuary.

The sculptor who had received Caesar's commission, Arcesilaus, was reputed to be the most highly paid artist in the world. He was mentioned in passing in Hieronymus's reports and had sent a note of condolence. Many years ago, I had met him at the house of the late Lucullus, a great patron of the arts. Arcesilaus had been young then, and quite handsome, with a reputation for vanity and hot-tempered genius. His hair had grown grayer, but he still had the big shoulders and biceps of a sculptor, and his temper still ran hot, if his reaction to our appearance in the sanctuary was any indication.

"What in Hades are you doing here?" he shouted. The

marble statue of Venus stood on a high pedestal at the rear wall. Arcesilaus was perched on a riser which allowed him access to the base of the statue, where he was tending to a finishing detail with a small hammer and a chisel.

I cleared my throat. "My name is Gordianus—"

"And I'm Diana, his daughter. And this is Rupa, his son."

I frowned at Diana's forwardness. Arcesilaus raised an eyebrow. I didn't care for the way his mouth twisted at one corner as he looked Diana up and down.

"You and I have met before," I said, "though it was a long time ago—"

"I know your name. I know who you are. And I remember when we met. That doesn't answer my question. What are you doing here? If the answer isn't, 'Caesar sent me and this is an emergency,' then all three of you can get out! Well, you two fellows, anyway." He looked at Diana again and narrowed his eyes.

"I *am* here on behalf of Caesar," I said, speaking a sort of truth.

"What can that man possibly want *now*?" Arcesilaus threw down his hammer and chisel. I flinched in anticipation of the impact, but the statue was surrounded by canvas drop cloths. The instruments landed with a soft thud.

Arcesilaus launched into a rant. "He says to finish the statue by the end of the year. 'Very well,' I say, 'that's possible.' Then he tells me it must be done by September. 'Impossible!' I tell him, 'It can't be done.' 'Ah, but it must be done,' he says. 'Make it possible.' And when I protest, he begins to recite his miracles on the battlefield, how he built a snare made of ships to catch Pompey at Brundisium, and tunneled under the walls at Massilia, and so on and so forth, always making the impossible

possible by sheer exercise of will. 'This is art, not war,' I told him. 'This is a statue, not a slaughter. I'm creating a goddess, not sacking Gaul!' "

He jumped from the platform and with a loud grunt bent down to pick up his tools. When he stood straight, he glared at me for a moment, then was distracted again by Diana. The fire in his eyes burned even hotter. His lips curled into a leer. When he was younger, men called Arcesilaus a lover; nowadays they called him a letch. I snapped my fingers to regain his attention.

His face went blank for a moment, then registered glum resignation. "Well? What does Caesar want now? Out with it!" When I hesitated, stumped for an answer, he threw down his tools again. "And don't tell me it has anything to do with *that* abomination!" He pointed past us, toward one of the corners of the sanctuary nearest the entrance. Partially wrapped in ropes and canvas, lying on its side, was the gilded statue of Cleopatra that had been displayed in the Egyptian Triumph.

"What is that doing here?" I said.

"My question, exactly!" Arcesilaus stormed over and stopped in front of the statue of the Egyptian queen. For a moment, I thought he might kick it. Instead, he glowered at the thing, stamped his feet, and came storming back. "What indeed is that—that atrocity—doing in this temple? Don't ask me. Ask Caesar!"

"Are you telling me Caesar intends to install it here, in the Temple of Venus?"

" 'As close to the statue of the goddess as possible'—his exact words. 'Without, of course, detracting from the integrity of your own work'—also his exact words. 'Without detracting'— as if such a thing were possible! The temple has been built to house the statue; the statue has been designed to fulfill the sacred purpose of the temple. The two things are one and indivisible. To introduce another element, especially a piece of garbage such as that thing—"

"The spectators at the triumph liked it well enough," said Diana. "People appeared to be quite impressed by it."

He scowled at her. "I preferred you with your mouth shut."

"That's uncalled for!" I said.

"Do you agree with your daughter, then? Do you think a drunken mob is capable of exercising artistic judgment? Is that what we've come to? Between chanting obscene ditties, they were momentarily awed by a gaudy statue, so now the thing deserves to be installed in a sacred temple, next to the work of the greatest sculptor in the world? Thank the gods, Lucullus is no longer alive to see this!"

He was close to tears. He grabbed my arm. Rupa darted forward, but Arcesilaus meant me no harm. He pulled me toward the statue of Venus.

"Look at her!" he commanded. "She isn't even finished yet—a few places need polishing, and no color has yet been added. But look at her, and tell me what you see."

I appraised the statue for a long moment. "I see the goddess Venus. She stands with one arm bent back to touch her shoulder, and her other arm slightly extended—"

"The pose is exquisite, is it not?"

I nodded. "Yes. One of her breasts is bare—"

"Her naked breast captures the exact weight and texture of actual flesh, does it not? You can almost feel the supple, warm skin beneath your fingertips. You can almost see her bosom rise and fall, as if she breathes."

"Yes," I whispered.

"And her face?"

"Serene. Wise. Beautiful." I thought of Arsinoë's face, when Rupa kissed her toe.

"And the molding of her gown, the way the folds bend and drape?"

I shook my head in amazement. "They look as if the slightest breeze might stir them."

"Exactly! What you see is made of stone, and yet, the longer you look at her, the more she appears to be alive, breathing, watching—as if she might step down from her pedestal at any moment."

The effect was indeed uncanny. I truly felt as if the statue of Venus gazed back at me. Unnerved, I lowered my eyes. At the base of the statue, I noticed the finishing detail which Arcesilaus had been adding when we entered. It was the artist's famous hallmark, an image of a rampant satyr.

"Now, come over here." He gripped my arm and led me to the statue of Cleopatra. "What do you see?"

I frowned. "It seems a bit unfair to make a comparison. The statue is lying on its side, after all."

"And would it look any less stiff and lifeless if it stood upright?"

"It's a different sort of statue," I argued. "It depicts a living human being, for one thing, not a goddess."

"And yet it seems *less* alive, *less* present in the room than does the image of Venus!"

He was right. The workmanship of Cleopatra's statue was decidedly inferior. The gilded bronze, which had been so dazzling under the hot sun, was less impressive in the dim light of the sanctuary; in fact, it looked a bit tawdry. The statue was not without beauty, but compared to the Venus, it was only a lifeless piece of metal.

"It hurts my eyes even to look at it!" declared Arcesilaus. "Yet Caesar insists that it be placed here in the temple, where it will upset the whole balance."

"Perhaps it will only point out the superior nature of your Venus," I said.

"That's not how it works!" he snapped. "Bad art diminishes good art. The closer the proximity, the greater the damage."

"Have you pointed this out to Caesar?"

" 'You've been working on the Venus for a long time,' he told me. 'I realize you're exhausted, and here I am, posing you yet another challenge. But you'll rise to it, Arcesilaus! You'll find the ideal spot for the queen's image. You can do it!' As if this were just another part of my commission, an opportunity to create something harmonious and beautiful, for which I should be *grateful*—instead of an insult to everything I've achieved in a lifetime of making art!"

I drew a sharp breath. How harmless was Arcesilaus's rant? Had he ever before expressed such rancor against Caesar? And had Hieronymus been there to hear it? I couldn't remember encountering any mention of the sculptor's animosity against Caesar in Hieronymus's reports.

"Why do you think Caesar wants this statue in the temple?" I asked. "Can there be a religious purpose? Cleopatra is linked to the Egyptian goddess Isis—"

"So she is," said Arcesilaus. "But Isis is a manifestation of the Greek goddess Artemis, our goddess Diana—*not* Venus. No, the image of Cleopatra cannot possibly be construed as another image of Venus. Isn't it obvious why Caesar wants that statue in a temple that honors his ancestress? He means to honor the mother of his own child."

"I think you're wrong there," I said, remembering my recent conversation with Caesar, and the absence of Caesarion in the Egyptian Triumph. And yet, a man like Caesar liked to keep all his options open. He also liked to keep people guessing.

"Perhaps you know Caesar's mind better than I do," granted Arcesilaus. "Why *did* he send you here today, anyway? It wasn't about this other thing, was it?" He indicated another corner of the sanctuary, where a large placard made of cloth on a wooden frame was propped against a wall. I drew closer and examined it. It was an image of a calendar painted in the traditional style, with the abbreviated names of months across the top and columns of numerals beneath marking the days, with the Kalends, Ides, Nones, and various holidays indicated. It was very artistically rendered in many colors, with exquisitely wrought letters.

"A calendar?" I said.

"*The* calendar," said Arcesilaus. "Hardly a subject worthy of my talents, but since Caesar means to announce his new calendar at the same time that he dedicates the temple, he wanted an image to unveil, so I made this thing myself. What do you think?"

"It's an object of beauty. Very elegant."

"I don't suppose you've come to check the accuracy? Someone is supposed to do that before tomorrow."

"No."

He frowned. "Why *did* Caesar send you here?"

"Send me?"

"That's what you said, that Caesar sent you."

"No, I said I came on his behalf."

"What's the difference?" Arcesilaus scowled.

"I wanted to check that the route from the Forum to the temple was safe for Caesar to traverse—"

"Is that your job?"

I considered how to answer. "Well, as a matter of fact, it's the sort of thing my son Meto does on Caesar's behalf; but Meto is away from Rome. And as long as I was here, I thought I'd have a look inside the temple." Not one word of this was a lie.

Arcesilaus was indignant. "Do you mean I've been wasting my time standing here and talking to you, and for no good reason? Get out, all three of you, at once!"

I took Diana by the arm and turned toward the exit. Arcesilaus's demeanor was so threatening that Rupa lagged behind, as if to make sure the artist didn't follow us. But when I looked back, he had returned to the statue of Cleopatra and was glaring down at it. While I watched, he gave it a hard kick, then shouted a curse to Venus. While the dull, hollow ring of the metal resounded through the chamber, Arcesilaus hopped about and clutched his injured toe.

X I X

For the rest of the day, Diana and I sorted and read through Hieronymus's notes. She questioned me about the material I had already read, and I did the same with her. We divided the material that remained unexamined, determined to read every word before the day was done.

Whether against my will or not, Diana had insinuated herself into my work, so it seemed pointless not to bring her fully into the process, to take advantage of her interest and of her sometimes surprisingly keen insight. She spotted certain meanings within Hieronymus's puns that had eluded me, and, being more abreast of current gossip, caught certain allusions to personal relationships and such that I had overlooked. But none of her insights added materially to our knowledge of who had killed Hieronymus, or whether that person posed a threat to Caesar, or when or how the killer might strike again.

Despite all our combined efforts, and a great deal of discussion and speculation, I went to bed that night believing I was no closer to knowing the truth than before.

The next day, along with everyone else in Rome, my family set out to witness the African Triumph. Since we would later be attending the dedication of the Temple of Venus Genetrix, a sacred ritual, I wore my best toga.

For a great many people, I suspect, attending Caesar's fourth and final triumph was done more from perseverance than pleasure. It is a Roman trait—to see a thing through to its end; the same dogged determination that has made us the possessors of a vast empire applies to every other aspect of life. Just as our generals do not raise sieges or surrender on the battlefield, no matter how great the casualties, so Romans do not walk out in the middle of plays, no matter how boring the performance; and those who can read do not begin a book without finishing it. And, by Jupiter, no matter how repetitious all the pomp and spectacle, the people of Rome did not attend Caesar's three consecutive triumphs without attending the fourth and final one as well.

Senators paraded (with Brutus and Cicero looking more bored and aloof than ever); trumpets sounded; and the oxen lumbered by, along with the priests and the camilli, the boys and girls who would take part in the sacrifices.

Captured treasures and trophies were presented. Caesar did not presume to show off the Roman arms he had captured in battle—even his most loyal partisans would not have approved of that—but there were a number of placards illustrating the ends met by his Roman opponents in Africa. We beheld a succession of suicides, each more wretched than the last.

Metellus Scipio, Pompey's successor as commander in chief,

after being defeated by Caesar at the battle of Thapsus, stabbed himself and leaped into the sea. The placard showed him in mid-jump above stormy waves, with blood trailing from his wound.

Another leader of the opposition, Marcus Petreius, fled after the battle of Thapsus and holed up for a while with King Juba. When the two realized they had no further hope, they held a sumptuous banquet and engaged in a ritual combat, so that at least one could have an honorable death. Juba won the contest. The placard showed Petreius lying dead of his wounds and the king in the act of falling on his own bloody sword.

Cato's suicide had been the messiest. He might have received a pardon from Caesar, but he did not desire it. After a quiet evening with friends, he withdrew to his chambers and attempted to disembowel himself. His effort was only partly successful, perhaps due to a wounded hand, and when he knocked over a table, his servants came running to find their master's belly bleeding and cut open, but with his bowels intact. A physician was called to stuff his entrails back inside and to sew him up, an indignity to which Cato, in a dazed state, submitted. But when he regained consciousness and saw what had happened, he tore open the wound, pulled out his bowels with his bare hands, and suffered an agonizing death.

The placard depicting the death of Cato was obscenely graphic. The crowd was already uneasy after viewing the previous illustrations. When the image of Cato passed before them, they grumbled sullenly and many began to boo.

The restiveness of the crowd was relieved somewhat by the animal show, which introduced an African beast never before seen in Rome. With their long necks, the creatures towered above the throng; the tallest of them loped by on eye level with those of us in the top of the stands. A crier explained that this was the camelopard, so-called because in some respects it resembled the camel, having long, spindly legs and a camel-like face, while its spotted skin resembled that of a leopard. But its extremely long neck made the creature unique. Children laughed and grown men gawked. The spectacle provided by the camelopards did much to restore the crowd's good mood.

There were no Romans among the paraded captives, only Africans, Numidians, and other foreign allies of the opposition. But here, too, Caesar provided an unexpected novelty. As Arsinoë had been the first princess to be paraded in a triumph, and Ganymedes and his fellow eunuchs were the first of their kind, so this triumph also featured a first: a baby. The last and most prized of the captives did not walk with the rest; he might have been able to toddle but could not possibly have kept up. Instead, he reclined upon a small litter carried by other captives. There were gasps and cries of astonishment as people realized what they were seeing: the infant son of the late King Juba.

I scanned the faces of the dignitaries in the box opposite our seats, curious to see their reaction. Among the staid ambassadors and diplomats, I saw a beautiful woman: Fulvia. The woman who intended to marry Marc Antony was still chiefly regarded as the widow of Curio, Caesar's lieutenant, whose head had been taken by King Juba as a trophy early in the war. Caesar had given Fulvia a place of honor to view this triumph, which celebrated Juba's downfall. As she gazed at Juba's tiny namesake among the captives, there was a look of grim satisfaction on her face.

But most of the women in the crowd—and most of the men, for that matter—had a different reaction. People frowned, muttered, and shook their heads. Some looked aghast. Did Caesar intend to have the child strangled at the conclusion of his triumph? Did he imagine that such a killing would be pleasing to Jupiter?

We were not kept in suspense for long. A crier announced that Caesar intended to show clemency to the infant son of Juba. The child would be spared, just as Arsinoë had been spared.

A sigh of relief spread through the crowd. "Caesar is merciful!" people shouted, and "Good for Caesar!"

I looked at Fulvia, whose face registered a different reaction. She lowered her eyes and clenched her jaw.

When had Caesar decided to spare young Juba? He apparently had planned to execute Arsinoë, and changed his mind only at the last moment in response of the crowd's reaction. Had he likewise planned to kill Juba's child, until the affair with Arsinoë made him realize that the mob would not stand for it? Caesar was not above slaughtering infants. How many babies had been among the forty thousand victims at Avaricum in Gaul? Caesar had taken no steps to spare those children, even to make them slaves.

At length, Caesar appeared in his gold chariot; even he seemed to be a bit tired of so much triumphing. Waging war and wrangling with political rivals wears on a man, but so does pomp and ceremony. The smile on his face looked forced and brittle.

Following Caesar, at the head of the veterans of the African campaign, rode young Gaius Octavius. He was outfitted as a decorated officer, even though he had taken no part in the African campaign, or in any other military operation. At the sight of him, people cheered; he made a dashing figure, and sometimes appearances are all that matter. The smile on his lips was ambiguous. Was he embarrassed to be receiving accolades he had not earned? Was he scornful of the masses who cheered him for no reason? Or was he simply a young man happy to be riding in the company of his distinguished older relative, pleased with himself and with his special place in the world?

The triumph concluded without incident. The prisoners (except young Juba) were duly executed, and a sacrifice was offered in gratitude to Jupiter atop the Capitoline. Then, without a pause, attended by a vast retinue of officer, senators, and priests, Caesar began to make his way down the Capitoline, heading for the new Temple of Venus.

After the triumph, my family and I remained in the stands for a while, waiting for the crowd to thin. As we began to descend, I saw a now-familiar figure mounting the steps, heading toward us. It was Calpurnia's messenger. The look on his face was grim. He was too out of breath to speak. Without a word, he extended a tablet toward me. I took it from him, undid the ties, and opened it.

The letters had been so crudely scratched in the wax—as if in haste or great agitation—that for a moment I could make no sense of them. Then, all at once, the words jumped out at me:

Porsenna is dead. Come to me at once. The messenger will bring you.

I lowered the tablet. Bethesda was staring at me. "From her?" she said.

"Yes. I must go with this fellow."

"Take Rupa with you."

"Of course. And you and the family?"

"We shall attend the dedication of the temple, as we planned. In the standing area, I presume." While Caesar had arranged for us to have seats in the stands for his triumphs, he had not followed up with any such arrangement for the dedication. I had tried to explain to Bethesda that the seating for the ceremony was strictly limited, but she was not happy.

"If you hurry," I said, "perhaps you can still find a good spot, not too far back."

Diana drew close to me. "What does Calpurnia say? Is there some sort of trouble?"

"The haruspex is dead. Murdered, I presume."

"I should come with you, Papa."

"I think not. The woman is quite particular about whom she'll allow into her presence."

"But Rupa is going with you."

"Rupa is my bodyguard."

"If I were your son instead of your daughter, you'd take me along without question."

Whether this was true or not, I was in no mood to argue, and the messenger was growing impatient. He deftly took the tablet from my hand, rubbed out the letters, and pulled at my toga.

"We should hurry, please!" he said.

"Davus, look after Diana," I said, fearful that she would try to follow against my orders. "Rupa, come with me."

We followed the man down the steps and into the crowd.

I had assumed that the messenger would lead me to the house of Calpurnia, but he turned in the opposite direction.

"Where are you taking us?" I said, suddenly suspicious.

"To the mistress, of course." He gripped my toga again. I knocked his hand away.

"This isn't the way to the Palatine."

"The Palatine?"

"Where she lives."

"She's not at home. She at the Temple of Venus. Please, hurry!"

Of course, I thought; the dictator's wife would have to attend the dedication, no matter what had happened to her haruspex. I followed quickly, realizing Diana and the family could have come at least partway with me, after all. But it was too late for them to rejoin me. We were separated by the crowd.

The open square before the temple was already thronged with people, and more were arriving from all directions. The standing area looked uncomfortably crowded—I had to wonder where Diana and the family would find space—but the benches nearer the temple were not yet filled; dignitaries are often the last to arrive. Some sat, while others milled about and conversed with their neighbors. The atmosphere was much like that at the theater before the crier announces that the play will begin.

In front of the seating area, at the foot of the temple steps, a large space was being kept clear by a row of lictors. Here, a marble altar had been erected for the ritual sacrifice. Close by the altar, a long ceremonial tent had been set up. Within the tent, those participating in the dedication could gather and prepare, unseen by the crowd.

The messenger led me toward the tent. The lictor at the entrance refused to let Rupa come inside. It seemed pointless to argue. The area within that tent was probably the safest, most secure place in all Rome.

I stepped from harsh sunlight into the diffused, warm glow of the tent. I smelled incense and flowers. As my eyes adjusted, the first thing I saw was the ox intended for sacrifice. It was a magnificent white beast, its horns garlanded with flowers and laurel leaves. It was circled by the young camilli holding shallow libation bowls to receive the spilled blood and the severed organs that would be offered to the goddess. Some of the boys and girls were washing the flanks of the ox with woolen cloths that had been dipped in warm, jasmine-scented water, while others were daubing the animal's hooves with cinnabar to stain them red. The ox stood quite still, its heavy-lidded eyes gazing straight ahead, seeming to bask in their attentions.

As my eyes continued to adjust, I saw others in the tent. Most were priests and lictors, but there were a few senators and other men in togas as well. Arcesilaus was also there, wearing a tunic covered with dust and spotted with paint. The large placard displaying the new calendar had been placed on a stand where it could be worked on, and he appeared to be making last-minute alterations with a set of paints, while another man—not a Roman, to judge by his Egyptian jewelry and pleated linen gown—looked on.

The artist glanced over his shoulder, saw me, and scowled. "You!" he said.

His perfunctory salutation canceled any need for pleasantries.

"Let me guess," I said. "The calendar contains an error, and this fellow is one of Cleopatra's astronomers from Alexandria, advising you on the necessary correction."

"And with plenty of time to spare!" said Arcesilaus sarcastically. "The fellow never showed up yesterday. Only now am I being told that the extra day in Februarius during a leap year is added *six* days before the Kalends of Martius, *not* eight. Ridiculous! So now, after all my painstaking effort, this little presentation will look as slapdash as if I'd turned it out on the spur of the moment. Caesar isn't paying me enough to endure this torment!"

His voice rose to a yell. He began to quake, vibrating like a plucked string, and raised his fists in the air, the veins in his biceps bulging like the vein in his forehead. The Alexandrian started back in fear, but Arcesilaus's attention was wholly on the placard. He looked as if he intended to beat it with his fists, and it was easy to imagine the delicate thing being totally demolished in a matter of heartbeats.

He was restrained by a hand on one shoulder.

"Don't do it, artist!" said Calpurnia. "Don't even think of it!" There was a shrill edge to her voice that made me shiver. Even the hot-blooded Arcesilaus was chilled by it. The vein pulsing across his forehead vanished, like a snake disappearing into the earth. Muttering, he turned back to the placard and resumed his work.

Before I could speak, Calpurnia gripped my arm and led me to a spot away from the others.

"My slave gave you the message?"

"Yes. Porsenna is dead?"

"Murdered! Stabbed, just like Hieronymus."

"When and how?"

"My messenger found Porsenna's body in his house on the Aventine less than an hour ago. Porsenna was to join me before the end of the triumph, so that we could come to the temple together—"

"You planned to appear with Porsenna in public, where Caesar might see the two of you together? I thought it was your wish that Caesar should never know you were consulting a haruspex."

"I don't care any longer what Caesar knows or doesn't know. The danger is too great—and this proves it! Yesterday, Porsenna was more certain than ever of the menace to Caesar. He told me that today would be the day of greatest danger, and the place of greatest danger would be here, at the dedication of the temple. And now, Porsenna is dead!"

"It was your messenger who found his body?"

"Yes."

"Call him over. Let me speak to him."

She summoned the slave.

"Your mistress sent you to the house of Porsenna on the Aventine. Had you been there before?"

"Yes," said the man, "many times." He had regained his breath, but his eyes had a haunted look. Clearly, he was recovering from a shock.

"Did Porsenna live alone?"

"Yes, except for a single slave."

"And what did you find when you went there today?"

"The door was unbarred. That was very strange. When I stepped inside, I found Porsenna's slave lying in the vestibule. His throat was cut. It took all my courage not to run!"

The messenger ventured a glance at his mistress, wanting her to take note of his bravery, but Calpurnia was not impressed. "Go on!" she snapped.

"I called for Porsenna, but there was no answer. I made my way to the garden. Porsenna was lying on his back, in a pool of blood. He had been stabbed through the heart."

"The heart?" I said. "Are you sure?"

"The wound was here." The slave pointed to his left breast.

"Was the blood wet or dry?"

He thought. "Mostly dry, but in places, still wet."

"Had there been a struggle?"

"I saw no signs of one."

I considered. "If the slave allowed the visitor into the vestibule, it may be that the killer was already known in the house. And Porsenna must not have feared the visitor, if he let the man join him in the garden, and then stood facing him, so that he could be stabbed in the chest."

"Conjecture!" said Calpurnia.

"Do you prefer conjuring tricks, like those Porsenna gave you? If his powers of prophecy were so great, how did he come to such an unexpected end?"

Calpurnia fell silent. Desperation mounted in her eyes. "Gordianus, what can we do?" she whispered.

"Surely Caesar has taken all precautions. I see lictors every-where—"

"It's not enough! Porsenna told me yesterday: 'Shields can-not protect him. Blades cannot protect him. Amulets and talis-mans cannot protect him. No circle of men can stop the one who seeks to harm him. Only *I* can help you!' "

"Porsenna can't help you now. What do you think I can possibly do?"

She seized my arm and pulled me to a narrow opening in the tent. She peered out at the milling crowd with nervous, birdlike movements of her head. "Which of them is it? Which of them intends to kill Caesar, Gordianus?"

"I don't know."

"Go out among them. Listen to what they're saying. Look them in the eyes."

I shook my head. "Calpurnia, I've done my best. Not just for you but for Hieronymus. I wish—"

"They call you 'Finder,' don't they? Or they used to. Be-cause you find the truth."

I sighed. "Sometimes."

"Others see but are blind, but when you see the truth, you know it! That's your gift. The truth is there to be found. The guilt is already written on someone's face. Go. Observe. Listen."

I took a deep breath. "I'll take a walk through the crowd," I said, partly because I was now desperate to escape Calpurnia but also because there was indeed a chance, however slight, that I might see or overhear something of significance.

"Go!" she said. "But return here before the ceremony be-gins. If something . . . goes amiss . . . I want you beside me."

I turned to leave. Calpurnia hurried across the tent to Uncle Gnaeus, who had just entered. He put his arms around her, and she hid her face against his shoulder. Uncle Gnaeus held her tightly and gave me a curt nod, as if to dismiss me and send me on my way.

X X

I left Rupa standing outside the entrance of the tent, telling him to await my return, then went to mingle among the dignitaries. Wearing my best toga, I did not feel entirely out of place among my betters.

The front row of benches had been reserved for the priests, camilli, and others taking part in the sacrifice and dedication ceremony, and for the dictator's immediate family. Most of these seats were empty, since their intended occupants were at present inside the tent, which made young Gaius Octavius and his family look all the more conspicuous. Dressed in spotless armor which had never seen the wear of a single battle, Octavius sat with his mother, Atia, on one side of him and his sister, Octavia, on the other. Aulus Hirtius stood over him, fussing with the straps of Octavius's breastplate; something about their adjustment was apparently not quite up to regulation. Octavius abruptly lost patience and waved Hirtius back. I almost laughed at the petulant look on his face, but when he glanced at me, there was nothing at all boyish in his malevolent gaze. I hurried on.

The foremost section of benches were reserved for the highest dignitaries, including senators. I noticed that Cicero had a choice spot on the aisle, with Brutus sitting next to him. Or perhaps the spot was not so choice after all, for beyond Brutus the entire row was filled with Gallic senators. The boisterous newcomers were talking loudly among themselves in a dialect that mixed their native tongue with Latin. It seemed to me that Cicero and Brutus were pointedly trying to ignore their new colleagues, even when the man next to Brutus repeatedly jostled him.

Cicero saw me and flashed a perfunctory smile, then trained his gaze on a figure behind me. I turned to see the playwright Laberius.

"Looking for a seat, Laberius?" said Cicero.

The playwright shrugged. "Not in this row, Senator. It will be something further back for the humble likes of me, I fear."

"Why, I should have been glad to have you join our ranks were we not already so *pressed for room!*" Cicero raised his voice and glared sidelong at the rowdy, oversized Gauls, none of whom took any notice of his sarcasm.

Laberius smiled. "I'm surprised that you of all people should be pressed for room, Senator. You're so good at straddling the aisle." Brutus barked out a laugh before covering his mouth. Cicero's face grew long. This was a barb aimed at his unseemly efforts to please both sides in the civil war.

Laberius looked pleased with himself, then caught sight of someone in the section reserved for the wealthy. "You must all excuse me while I go pay my respects to Publilius Syrus. Look at him over there, consorting with the millionaires! As if he plans to join their ranks quite soon. Do you suppose the dictator has already promised him the grand prize, before we've even performed the plays? Well, Pig's Paunch shouldn't count his million sesterces yet!"

Laberius stalked off.

I was about to say something to the two senators, then realized they were paying me no attention. "What in Hades *are* they babbling about?" muttered Brutus, speaking to Cicero and referring to the Gauls.

"Hard as it is to follow their uncouth dialect," said Cicero under his breath, "I think I actually heard one of them say something like, 'He spared the Egyptian princess, and he spared little King Juba—you'd think he might have spared Vercingetorix as well!' But I couldn't tell whether the man was joking or not." He groaned. "Hercules give me strength, the sooner this is over, the sooner I can return to the arms of my dear Publilia."

Having had enough of Cicero's oblivious self-concern, I moved on.

In a special section reserved for her retinue, I saw the queen of Egypt, resplendent in a multicolored robe and wearing a nemes headdress with a golden uraeus crown in the form of a rearing cobra. For this occasion of state, she sat in a formal pose, holding the emblems of her royal status, the flail and the crook, crossed over her breasts. She was surrounded by many consorts. That the queen should be present, and in such an ostentatious fashion, was perhaps not surprising; Caesar was installing her statue in the temple, and it was scholars from the queen's library at Alexandria who had devised the new calendar, which was to be formally presented that day. With some surprise, I saw the boy Caesarion seated next to his mother, dressed like a Roman child in a simple white tunic with long sleeves. Caesar must have approved the child's appearance at the event. It seemed to me that the contest of wills between Caesar and the queen regarding the boy's status might yet go one way or the other.

Where was the queen's sister? Arsinoë was still in Rome, presumably, and still a prisoner. Having brushed so close to death, and having survived, what role would she play from this point onward?

"Gordianus!" I heard my name called from nearby, and turned to see Fulvia waving to me. Caesar had granted her a special seat at the triumph, and also at the dedication, it seemed. She appeared to be in unusually high spirits. Seated next to her, I saw the reason: Marc Antony, looking quite handsome and surprisingly sober in his senatorial toga.

I greeted the two of them. Fulvia smiled. "You needn't look so surprised, Finder. Antony and I are old friends. Aren't we, Antony? And Cytheris does occasionally let him off his leash."

"You were missed at the triumphs," I said to Antony, simply to make conversation. "The people expected to see you."

"That's exactly what I told him!" said Fulvia. "It was foolish, missing the opportunity to show himself off, especially since he earned a place of distinction in every one of those triumphs."

Antony smirked. "Technically, I didn't serve at all in the Egyptian campaign, or in—"

"And Gaius Octavius never served in Africa," said Fulvia, "yet Caesar saw fit to shower the boy with honors and show him off, as if Octavius himself put an end to King Juba. You may not have been by Caesar's side at every moment and in every battle, but you were always in his service. It was you who made it possible for him to wage war all over the world, because it was you who kept his name and his authority alive here in Rome—"

Antony clutched his head. "Please, must I hear all this again? Is it not enough that I'm here, as you wanted?"

"Caesar sent you a special invitation to attend this ceremony. You could hardly have refused without insulting him. Don't you see? This is his way of initiating a reconciliation with you. You couldn't turn your back on such an opportunity. Nor could you bring *her* with you, for all Rome to gawk at!" Apparently Cytheris had been left behind at the House of the Beaks—to brood, to pout, to plot her own next move? It looked as if Fulvia might be gaining the upper hand in her campaign to become Antony's wife. Where would her ambitions take them both?

I looked to see Antony's reaction, but he was distracted by someone nearby. I followed his gaze and saw that he was staring at Cleopatra. His expression was one of curiosity more than anything else. I recalled that he had met her years ago in Egypt, when she was hardly more than a child. Having been estranged from Caesar, he had not gone to visit the queen at Caesar's villa. This was his first look at Cleopatra in many years.

Fulvia followed his gaze. "The queen of troublemakers, I call that one," she muttered. "She leaves for Egypt soon, and without having achieved either one of her goals here. Her sister still breathes; her son is still a bastard. But I'll wager we haven't seen the last of that one!"

"I hope not," whispered Antony. Fulvia looked at him askance.

I left these two and continued to stroll among the crowd, searching every face I passed.

The sun was still high. The heat of the day sapped my strength. My instinct and reason were equally at a loss. Lurking behind every pair of eyes was a different consciousness with an unknown agenda. Every face might be utterly innocent; every face might be that of a murderer.

I looked at the rich and powerful, who milled among the benches, but also at the common people in the crowd beyond. They had suffered from the war and its reversals of fortune no less than their betters. How many of these men and women had lost a loved one, fighting for Caesar or against him? How many of them harbored feelings of hatred and resentment against the dictator? How many among that vast crowd, if they could have killed Caesar with a thought, would have done so?

A priest on the temple steps blew a shrill fanfare on a pipe, signaling that the ceremony was about to begin. People took their seats. The standing crowd pressed closer. I looked among them for Bethesda and Diana and the rest of my family, but saw them nowhere.

Calpurnia had instructed me to return to her, and so I did. She had moved from the tent and had taken a seat in the front row, not far from Gaius Octavius and his family, but I saw no empty seats around her. A hush was falling on the crowd, so I spoke in a low voice.

"Calpurnia, if you wish me to stay near you, I suppose I could stand over there, beyond the tent. That is, if the lictors will allow it." I frowned. "Where has Rupa gone? I left him at the entrance to the tent."

"I dismissed him," she said. "He couldn't stay there. Now hush, and sit here beside me."

I pointed out the obvious. "Your Uncle Gnaeus is sitting there."

"Not for long. He's performing the sacrifice, so he'll spend most of the ceremony at the altar."

"The sacrifice?"

"The slaughter of the ox. Why not? Uncle Gnaeus is as qualified as any other priest, and it seemed fitting that someone from my side of the family should play a role in the ceremony. This day shouldn't be entirely about Caesar and the Julii and their divine ancestress and—and that queen whose statue he insists on putting in the temple, next to Venus."

With a haughty flourish, Uncle Gnaeus stood and offered me his seat. I sat between Calpurnia and a man I had never seen before, presumably another of her relatives. Uncle Gnaeus strode toward the altar, pulling the mantle of the robe over his head.

Beside me, Calpurnia continually fidgeted, grunted, and pulled at her fingers.

The crowd fell silent. The ceremony commenced.

The camilli led the ox from the tent. Like the beast, the children were strewn with garlands of flowers and laurel leaves. While the ox lumbered forward, some of the camilli laughed and sang and danced in a circle around it. Others carried trays of smoking incense. They cajoled the creature into ascending a ramp, where the priests used hooks to pull it onto its side on the altar and quickly tied its limbs. The ox began to bleat in alarm. Some of the boys and girls assembled on the temple steps and sang a hymn to Venus while priests played upon pipes. Uncle Gnaeus stepped forward, holding aloft the ceremonial knife.

The heat of the day, the smoking incense, and the chanting

of the children acted on me like a drug. Weariness descended on me. I bowed my head. I closed my eyes . . .

I gave a start. I opened my eyes. I looked around me, dazed, and saw a most remarkable thing.

The stranger sitting next to me had vanished. In his place sat my friend Hieronymus.

X X I

The chanting continued, but seemed strangely distant and muted. The smoky haze of the incense was thicker and more intoxicating than ever. I blinked and rubbed my eyes, but there was no doubt: Hieronymus was sitting next to me.

He was wearing his favorite pale blue tunic with a black border in a Greek key pattern. He looked quite strong and fit and younger than I remembered him. All gray was gone from his hair, and his face had no wrinkles. He fixed me with a sardonic gaze.

"What are you doing here?" I whispered. No one else seemed to have noticed his presence, not even Calpurnia.

"That's hardly a suitable way to greet a man who's back from the dead."

"But this is . . . unbelievable!"

"What's unbelievable is the manner in which you've conducted this so-called investigation into my death. Really, Gordianus, I had no idea you were capable of such incompetence.

You're too old for this sort of thing. Time to pass the baton to that eager daughter of yours."

"Don't speak of Diana!"

"She's a beautiful girl, isn't she? And smart! Not like that husband of hers; poor Davus has a brick between his ears. But he's strong enough. They'll make a good team. He can go along and protect her when she sticks her nose into other people's business, the way young Rupa's been protecting you." He craned his long neck and peered around. "Where has Rupa got to, anyway? And where is Diana, for that matter?"

"Stop this talk!" I whispered. I glanced at Calpurnia, who was wringing her hands and muttering to herself.

"The poor woman's at her wits' end." Hieronymus clucked his tongue. "Married to the most powerful man in the world, and not able to enjoy a moment of it. Listening to soothsayers, crying on her uncle's shoulder, and hiring the likes of me to uncover the truth for her. Mind you, I did uncover the truth, and all on my own—which is more than I can say for you, Gordianus."

"If you found the truth, then why isn't it anywhere in your writings?"

"Didn't you read that passage in my journal? 'But I could be wrong. Consequences of a false accusation—unthinkable! Must be certain. Until then, not a word in any of my official reports to the lady and her soothsayer.' Well, as it turned out, my suspicion was correct." He sighed. "Which is why this happened."

I looked at him again, and saw a huge bloodstain on his breast, above his heart. His flesh had turned as pale as ivory, but his expression was as sardonic as ever. He saw my consternation, and laughed.

"But who did this to you, Hieronymus?"

"That is what *you* were supposed to find out, Gordianus!" He rolled his eyes.

I was stung by his sarcasm. "Help me!" I pleaded.

"I've already given you all the information you need."

"Nonsense! The material you left behind was worthless. Worse than worthless, because there was so much of it. Report after report, all written in that thorny, cryptic prose—nothing but words and more words, and nothing of substance for me to grasp!"

"Calm yourself, Gordianus. Emotion will lead you nowhere. Think!"

"You're not Hieronymus. You're a daemon, an evil spirit come to taunt me."

"No, Gordianus, I *am* Hieronymus—or at least, I'm the sum of all you ever knew about Hieronymus. All we can know of another human being is the image before our eyes and the voice in our ears. What you see and hear now, beside you, is as much as you ever knew of Hieronymus, as real as the man himself. Here I am!"

"Crazy Greek! You confuse me with philosophy!"

"Simpleminded Roman! Always so literal, so mired in facts and figures!"

"Tell me who killed you. Say it plainly!"

He sighed. "First of all, accept the proposition that Calpurnia is right. Someone *is* plotting to kill her husband. I figured out who that person was, and I discerned the motive as well. And because of what I deduced, I was killed."

I was distracted by the lowing of the ox. Uncle Gnaeus was about to cut the creature's throat. Facing the crowd, he raised the knife for all to see. The blade glittered in the sunlight, looking huge and very sharp. He struck the blow: metal sliced into flesh. The ox thrashed its bound limbs. Scarlet poured from the wound. Camilli rushed forward with their libation bowls to catch the spouting blood.

"Have you considered the suspicious behavior of Agapios, the door slave at the building where I lived?" said Hieronymus, watching the slaughter without emotion. He had never been squeamish.

"What do you mean?"

"Really, Gordianus! When a fellow that young flirts with a fellow your age, it can only be because he has an ulterior motive."

"Not necessarily. The vagaries of human nature—"

"Are reducible to the narrow parameters of self-interest. Young Agapios is a spy. In addition to his regular duties, he also kept an eye on me. He was always stopping me on the stairs to chat, especially when I'd come home a little drunk after a party. Who knows what information he got out of me? I suspect he also looked through my journal occasionally, despite my efforts to hide it."

"A spy for his mistress, you mean?" I looked sidelong at Calpurnia, who was watching her uncle perform the sacrifice. What sort of madwoman set a spy to watch her own spy?

Hieronymus shook his head. "Agapios is the property of Calpurnia, but he didn't report to her. He reported to Uncle Gnaeus. That's why the old priest was so angry when he found that Agapios had given you the key to my rooms without his knowledge."

The sacrifice was proceeding. Wielding the huge knife, his

hands smeared with blood, Gnaeus Calpurnius was carving the ox, removing one organ after another. The camilli gathered around him with their libation bowls to receive the kidneys, the heart, the liver, and the rest. One at a time, with prayers and chants, these were offered to Venus, then placed upon a pyre. The organs popped and sizzled, transformed by the flames into divine sustenance for the goddess.

"I found your journal, Hieronymus. By now, I must have read every word of it, and so has Diana. We discovered nothing!"

"Untrue. You found the key! Don't you remember? 'To any seeker who finds these words and would unlock the truth, I shall leave a key—' "

"Yes, yes, I remember. 'Look all around! The truth is not found in the words, but the words may be found in the truth.' But where was this key? I never found it."

"The words themselves were the key. Where did you find them?"

"In your journal, of course!" I snapped, exasperated.

"But where did you find the journal? What was *all around* it?"

"The pages were inside a scroll."

"And what was that scroll?"

I tried to remember. I shook my head.

"Think, Gordianus! I was with you even then. I spoke inside your head. What did I say?"

I remembered now. I had found the journal because I saw my copy of Manius Calpurnius's *Life of King Numa* among the books on Hieronymus's shelf. I was peeved that he had taken it without my permission, so I reached for it, and inside it I found the pages of his private journal. I had sensed that Hieronymus was watching. I had imagined his voice in my head: *How predictable you are, Gordianus! You saw your precious copy of* Numa *and felt compelled to check at once that I hadn't damaged it—you did exactly as I intended! You found my private notes, intended for my eyes only, while I lived. But now that I'm dead, I wanted you to find my journal, Gordianus, tucked inside your precious* Numa. . . .

The sight of the *Numa* had lured me to find the journal. But the *Numa* itself was the key—the truth within which the words were found. Its author was a Calpurnius, one of Numa's descendants, like Caesar's wife and her uncle. No one cared more about the legacy of Numa than Uncle Gnaeus, and Numa had left no greater legacy than his calendar, which was meant to fix for all time the sacred days and the manner of reckoning them. . . .

"And what about my notations regarding celestial movements?" said Hieronymus. "Didn't you connect those to my interest in the calendar?"

"Yes, but where did you learn all that?"

"From Uncle Gnaeus, of course. It was when I saw how he ranted against Caesar's intention to change the calendar that I first became suspicious of him. After that, my continuing curiosity about the calendar made *him* suspicious of *me*."

"But I asked Uncle Gnaeus whether he instructed you about astronomy, and he denied it. He said he wouldn't waste his effort on his niece's foreign-born minion."

Hieronymus snorted. "And you believed him? That man would gladly lecture anyone who asked about the calendar— slave, freedman, foreigner, or even female—for hours on end!" He shook his head ruefully. "You used to appreciate a puzzle,

Gordianus—the more baffling, the better. What's become of your powers of deduction? Gone to Hades, along with your powers of observation, I suppose."

"What is that supposed to mean?"

"What a fuss Calpurnia made over you earlier. How did she put it? 'Others see but are blind, but when you see the truth, you know it!' Yet earlier today, at the triumph, it was what you did *not* see that mattered. But at the time, you took no notice, and now it's completely slipped your mind."

"What are you talking about?"

"Who was not in the procession who should have been?"

I shrugged. "Marc Antony?"

"Please, you can do better than that!"

I thought. Cicero and Brutus had been among the senators. Gaius Octavius had ridden with the troops, as intended. And amid the priests—

"By Hercules! Uncle Gnaeus didn't march with the other priests today. I saw the priests, and he wasn't among them. You're right; I took no notice of that. I saw, but I did not observe! It's only now, thinking back, that I realize he wasn't there."

"And where might he have been?"

"At the house of Porsenna, murdering the haruspex!"

Up at the altar, Uncle Gnaeus, having completed his dismemberment of the ox, was wiping the blade with a piece of wool, staining the cloth bright red and making the knife ready for its next victim. His clothing daubed with blood and viscera, Uncle Gnaeus left the altar and stepped into the tent, where the camilli would wash his hands and dress him in new, spotless vestments.

Hieronymus nodded. "That's the very knife he used to kill

Porsenna, earlier today—the same knife he used to kill me, when I went to report to Calpurnia that night. In fact, I still wasn't quite ready to share my suspicions of Uncle Gnaeus with her, but he saw the signs and knew I was drawing close. He was lying in wait for me, in the darkness. The old man is stronger than he looks. He knows how to use that blade, and he knows exactly where a man's heart is located."

I averted my eyes from Hieronymus. "Your murder I understand. But why Porsenna?"

"We can conjecture that the two of them were in league from the start, each working upon Calpurnia to gain her trust and to garner her intimate knowledge of Caesar's intentions. Uncle Gnaeus believed that the Etruscan soothsayer was on his side, a fellow proponent of old-fashioned religion and a defender of the old calendar. Porsenna's job was to fill Calpurnia's head with false suspicions, to deflect her attention from the real threat: her own uncle. But Porsenna was playing his own game. What if, at the very last moment—today—the haruspex revealed what Uncle Gnaeus was up to and saved Caesar's life, thus proving his powers of divination and his devotion to the dictator? Calpurnia would fall even more deeply under his spell; he might win even Caesar's trust. What soothsayer doesn't lust after that kind of power and influence?"

I nodded. "But Uncle Gnaeus grew suspicious of his partner. . . ."

"Yes. Porsenna was the one person remaining who could ruin his plans. So Uncle Gnaeus decided to put an end to him. During the triumph, he slipped away from the procession and murdered the haruspex in his home, then hurried here, in time for the ceremony."

I frowned. "The one person who could ruin his plans? What about me?"

"Uncle Gnaeus considered killing you. He very nearly did."

"When?"

"Two days ago, in the public latrine, during the Asian Triumph. Did you think it was a coincidence that he happened to join you? He was marching by in the procession and spotted you in the crowd. When he saw you slip into the latrine, he followed you. You thought he was fiddling with his robes, attempting to relieve himself—when in fact he was reaching for his knife, deciding whether or not to kill you."

"Why didn't he?"

"You were very close to death, Gordianus—as close as you've ever been. You felt it brush against you; you shivered. But Gnaeus Calpurnius decided you were harmless. You knew nothing. Or rather, you knew all you needed to know, yet you still did not suspect him. He chose to let you live." Hieronymus looked at me sadly and shook his head.

"The accident that occurred during the first triumph, when the axle of Caesar's chariot broke—was Gnaeus Calpurnius responsible for that?"

"What do you think, Gordianus? Caesar himself suspected sabotage."

"As a priest, Uncle Gnaeus would have had access to the sacred chariot . . . but I can't imagine him crawling under the carriage and sawing through the axle."

"Perhaps not, but he could have suborned some mischievous young camillus to do so."

"But what was the point? Caesar was unharmed. Such an accident could hardly be counted on to kill him."

"Uncle Gnaeus's intent was not to harm Caesar but to turn the people against him. Uncle Gnaeus is a very religious man; he expected the crowd to be awed and shaken by such an ill omen. How frustrating it must have been for him that the incident actually lightened the mood of the spectators. He became more determined than ever to take matters into his own hands."

Hieronymus turned his gaze to the tent and smiled.

"But look!" he said. "There's Caesar now, stepping out of the tent and mounting the steps. Listen to the people cheer!"

Caesar still wore the gold-embroidered toga and the laurel crown of a triumphing general. He walked to the top of the temple steps, where he could be seen by the crowd. The cheering was thunderous. Caesar raised his hands. The tumult subsided.

He delivered a brief speech. I couldn't follow the words; they seemed muffled and garbled, as if my head were underwater. I heard only snatches—something about "Venus, my ancestress" and "the promise I made at Pharsalus" and "the dawn of a new world, a new age, even a new way of reckoning the days that are sacred to the gods."

From the tent, the placard inscribed with the new calendar was carried by priests to a place on the steps just below Caesar. The people of Rome beheld their dictator and his new calendar. The image conveyed an awesome truth: Caesar, the descendant of a goddess, was master not just of space but also of time. On the steps of the temple he had made, in front of the calendar he had decreed, his divine power was made manifest.

But even demigods are not immortal. And now, for the crime of sacrilege, for presuming to replace the ages-old calendar of

Numa, Caesar would die, and the agent of the gods' wrath would be Gnaeus Calpurnius.

The old priest, attired in spotless vestments, stepped out of the tent and quickly mounted the steps. No one tried to stop him; he had been the priest in charge of the sacrifice, after all. Even Caesar, seeing his in-law approach, thought nothing of it.

Uncle Gnaeus pulled the sacred blade from his vestments and thrust with all his might. Caesar never even flinched.

It requires only a single blow to the heart to kill a man. Caesar could be made to die just as easily as all the men and women and children whom he himself had killed in a long life of killing—all the Gauls and Massilians and Egyptians and Romans and peoples of Asia; all the kings and princes and pharaohs; all the consuls and senators, officers and foot soldiers, struggling commoners and starving beggars. Every man dies, and Caesar, thanks to Uncle Gnaeus, was shown to be no exception.

Caesar might be forgiven for all the death and suffering he had inflicted on others; warfare is the way of the world, after all. But for what he had done to Numa's sacrosanct calendar—corrupting it with Egyptian sorcery and false religion—he could not be allowed to live.

Caesar staggered, lurched, and fell forward against the placard. The weight of his dying body broke the wooden frame and ripped the fabric down the middle. Caesar tumbled down the temple steps. Triumphant, Uncle Gnaeus raised the knife and slashed the bloody blade against the remains of the calendar, destroying the hated object in a religious frenzy, all the while crying out the name of his ancestor King Numa.

The spectators gasped, wailed, cheered, screamed. Calpurnia shrieked, ran to Caesar's lifeless body, and tore at her hair like a madwoman. Hieronymus, imperturbable, fixed me with his sardonic gaze.

"Gordianus, Gordianus! How is it that you failed to anticipate this event and prevent it? Even your daughter, turning the facts over and over in her mind, has come to realize the truth. I told you she was smart! Not knowing where you are, failing to find you in the crowd, she thinks to warn Caesar herself. Look, there she is, at the entrance to the tent!"

Sure enough, I saw Diana, pleading and arguing with a lictor to let her enter. Above the tumult, I was able to hear her voice and catch a few phrases: "But you must . . . to warn him . . . Caesar will know who I am—tell him it's the sister of Meto Gordianus. . . ."

Hieronymus laid his hand on mine. I could not feel his touch. "I was never here, old friend," he said. "Yet I am always with you."

I was blinded by tears. I closed my eyes.

I gave a start. When I opened my eyes, Hieronymus was gone. I blinked and looked around, dazed.

The sacrifice was over. The priests and the camilli had vanished. The temple steps were vacant.

"Where is Uncle Gnaeus?" I whispered.

Next to me, Calpurnia raised an eyebrow. "Why, he's in the tent, of course, changing his vestments. He did a splendid job with the sacrifice. Haven't you been watching?"

"I must have . . . closed my eyes . . . for a moment. And Caesar?"

"He's in the tent, too. He should be stepping out to speak

any moment now." Calpurnia frowned. "But isn't that your daughter over there, arguing with the lictor?"

Sure enough, Diana was at the entrance of the tent. It must have been the sound of her voice that woke me. "To warn him," I heard her say. "Don't you understand? If only my father were here, Caesar would . . ."

The grim-faced lictor was unmoved. Diana finally relented. She slumped her shoulders, defeated, and stepped back. The lictor let down his guard. Diana bolted past him and disappeared into the tent.

Caesar was in the tent. So was Uncle Gnaeus, with his knife.

I rose from the bench and ran toward the tent. The lictor, following Diana, had abandoned his post, and I was able to slip inside unopposed.

My eyes were slow to adjust to the filtered light. I saw a confusion of people and objects—priests, camilli, garlands, sacred vessels. At the far end of the tent, I saw the calendar. Arcesilaus was still working to complete his last-minute corrections. Caesar, his back to me, was hovering over the artist, his arms crossed, tapping the ground impatiently with one foot.

"Papa!"

Diana had been apprehended by the lictor, who was roughly escorting her back toward the entrance. But Uncle Gnaeus, still dressed in his bloodstained vestments, seized her arm as she passed by.

"Leave the girl with me, lictor." His voice was low but insistent.

"Are you sure, pontifex?"

"Yes. Go back to guarding the entrance."

"What about this fellow?" The lictor indicated me.

"He'll be leaving very soon. Very quietly. Isn't that right, Gordianus?" Uncle Gnaeus spoke through clenched teeth. His grip on Diana's arm was very tight. In his other hand, he held the knife.

My heart pounded in my chest. The moment felt unreal— far more unreal than my dream-conversation with Hieronymus. I spoke in a whisper. "Gnaeus Calpurnius, you can't succeed. I won't let you. I have only to shout a warning to Caesar."

"But you won't do that. Not while I'm holding your daughter. Now, go. Quietly!"

I shook my head. "If you hurt Diana, if I shout— Don't you see, it can't happen now, not the way you intended, not in the middle of Caesar's presentation, for all Rome to witness. Your grand gesture has been spoiled."

He considered for a moment, then nodded. "You're right. It can't happen as I planned. I'll do it here in the tent, then. What matters is that the thing is done, not how or where or who sees it. As long as you and the girl keep your mouths shut, I needn't harm either of you. It will take only a moment for me to cross the tent and do what I have to do. Stay silent, Gordianus. And you do the same, girl, while we walk together toward Caesar."

I stood frozen to the spot. What did I owe to Caesar? Nothing. Was he worth my daughter's life? Certainly not. How many crimes had Caesar committed? How many deaths had he caused, how much suffering had he inflicted on others? Was there any reason at all that I should try to save his life?

I heard Diana's answer in my head. "People are beginning to live again—to hope, to plan, to think about the future . . . If Caesar were to be murdered . . . the killing would start all over again. . . ."

Amid the preoccupied priests and camilli who chattered among themselves, preparing for the next part of the ceremony, Gnaeus Calpurnius was making his way across the tent, taking Diana with him. Caesar stood with his back to us. He and Arcesilaus were exchanging heated words about the calendar—why was it not ready, and who was responsible for the mistake? How strange that the conqueror of the world should be spending his last moments on earth wrangling over such an insignificant detail!

I stood dumbfounded. It was going to happen—not as I had dreamed it but as circumstance and the will of Gnaeus Calpurnius decreed. In a matter of heartbeats, Caesar would be dead, and the fate of the world would diverge from whatever course Caesar had intended.

"Gordianus! Uncle Gnaeus! What's going on?"

Sweeping past the lictor, Calpurnia followed me into the tent. She spoke in a loud, gruff whisper. Caesar didn't hear, but Uncle Gnaeus did. Distracted, he turned and looked at his niece.

There was only an instant in which the thing could be done. I acted without thinking. When men do such things, we say that the will of a god animates them, but I felt nothing, experienced nothing, thought nothing as I seized a libation bowl from a camillus standing nearby, flipped it upside down, and flung it at the man who held my daughter.

The shallow bowl hurtled spinning through the air and struck Uncle Gnaeus squarely on the forehead. He lost his grip on Diana; she slipped away from him in the blink of an eye. With a stupefied expression, he staggered backward, then forward. He lurched toward Caesar, out of control. He still held the knife. For a dreadful moment I thought he would yet sink the blade into Caesar's chest—for Caesar had turned and now stood facing him, looking confused. But Uncle Gnaeus careened past Caesar, past Arcesilaus, and hurtled headlong into the calendar.

The placard was ripped asunder—that part of my dream, at least, came true. Uncle Gnaeus tumbled head over heels. The knife flew from his grasp. He came to a halt and lay groaning and dazed on the ground amid the ruined remains of the calendar.

Red faced and sputtering, Arcesilaus looked ready to explode. Calpurnia let out a little scream and swooned; the lictor caught her. Diana ran into my arms; she trembled like a doe. The priests and camilli cried out in confusion. And Caesar . . .

Caesar alone, of everyone in that tent, appreciated the absolute absurdity of the moment. Resplendent in his gold-embroidered toga, wearing his crown of laurel leaves, the descendant of Venus and master of the world put his hands on his hips, threw back his head, and laughed.

XXII

I sat in my garden.

By the calendar—Caesar's new calendar—exactly a year had passed since the dedication of the Temple of Venus Genetrix.

In fact, the days that had transpired numbered substantially more than a year; before the new calendar could begin, some sixty or so days were simply added to the old calendar of Numa, which then expired forever.

The correction had successfully realigned the days with the seasons. And so, on the twenty-sixth day of September, six days before the Kalends of October, in the year one of Caesar's calendar, I sat in my garden, enjoying the mild weather of early fall, noting wistfully how short the days were growing.

It seemed strange, in a way, that September should again be an autumnal month and not the middle of summer; but a part of me, deep within, felt gratified beyond words. Man's calendar and the calendar of the cosmos had been reconciled. A flaw in the man-made world had been set right, and we had Caesar to thank for that.

Sitting in my garden, I thought back to the events of a year ago.

Immediately following Gnaeus Calpurnius's unwitting destruction of the placard, confusion reigned. Caesar laughed. Arcesilaus raged. Lictors sought to remove Diana and me from the tent, but I managed to make my way to Calpurnia. In a hurried whisper, I told her all I had realized about Uncle Gnaeus. She was in such a state that I couldn't be certain she understood me. The lictors swept me away.

The ceremony proceeded. On the temple steps, showing not a trace of discomposure, Caesar announced the introduction of his new calendar, but without the placard and without Uncle Gnaeus, who was nowhere to be seen. Calpurnia, too, had vanished.

Days passed. I attempted to visit Calpurnia. I was not admitted. Nor did I hear from her.

I did not hear from Caesar, either. He might at least have thanked me for saving his life.

I brooded in silence, until finally I wrote a message to Calpurnia. I pointed out that my purpose in assisting her had been, first and foremost, to discover the killer of Hieronymus and to obtain justice for my murdered friend. Did she understand what I had told her in the tent? Did Caesar understand what had occurred? What did the two of them intend to do about it? Rashly, perhaps, I demanded that the killer of Hieronymus must be punished. I told her I had no intention of seeing the matter swept under the carpet.

The next day I received her reply:

I regret to inform you that Uncle Gnaeus is no longer with us.

The night of the dedication, he succumbed to a sudden illness—
a fever followed by delirium, copious sweating, and a seizure which
stopped his heart. He died like a proud Roman, praising the achieve-
ments of our ancestors to his final breath. "Numa" was the last word
he spoke.

You may remember his unfortunate fall in the tent, earlier that
day. There are some who claim they saw a person throw an object at
Uncle Gnaeus; Caesar himself did not witness the onset of my un-
cle's staggering fall, but I did, and I have explained to Caesar that it
appeared to be caused by a sudden fit or spasm. Caesar apologized
profusely for laughing at Uncle Gnaeus's clumsiness. He thinks this
strange spasm must have been the first symptom of my uncle's ill-
ness. Caesar is surely right, as I am certain you will agree, should
Caesar ever discuss the matter with you.

The funeral was conducted in a very private manner, as my un-
cle would have wished. I made no public announcement, as I did not
want sad news to spoil the people's enjoyment of Caesar's generous
entertainments.

As for the matter you raised in your last message to me, we shall
never speak of it again.

Along with the note, the messenger delivered a small but very
heavy box. I considered sending it back—I had told Calpurnia I
would accept no payment—but Bethesda had seen the box and
demanded to know what was inside. I let her sort the coins and
tally their value. The task gave her great pleasure.

Justice, of a sort, had prevailed. A year had passed, and in all
that time I had received no more visits from Hieronymus, in my

dreams or otherwise. Did that mean his lemur was at peace? I hoped so.

The triumphs of Caesar marked the end of the old world and the beginning of the new, but the dedication of the Temple of Venus Genetrix was only the midpoint in the festivities. The days that followed were full of yet more feasting and celebration, as the people of Rome were presented with a dazzling array of diversions, including plays, which were staged all over the city. Syrus took first place among the playwrights, and the prize of a million sesterces. Laberius—who presented his satire uncut, including the thinly veiled references to Caesar—came in second, and received half a million sesterces. Caesar's fawning admirer and his sardonic critic both became wealthy men, thanks to the largesse of the dictator.

There were chariot races, athletic competitions, and equestrian exhibitions in the newly expanded Circus Maximus. There were contests in which gladiators were pitted against wild beasts. Spectacular reenactments of famous battles were staged in a special enclosure on the Field of Mars, in which hundreds of captives and condemned men fought to the death. A naval battle was waged on a man-made lake created especially for the purpose, using a thousand men on each side. Many died fighting or were drowned when their ships were set afire and sank.

The citizens of Rome grew sated with spectacle. The gory gladiator contests and staged battles created carnage on such a huge scale that some spectators began to question whether

Caesar had not already caused enough bloodshed. Others were outraged at the profligacy of Caesar's expenditures. It was said that the dictator had robbed the whole world of its wealth and was now squandering his ill-gotten gains like a drunken brigand.

Most dissenters did no more than grumble, but at one point a group of disgruntled soldiers staged a small riot in the Forum. Caesar, chancing to come upon the disturbance with his lictors, apprehended one of the ringleaders with his own hands. The priest of Mars declared that three of the rioters must be put to death. The executions were carried out as a religious rite—yet another occasion for celebration. The men were sacrificed on the Field of Mars. Their heads were placed on stakes in the Forum. Did their grisly punishment remind people of the atrocities of Sulla? Such thoughts were spoken only in whispers.

Eventually, the celebrations came to an end. Life went on.

To deal with the last remnants of the Pompeian opposition, Caesar left Rome for Spain. Gaius Octavius had fallen ill and could not travel with him. In the month of Martius (by the new calendar), a decisive battle took place on the plains of Munda. Caesar lost a thousand men. The enemy lost thirty thousand. The opposition was crushed. Young Octavius arrived too late to take part in the slaughter.

Back in Rome, Marc Antony put aside Cytheris and married Fulvia. She encouraged him to travel to the Spanish frontier, where he placed himself at Caesar's disposal, and the two men were reconciled.

Brutus completed his term as governor of Cisalpine Gaul,

then was appointed by Caesar to serve as a praetor in Rome. Just when he appeared to be solidly in Caesar's camp and rising in the dictator's favor, he married Porcia, the daughter of Cato—a union that must surely have displeased Caesar. Beyond his glib facade, there was an independent and unpredictable streak in Brutus's character.

Cicero was suffering a terrible year. First, his beloved daughter died in childbirth. When Publilia made some tactless comment about the tragedy, Cicero summarily divorced her. Alone and miserable, with his personal life in shambles and his political ambitions at an end, he had withdrawn to one of his country estates to seek the consolations of philosophy.

Cleopatra was back in Egypt. By all accounts, she was a competent ruler and a steadfast ally of Rome. She was said to be planning another visit to Rome in the coming year. Her son remained unacknowledged by Caesar.

Arsinoë was residing in exile in Ephesus. At Rupa's insistence, I sent her a letter asking after her health. She never replied. Perhaps the letter was seized by her keepers.

Despite Caesar's apparent invincibility, his wife's morbid dread of the future was as acute as ever. Following the death of Porsenna, Calpurnia found a new haruspex. His name was Spurinna, and he appeared to exercise an equally powerful hold over her.

Now Caesar was on his way back to Rome, where preparations were underway for his Spanish Triumph. The event was to be stupendous, eclipsing even last year's triumphs. I would have dreaded the forthcoming pomp and ceremony, but for one reason: to take part in the planning, arriving ahead of Caesar, my son Meto was finally returning to Rome.

I expected him at any moment. Diana had promised to

show him immediately to the garden upon his arrival, so that I might see him alone for a little while before the rest of the family greeted him and claimed his attention.

Shadows were lengthening. The September air grew chill. I wrapped my cloak around me. I was beginning to despair of his arrival, when Diana appeared. I read the smile on her face. Meto stepped from behind her. Diana withdrew.

I rose to embrace him. For a long moment, neither of us spoke. When at last I stepped back, I did what I always did upon seeing him after a long absence: I surveyed his body for any new scars and checked his limbs for any signs of lameness. But the gods continued to protect him, despite the terrible risks he took in battle. He was as sound and whole as when I last saw him.

How remarkably handsome he had become! I can say this without vanity, since he was not of my making.

Mopsus brought wine and water. Meto asked about the family.

"All are well," I said. "They'll join us soon. Even your brother is here, if you can believe it. I almost never see Eco these days. He got back just yesterday from a job that took him all the way to Athens."

Meto laughed. "Eco the Finder! He must stay very busy, seeking truth and justice for the people of Rome while you sit here in your garden, Papa, basking in your retirement."

I merely nodded.

Meto inquired about events in Rome. I told him the latest news, then asked about his life on the battlefield.

"Actually, now that the fighting is over, I've put aside my sword and picked up my stylus," he said. "I spend most of my time working on the latest volume of Caesar's memoirs."

"It must be a great challenge, to distill such extraordinary experiences into a few words."

"Indeed! But the research is the biggest challenge."

"Research? It's a memoir, not a work of history. You lived every moment of it. Or rather, Caesar did."

"Yes, but Caesar is very keen to verify every factual statement and all the various claims he makes. For example, did you know that he's fought a total of fifty pitched battles? Fifty! That's a record, as far as I can determine—more than any other commander in the history of Rome. The closest competitor I can find is Marcus Marcellus, the conqueror of Syracuse, who lived a hundred and fifty years ago. And he fought only thirty-nine battles."

"How remarkable," I said. "Fifty battles . . ." How many men had died in those battles? How many had been maimed for life? How many women and children had been enslaved? Fifty was a large, round number. It would look very impressive in Caesar's memoirs.

"And here's another remarkable figure," said Meto. He spoke in a hush. He was excited to share his work with me, and I was touched. "Of course, it isn't exact, because making such a calculation presents all sorts of difficulties and possibilities for error—overcounting, undercounting, and so forth—but I did the best I could, and I think I did a pretty good job."

"A good job with what?"

"Caesar asked me to calculate the number of those who died as a result of all his campaigns—well, those who were actually killed in battle, not counting citizens who died from hardship and disease and such; although we have some idea of that figure from the census he commissioned last year that shows the population of the city is only half what it was before the civil war."

"Only half?" I whispered. Half the population of Rome, wiped from the face of the earth . . .

"Anyway, after I gathered all the information I could, and sorted through all the various estimates, the number I came up with was one million one hundred and ninety-two thousand."

I wrinkled my brow. "What exactly does that number represent?"

"The number of people killed by Caesar in his fifty battles."

"How extraordinary," I said; though, in fact, the number meant nothing to me. How could anyone grasp such a number? I tried to imagine seeing the faces of all those 1,192,000 who had died, one at a time. It was inconceivable. No mortal could hold such a number in his head. A great many people had died; that was all one could say, really.

Apparently Caesar agreed. Meto shook his head ruefully. "And after all that work, all my careful calculations, Caesar has decided he doesn't want the number to appear in his memoirs. Can you imagine that?"

"Actually, I can," I said quietly.

"Ah, well, that number's likely to be superseded in the near future, anyway," said Meto. "Now that he's conquered the whole of the Mediterranean, it's almost inevitable that Caesar will look east and invade Parthia. That means mounting a huge expedition, probably by way of Egypt, perhaps as soon as next year."

"More battles, to spoil that perfect round number of fifty?" I said.

"Yes, many more battles."

"And more deaths?"

"A great many deaths, undoubtedly," said Meto.

Exactly a year ago, I had made a choice that saved Caesar's life. Thinking back to that moment, I felt a twinge of something like regret. How many more men would die before Caesar breathed his last?

But in the next instant the feeling vanished, for suddenly Bethesda appeared, with a broad smile on her face. At the sight of Meto, she trembled with joy.

"Husband, we can wait no longer. It's our turn now to welcome Meto home!"

A moment later, they all came running into the garden—Diana and Davus and their squealing children, Eco and Menenia and the golden-haired twins, silent Rupa and the laughing slave boys.

Those I loved were still alive, and we were all together.

AUTHOR'S NOTE

Our information about the triumphs of Caesar in 46 B.C. comes from various sources. These are the principle citations:

Appian, *Roman History,* 2: 101–102
Cassius Dio, *Roman History,* 43: 14, 19–24, 27; 51: 22
Pliny, *Natural History,* 7.92, 9.171, 14.97
Plutarch, *Caesar,* 55
Suetonius, *Augustus,* 8
Suetonius, *Caesar,* 37–39, 49, 51, 52, 78

Regarding the exact dates of the triumphs, the best supposition I have found is by Chris Bennett at his Web site dealing with Egyptian royal genealogy (www.geocities.com/christopherjbennett). His notes on Cleopatra's sister Arsinoë IV make the most clearly argued case I have read for determining the dates of the four triumphs.

Our knowledge of the playwrights Laberius and Syrus, and some fragments of their works, can be found in the *Saturnalia* of

Macrobius (2.3.9–10; 2.6.6; 2.7.1–11; 6.5.15; 7.3.8), the *Satyricon* of Petronius (55), Suetonius (*Caesar,* 39), and some letters by Cicero (*ad Familia* 7.11 and 12.18.2; *ad Atticus* 14.2). Pliny (8.209) tells us that Syrus's nickname was Pig's Paunch.

The "King of the Hill" ditty in Chapter XVI is adapted from Horace's *Epistles* (1.1). Arcesilaus the artist previously appeared in my short story "The Cherries of Lucullus" (in the collection *A Gladiator Dies Only Once.*)

Plutarch (*Caesar,* 55) and Appian (2: 102) tell us that the census commissioned by Caesar found that the population of Rome had been reduced by half as a result of the civil war. Pliny (7.92) cites Caesar's fifty battles and provides the number of the dead mentioned by Meto in Chapter XXII.

While working on *The Triumph of Caesar,* my favorite books by modern historians were Arthur Weigall's *The Life and Times of Marc Antony* (G. P. Putnam's Sons, 1931) and Jack Lindsay's *Marc Antony: His World and His Contemporaries* (Routledge, 1936). These two authors never fail to stimulate and entertain.

For visual inspiration, we can turn to one of the great masterpieces of the Italian Renaissance, *The Triumphs of Caesar,* a series of nine monumental paintings by Andrea Mantegna (ca. 1431–1506). Inspired both by literary accounts and by the collection of antiquities owned by his patrons, the Gonzaga family of Mantua, Mantegna created one of the first major attempts to visualize the ancient Roman world. The paintings are on permanent display at Hampton Court Palace in London.

Erich Gruen has speculated that the statue of Cleopatra in the Temple of Venus Genetrix was placed there not by Julius Caesar (as Appian explicitly states), but later, by Augustus, as a trophy after the queen's defeat and death. This is an eminently sensible idea; nevertheless, I prefer to take Appian at his word. Caesar's installation of the statue presents us with a puzzle, to be sure, but so do many actions taken by our own leaders. Because an act by, say, a president of the United States did not make sense to a reasonable person does not mean that the act did not take place. I would suggest that the type of man who thinks he can rule the world is not, by definition, a reasonable man, and the actions of such men inevitably leave us with vexed questions that defy sensible explanation by sensible historians. Gruen's essay "Cleopatra in Rome: Facts and Fantasies" can be found in *Myth, History and Culture in Republican Rome: Studies in Honour of T. P. Wiseman,* edited by David Braund and Christopher Gill (University of Exeter Press, 2003).

For reading and commenting on the first draft, my thanks to Penni Kimmel and Rick Solomon. For all his hard work, high spirits, and unfailing sangfroid, my thanks to Alan Nevins, my agent. And my heartfelt thanks to my longtime editor, Keith Kahla, to whom this book is dedicated. Since the days of *Roman Blood,* Keith, Gordianus, and the Finder's creator have gone through many trials and triumphs together.

Caesar and his legacy present a complexity that mirrors that of our own times. Like Gordianus, I find myself endlessly fascinated by the man, and endlessly perplexed. The life of Caesar provides generous inspiration to both the historian, who deals in facts, and the novelist, who deals in the ironies and ambiguities of human existence and the tenuous nature of all knowledge.